Sent Rising

Dove Strong Trilogy #3

Erin Lorence

Contact Information: titleadmin@pelicanbookgroup.com

Cover Art by *Nicola Martinez*

Watershed Books, a division of Pelican Ventures, LLC
www.pelicanbookgroup.com PO Box 1738 *Aztec, NM * 87410
Watershed Books praise and splash logo is a trademark of Pelican Ventures, LLC

Publishing History
First Watershed Edition, 2019
Paperback Edition ISBN 978-1-5223-0230-8
Electronic Edition ISBN 978-1-5223-0218-6
Published in the United States of America

Dedication

To my Brooke. Your laughter keeps me smiling. Your hugs give me strength. Thanks for sharing your joy with me!

Dove Strong Trilogy

Dove Strong
Fanatic Surviving
Sent Rising

1

My fistful of carrots flopped onto the pasture's dead grass. I paused with the spear's red-stained tip two paces from my heart.

A couple dozen pointed poles and pronged branches stuck out horizontally from the giant juniper bush at the edge of the forest, positioned to impale the unlucky trespasser who stumbled too close. While I'd harvested the summer's early vegetables from Wolfe's backyard, my brother had been busy beefing up Micah Brae's home security.

I scratched the red wooden point with my fingernail. Not blood. Beet juice...from our garden patch.

"Gilead, this paranoia of yours is stupid. We're here to live peaceably with these people. Not skewer them."

His humming dropped off, though he continued to secure another spear. "Don't stand there hollering in the open, Dove. You'll attract the enemy. On second thought, keep hollering. I wouldn't mind trying out his new defensive boundary while it's still light."

Trinity paused in the act of hanging what appeared be a glass wind chime above Micah's prickly doorway. She jingled it at my lifted brow. "Burglar alarm. To wake Micah if anyone tries to sneak in while he's sleeping. Plus, it's the color of smoke."

"And the color of your eyes. Subtle." I snorted. Trinity had strewn reminders of herself everywhere in our neighbor's cramped, juniper-bush dwelling—from a corn silk pillow the exact hue of her hair to duplicates of her tattoos scratched in the forest floor. She'd planted these subliminal messages in hopes that he would stop being blind to the fact that he liked her in the same way that she liked him.

Gilead fastened a spike next to the wind chime. He paused suddenly, and his expression threw daggers at the pole in my hand. "Sky alive, Dove! You didn't dismantle the defensive perimeter I put up at our place, did you?"

"Only a few spears." I didn't add that I'd tried to remove all of them but hadn't been able to wrestle them off the shelter that he, my cousin, and I shared. "You put them up, so you get to take them down."

"Don't be an idiot. We need them intact."

"I'm the idiot? Your perimeter won't stop fire. Arson is our biggest threat."

He bent to straighten a pronged stick. "It's too dry this season for intentional arson. Even the most brainless demon from this town will think twice before turning our shelter into a fireball. They'd burn up their own homes, too."

I couldn't argue. Even now, the brassy sun seared my exposed skin like a cooking fire and stole the moisture from my lips. "Fine, Gil, but your spikes won't stop any dogs. You've positioned them too high."

"My second perimeter—the outer one—will take care of any dogs or creatures without foot protection. Haven't you noticed the burr rings I've set in the weeds? They begin ten yards out and get thicker the closer you get to our place. The hounds will go limping home if they try to nose around."

I'd spent a painful hour this morning digging a barbed spike-ball out of my palm. My brother had planted the tiny, torturing bits of nature near our front door on purpose? I swung the blunt end of my pole at his shaggy head to thump some sense into him. He caught it without looking.

The glass tinkled above Trinity's upstretched arms. "Not cool, Gil. I had to cut half my braid off to get two burrs out yesterday. Keep it up, and I'll end up looking like her." She thrust a piece of wind chime in the direction of my blonde, chopped-to-shoulder-length hair.

Micah aimed a pair of wistful eyes at me.

I let go of my tug-of-warring pole and pointed in the direction I'd come. "Gilead, you and Trinity should have been waiting at our place today. What if you all missed Uncle Saul when you were messing around here? You were supposed to be on the lookout for him."

"He'd check here at Micah's—or at *his* place—before giving up on finding us. Isn't that where you were? *His* place?"

Gilead meant Wolfe's property. Since relocating to Sisters, he had yet to call my non-Christian friend by name.

I gazed at the treetops to the east, in the direction of my family's out-of-sight home in Ochoco. "Saul said he'd bring us news from home every Saturday. It's been three Saturdays since we saw him...I think."

Gilead shrugged, but Micah disappeared inside his juniper bush.

"Eleven...twelve...thir-thirteen..." His labored counting continued. The Brae guy kept a tally of each day in this enemy territory where we'd agreed to live for a year as part of the Christian Sent.

His dark head poked out and set the wind chime jingling. "Twenty-two. Twenty-two days since Saul's last visit. You're right, Dove. You're absolutely right." He eyed me. A dog wanting a pat from its master.

Gilead secured another horizontal pole to the prickly bough. "Well, did *he* give you any useful information about what could have stopped Saul? Any report of accidents? Wildfires between here and Ochoco? Attacks?"

I shook my head. Wolfe didn't like to relay bad news. What I knew about the famine, high food costs, and the devastating nation-wide drought, I'd learned from his kid sister, Jezebel. She reported information better than our radio back home.

My brother pulled out his hunting knife and began to whittle a branch's tip. "What a good-for-nothing guy. What a worthless, waste of a human—"

"Probably your uncle went crazy again. He probably forgot where you live now." Jezebel popped up from behind a boulder where she'd been spying. "He'll show up when he remembers. But Dove and I'll go ask my brother if he's heard anything...since the rest of you are too chicken to leave your forts to find out."

In three strides, Gilead towered over the girl. He cracked his knuckles. "OK, Spy. Let's find your brother. Now!"

Trinity dropped the vine supporting her glass pieces. "Chill, Gil. She's like five years old. Anyway, my dad's not crazy."

"Who's five?" Jezebel's bottom teeth clamped over her upper lip in a fierce underbite while she rolled to her sandaled feet. The brown grass clump from her hand rained against my brother's earth tone pantleg.

"C'mon, Dove."

Trinity came to stand at my shoulder. "I'll come, too. Micah? Want to go check why my dad's delayed?"

"No. No, I'll, uh...I'll finish up here. I'd like to find out what's going on, but I'd better finish the perimeter. The perimeter is the most important part of security. But you could bring me some corn. Or some strawberries."

Strawberries. Trinity's dreamy, wide-set eyes crinkled in a smile. She touched her wrist where years ago she'd inked on the strawberry plant. A matching drawing ran the perimeter of his shelter's floor.

"It's working," she mouthed.

Gilead, gripping a whittled branch, marched through the center of the field with Jezebel instead of slipping through the bordering foliage toward the paved road that led to the Picketts' home. He barreled through a herd of cows, slapping one on its bony rump. *Who's a coward?*

Trinity and I followed, staying closer to the forest's edge and away from the vast, gray roofs of the godless houses that loomed through patches of dying vegetation. As we passed by our own shelter, we were careful to avoid my brother's planted burrs.

My eyes narrowed at my temporary home. Trinity's swags of dandelion chains and old-man's-beard moss drooped in artistic intervals around the top of our bushy enclosure. Gilead's wicked spikes encircled the entire copse of arborvitae trees at chest and throat level, complete with a jagged, teethlike collection of poles at our semi-secret entrance.

Had the Heathen who lived in those boxy homes noticed the unnatural changes—poles and flowers— to this arborvitae copse? How long until a resident of

Sisters guessed that this tight knit group of abandoned landscaping trees in the field housed three people?

I hopped the cow fence and faced signs of Heathen life in Sisters. Enormous homes. Sleek cars. And staring humans.

We stepped among them. I no longer searched for hiding spots like I used to when I walked the nonbelievers' turf. I was part of the Sent, and we Sent weren't in the Enemy's territory to hide. We were here to represent Christ for our nation's spiritual revival—a type of nonviolent war fought by us showing our love of Christ.

I alone of my cousin, brother, and Micah—also the Sent—ever remembered our mission.

Gilead marched along with stiff, raised shoulders. Uncomfortable and on guard. Trinity shuffled behind, hunched over with her eyes darting up to the sparse trees like mine used to.

Nowadays, I focused on the pavement in hopes I wasn't recognized as the girl from the television show. My family was clueless about my two-week survival in the Texan desert last spring—all for Heathen viewing pleasure. They'd never travelled the road out of town, so they didn't see my face on the billboard. They blamed Wolfe for the extra attention I received from nonbelievers.

"Rainbow," Trinity muttered. "Ten o'clock."

To my right, a nonbeliever aimed a jet of hose water away from himself. Defensively. As if to force us to keep our distance from his dripping, squashed-egg car. The faded arc of colors wavered from the hose's blast that splattered from the edge of our path.

He hooked a finger at Jezebel. "Hey, kid. You know you're walking with freaks? Why don't you get away from—hey!"

The water trickled to a stop. *Clunk.* Gilead tossed the hose he'd knotted onto the front of the vehicle and glared down into the stranger's flushed, pop-eyed face. The man's factory-made shoes stayed rooted to the wet pavement, but his upper body bowed backward, retreating from my brother's fierce bulk.

I jerked Gilead's arm to get him walking. "You may as well go back to Mom and Grandpa if you're going to pull stuff like that. We're supposed to be likeable, not jerks—ow!"

Unexpected sharpness jabbed between my shoulder blades. With a sharp exhale, I whirled around.

A familiar female with purple irises stood with feet apart, levelling an arrow from a medieval bow weapon at my collarbone. My brother yanked me away from its trajectory. "Beat it, Diamond. I've no time for your games, so step aside."

She adjusted so its lethal tip pointed at my brother. "You should really listen to that smart man, Jezebel. Stay away from freaks."

2

Diamond, Wolfe's neighbor who'd eagerly beaten me to a pulp in the past, now seemed to hesitate to murder me, my brother, and my cousin. She blinked in the bright sunlight and threw a glance at the man whose knotted hose dangled from his motionless hands.

"Walk." Her crossbow shepherded us into the gloomy shadows next to Wolfe's boxy home.

Not a surprise. Satan's minions prefer, if given a choice, to act against Christians in the veiling darkness. This was the reason I retreated to my hidey-hole tree copse with my family before each sunset to remain until sunrise.

"Halt."

Our feet crunched to a stop in the cropped, brown grass. I kept my hold on Trinity, so she wouldn't make a running fly for the forest beyond our garden. Of course, at any moment now, my brother's arm would strike and relieve Diamond of her weapon. At any moment...

Diamond's index finger continued to rest on the trigger. "It appears you've got nothing else to do other than grow beans and poison people's property. So? Which of you destroyed mine? Or was it a group activity? It was you, wasn't it?"

The arrow's point swung toward me.

"Don't think I don't understand how you work—

tricking people like my cousin and the Picketts into believing that you're harmless. Using Wolfe as a shield. Always cozying up with him any chance you—"

There was a blur of movement. Gilead now held the crossbow.

He directed its trajectory at Jezebel's brother, who emerged, laughing, from the sunlit corner with the little girl. "What kind of cozying have you been doing with my sister?"

"Wha...what? Nobody's been cozying. No cozying." Wolfe tripped backward to get out of the projectile's range.

"Watch your big feet, Woof." Jezebel scrambled up and galloped to face my brother. The arrow now pointed at the small bit of pale scar peeking from the top of her skimpy shirt.

Her hand found her hip. "Because you're huge, you think you're scary. Well, you're wrong. Dove's other boyfriend is a lot bigger giant than you and has more muscles. And I hit him in the head with a banana slug. Hard. *Bam-o!*"

Jezebel extracted the bow from my brother's frozen grip. Wolfe chuckled.

Carrying the vision of a slimy mollusk entwined in the traitor's ashen strands, I smiled and left the shade for the sunlit vegetable beds. Jezebel's unexpected word-bomb about Stone Bender had blasted away the paralyzing current of suspicious hate holding everyone.

Gilead caught up to me when I stepped off the brittle grass and into the ankle-high, green blades at the perimeter of my garden. "Another boyfriend, Dove? Who is this other loser? I don't like the sound of him."

Jezebel scampered up the triangular woodpile. Balancing like an oversized weathervane, she aimed the arrow-less crossbow at Diamond. "And Di, for your information, no one's poisoning your garden. You're just a total delinquent at growing things."

Her neighbor's face flushed beet-juice bright. Diamond pulled a miniature knife from her back pocket and began to hack shavings from a piece of kindling.

Gilead drew out his own six-inch hunting blade from his waistband and copied her. His glare flickered between us.

Jezebel stomped her foot so hard a wedge of wood tumbled off the stack. "I'm sick of it! Sick. Of. It. Even all the way to California it's the same thing. Everyone is all mad at Sent people like Dove, who are minding their own business...digging in the dirt and growing potatoes. And then, Dove, your people get all fired up because radicals like your uncle go missing. And they break people out of the CDTCs...which is, OK, sort of cool, but not helpful to me when I want everyone to get along. So, you all need to cool it. That's all I have to say. Dove, go help Diamond grow potatoes."

I paused in plucking a worm off a berry leaf and met Diamond's eyes. *Help you grow potatoes?*

Offer to do that and you'll find this wood impaled somewhere in your body, her purple irises promised.

Wolfe tripped between us, snapping a young corn plant in half. "Oops."

Trinity growled, an anguished sound. She wandered to the swirl of marigolds whose sunshine heads grew like heavy oranges. My cousin's artistic mastermind revealed itself in the layout of the small garden Wolfe's grandma allowed us to keep on her property. The complicated design of colors, leaf shapes, and plant heights depicted a fire-breathing dragon.

Wolfe quit trying to prop up the severed corn stalk and extended his arm, as if to fit it around my shoulders. "Is it true? Your uncle still hasn't shown up? I thought he had. I mean you never said he hadn't, and—"

My brother wedged himself between us, his knife aloft. "Move back from my sister."

"No. You move back." Diamond flung herself in front of Wolfe. Her blade hovered near my brother's blonde, bearded throat.

"I said cool it!"

Both razor-edged weapons lowered at Jezebel's command.

Wolfe craned over Gilead's shoulder. "Is it true about your uncle?"

I nodded. "And is it true, what Jezebel said about other Christians going missing between here and California? That it's not only my uncle who's disappeared?"

He bit his lip.

"Wolfe. Don't be a spineless slug. Tell the truth."

His shoulders sagged. "OK. Fine. Yes. I figured there was no need to mention the missing-Christians stuff since your uncle had shown up. The disappearances are happening up in Washington state too. And what the brat said about your people breaking into the Christian Terrorist Detention Centers wasn't a lie either. Not that they've found any of the missing believers there...but the attacks on the centers have been pretty regular lately."

I pictured the pink cracked walls from the week

I'd spent in the detention center for religious terrorists last spring. Was my uncle there right now? Had he been arrested by nonbelievers for some trivial illegal deed? Was he now stuck inside with no hope of getting out?

Gilead returned his knife to the rope loop he used for a belt and hummed a few bars of my grandma's favorite hymn. His fingers shot out, gripped Wolfe's black shirt, and reeled him in. "Where is Ochoco's closest detention center? Give me directions for the fastest way to get there."

Diamond stuck her knife between her teeth pirate-style. But before she could launch herself onto my brother's back, Trinity's calm voice piped up from the flowers.

"Or...my dad's merely at home. Resting and recovering from the flu or a busted ankle. Before we go bashing down the door of the Heathens' detention center to free him, we'll check home first. If he's not there, Grandpa will know where to look."

Gilead's grip relaxed at my cousin's obvious wisdom, and Wolfe was able to yank his shirt free. As the potential for a fight passed to nothing, excitement drained from Diamond's eyes. She straightened from her crouch, wiped the spit from her switchblade, and moved back to the woodpile.

I scrubbed my dirty palms against my home-sewn pants that used to be Gilead's and headed toward the front of the painted home where the familiar white Jeep waited. "You're driving us, Wolfe. I mean...uh, please?"

"On it." The keys jangled in his tanned fingers. He swung past me to open the ancient vehicle's dented door. "First stop for doughnuts?"

I groaned. No more doughnuts. I'd ingested more of that sweet pastry in this town than I'd eaten squirrel my whole life growing up in Ochoco.

"No. First stop is Micah's place." Trinity clambered past me into the backseat area. One hand cradled red strawberries.

"Right." He began to whistle my brother's hummed hymn.

I planted myself at the Jeep's open door. With a sigh, I shook my head. "Gilead, get in. Jezebel, get out."

Still whistling, Wolfe extracted his struggling sister from the seat next to Trinity.

She kicked the air and writhed to break his grip. "Lemme go, Woof! It's not fair! I'm coming to Dove's house, too!"

"Not this time, brat. You're not invited." He thrust her at Diamond, whose wiry arm came around the little girl's scrawny middle like a snare.

I crossed my arms. "Gilead? We're waiting on you. You were the one in the big hurry to find Uncle Saul."

My brother quit studying the distant treetops and frowned. "Not in that death trap, and not with him driving. If you and Trinity had any decency, you'd refuse his ride, too."

I plunked down on the hot seat and slammed the door.

His lowered head filled the window's opening. "Fine. Micah and I will meet you at our property in a couple days. Wait for me there."

"Fine." I hit a button and the glass rolled up.

Wolfe quit whistling and leaned over. He spoke in a low murmur. "Maybe this is bad timing, but the guy called Lobo left a message for you. He'll be here tomorrow morning to collect you with Jessica. He hinted about werewolves, gators, and a dead voodoo princess. Which means ten-to-one your next survival is in the Manchac Swamp. That's Louisiana. You have experience dealing with haunted swamps, I hope?"

"Shish." I glanced back, but Trinity was in her own world of shapes and colors. Her slim fingers held a heart-shaped berry in the sunbeam. The red glowed like a ruby. "How would I know about swamps? You know I've been in Ochoco all my life and haven't gone anywhere else. Well...except Texas. And New Mexico. And Colorado, Utah, and Idaho."

Being God's messenger had made me quite well-traveled, when I actually listed the places I'd been. But I hadn't been to Louisiana.

What would it be like there? A swamp with alligators? The werewolf and voodoo stuff...not a big deal. I faced Satan's obstacles every day as part of the Sent. Did it matter what form evil came in? A dead voodoo princess or Diamond with a crossbow? Nope.

I shrugged. "It'll be Lobo's problem tomorrow. Not mine. If I'm not here, I'm not here, and I can't go."

Wolfe guffawed. "Sure. No problem. And when you're arrested for breach of contract again, I'll just come bust you out of the CTDC like the rest of the Christians are doing."

I rolled my eyes. Still...

I bit my lip. Jessica was coming here. I'd been watching for her in town all June, and now she arrived tomorrow. Jessica and Diamond were cousins, and the only true difference between them was that Diamond glared and threw pointed elbows...whereas Jessica glared and threw out pointed questions, revealing a burning curiosity to know more about the true God.

If I found my uncle at home today, Wolfe could have me back in town in time to go to Louisiana for *Fanatic Surviving*. If my uncle wasn't at home...

I strapped the safety belt around my waist. God alone knew whether or not I'd be here in Sisters tomorrow to meet Jessica and Lobo. So why whine about it?

"Wolfe? Are you driving me home sometime today? Please?"

"Sure." He turned on the engine and peeled his gaze from my brother, who loomed next to his window.

Gilead continued to drag a slow finger across his throat. His message was clear.

Touch my sister...I kill you.

3

My stunned body pivoted in a slow, full circle. I forced my eyes to stay open instead of squeezing shut to block out the harsh reality illuminated by the sun's tawny rays.

Oh, God, how...

My unfinished prayer trailed off. Fat flies speckled the ruined zucchinis. The green squash—swollen to the size of eggplants—rotted back into the parched soil. My rotating feet trampled their vines' limp leaves that had overgrown and swallowed up the path before dying of thirst. The extreme heat had destroyed every crop my family had planted. Why hadn't anyone watered them?

A shifting, metallic noise broke through the insect hum. Wolfe picked up one of the bike-chain lanterns that sprawled in its own broken glass at the foot of the tin-can rainbow. He cradled it, and with another clank, rehung it on its hook.

Trinity hadn't moved since entering our family's ruined garden. Every few moments, she exhaled one word.

"Dead...dead...dead..."

I filled my lungs with the hot aroma of spoiled vegetables, baking dirt, and pine. No bell pealed overhead. No shaggy-haired boys tumbled over each other like puppies or shouted. No mothers hurled themselves down the ladder to hug their daughters.

A crow's angry caw interrupted the too-silent—yet familiar—nightmare. I let the black-feathered scavenger return to his zucchini meal at my shoe and steered Trinity to the maple's ladder.

We never used the ladder, but now my muscles felt as solid as the rotting squash behind me. If I climbed my usual route of leafy branches up to the platform, I'd fall.

I balanced on the edge of the living space platform and allowed myself a long blink—a tiny reprieve from the new terrible scene I faced. Trinity whimpered.

"Oh no...no."

"What?" Wolfe had trailed us up the ladder to our home's back entrance. He nudged me out of the doorway. "What's the trouble?"

His wide, brown eyes lifted to the sturdy ceiling beam that had held him aloft by his ankles months ago. He wandered into the middle of the empty space. His arms spread wide. "I don't see anybody...or a sign of a fight. Dove? Trinity? What's wrong?"

I shook my head. The terror that gripped my cousin and me sprang from the fact that there wasn't anybody to see. That there was no sign of recent activity—a fight or otherwise. The nothingness...the abandoned air...the undone chores and housework—that was what made my lids squeeze shut and Trinity struggle not to cry. Our family had nowhere to go. They couldn't have left. But they had.

Where, Lord? Why?

I walked in a straight line past the empty willow chair, refusing to focus on the familiar seat whose occupant had died last spring. I paused at the platform's opposite railing. My grandpa's lookout platform perched near the upper canopy of the neighboring tree. The large, rusted bell hung silent. A thick layer of leaves covered his rumpled blanket on the weathered boards.

Trinity's running footfall echoed from nearer floorboards. She checked the sleeping porches. Then a balcony. Trudging steps returned to where I waited.

"They didn't leave a message or note. And there's this. Your mom didn't take it with her." She handed me an ancient willow frame.

My fingertips traced the warm smoothness through the dust. The yellowed paper with my parents' signatures glinted at me under the glass. "No. She would never have left her marriage certificate behind, wherever she went. Not on purpose."

"I know. My parents' is still next to their hammock too. Next to the family portrait I carved before we became Sent that my mom said she'd cherish forever. *Forever*. No way she'd have left it."

Silence pressed down.

"Dove, they...they could be visiting the Braes' home. Or maybe they're with the Joyners. Maybe they'll be back tonight."

The state of the garden and the tree debris scattered across the floor and wedged in crevices shouted the truth. They'd been gone for a week or more. Not out visiting neighbors for the day.

Trinity's unsteady finger scrolled a wavy heart around my parents' handwriting. "Let's check. I'll go to Micah's home. I...I wanted to see what his mom is like anyway. You visit the Joyners."

I nodded, grateful she suggested I go to the Joyners' because I couldn't stay here in my abandoned home tonight while we waited for Gilead. I'd end up in Gran's chair, a blubbering mess. And I also couldn't face the Braes' claustrophobic tunnels and Micah's parents. And the other Brae girls.

My insides clenched. They were miniature Melodys...Melody, the friend I thought I could trust. But she'd turned out to be a traitor like Stone, choosing to side with Warrior Reed whose ultimate goal was to push our country's Christians into a bloody war with non-believers called the Reclaim, even if it meant us sinning to do it.

Wolfe gave a hearty clap. "Great. And where do I check?"

"Go with Dove. She'll need help making sure the zip lines are secure."

"Zip lines! Isn't riding them like flying?"

My lips tightened at his excitement. This terrible situation was exactly like my old, reoccurring dream with the dove...except without the dripping red and I had no ability to fly. My family was gone. How could he smile?

He caught my dagger-look and returned it with a hang-dog expression. "I mean...I've got your back on securing the zip lines, Dove. And we'll find your family. I promise. Like Trinity said, they're probably off visiting neighbors. My grandma disappears for days sometimes. Weeks. So do I. But we always find our way home. Eventually."

I turned my back on him and his unfounded optimism. "I'll come with you to the Braes' entrance, Trinity. Getting there is tricky."

She shook her coiled hair and shouldered her satchel. The dried roses she'd stitched on the bag's sides rustled with a faint cloud of scent. "No need. Gil and Micah created a shortcut that comes to the edge of our property, and I know where the tunnel's entrance is. You should get going now so you can reach the Joyners' before dark. You can't check zip line cables if you can't see them."

"Meet you back here tomorrow? No matter what?"

"No matter what."

I glared into her smoky, wideset eyes. "Don't go and get yourself trapped underground in an avalanche."

"And you don't slack off. Otherwise you'll break your neck."

We ended our brief hug when Wolfe joined in.

"What? No one cares if I fall, too? We'll find your family, girls, I promise. Now lead the way to the zip lines."

4

The pines blurred past, indistinct brown and green pillars in the golden light. Ahead, Wolfe's figure at the far-away tree where the cable ended swelled from a speck into a life-sized person. He balanced on a limb, his tall self blocking the exact spot of the trunk I would use to stop myself. His bare arms were open, as if to catch me at the end of my final zip line.

I shouted to be heard above the screaming *whir* of Gilead's handmade trolley-device flying down the cable. "Move yourself! Drop down. Down!"

I gripped my handle-hold tighter, and the metal trolley hit the block of wood on the line. With a whiplashing motion, my body swung forward. My legs caught and gripped the trunk inches above Wolfe's hair.

He pulled himself up straight. "I can't help that I'm so chivalrous."

I batted away his attempt to unfasten my harness. "Yeah, that was real helpful. We both almost died...well, mostly you."

"Hey. Don't forget I was the one who noticed the cable separating from the ginormous, pitchy tree back at the beginning. And I rode first each time to make sure the cables would hold. I kept you safe like Gilead would have."

"Except my brother doesn't shout 'yee-haw' and 'let's do this' when he rides."

He grinned and stepped from the branch onto the Joyners' porch that was twice as wide as the actual home. He offered me a hand. "So, this is it? The Joyners live here?"

I nodded. Despite the fact I'd never visited before and that this was all unfamiliar territory, we were at the right place. We only had one tree-dwelling neighbor.

"Cozy." His six-foot frame blocked my beeline to the green-stained door. "Half a sec. Is there anything—anyone—you need to tell me about before we drop in unannounced?"

"Huh?"

"Is there a neighbor living here who is, you know, someone you're special friends with? A special guy?"

"Sky alive, Wolfe! Mr. Joyner is super old—probably almost thirty. He's married, and they have a baby girl. Now move aside. My mom might be in there."

I yanked the oval door open. "Shalom?"

The Joyners' enclosed space was at least five times smaller than my home's, yet it contained the same abandoned air. Too quiet. Too still. Forest debris littered the floor planks.

"Hello? We come in peace. So, don't attack us." Wolfe's messy strands brushed the rafters of the living space that included a kitchen, a crib, and a double-wide hammock.

A terrible thought made my heart slam. I sprinted to the crib and peered inside.

It was empty except for a stuffed raccoon toy and some pine needles.

My breath escaped in a gust of relief. I sank down onto Mrs. Joyner's rainbow, knotty rug while Wolfe flung open a shutter. He leaned out with cupped hands.

"Hello—oo! Dove's mom? Saul? Mr. and Mrs. Joyner? Are you out there?"

He gave up and walked the perimeter of the room. "It's a small place. Doesn't seem to be any other spots to check, does there?"

"No."

"Hey." He sank down next to me. The weight of his forearm came across my shoulders. "Hey. Dove. Don't be like that. It's OK. They're probably over at the Braes'. Trinity's talking with them right now, and they're all hugging and laughing at you and me for making the long trip out here. No, listen to me. Trinity said Gilead made a tunnel from your property to their place, right? And you've got a whole herd of kid cousins? Where's the most likely place they'd evacuate to if they felt they needed to go somewhere fast?"

His eyes smiled into mine.

"Exactly. They'd go to the Braes'. Because it's closer and easier to get a bunch of kids through some tunnels than having to zip line over here one by one. Right? So that's where they'll be. I bet the Joyners are there, too. No doubt they heard about the recent Christian disappearances and decided to lie low for a couple weeks and hide. Think about it—out of all three homes, which is the most hidden?"

"The Braes'."

"Exactly. So that's where they headed. They're not all as lamebrain as you, Dove. They're doing what they're good at—surviving. Taking care of themselves. Playing it safe."

He was right. My grandpa always had a plan to protect the family. If plan A didn't work, he'd switch to plan B...and so on, right on to plan Z.

For the first time since arriving in Ochoco, I made my own worries shut up and listened to God.

What do You want me to do? Return home? Keep searching? I'll do it...whatever You say.

Silence. Yet a detailed scene of my own making played out behind my closed lids. In the deepening twilight, I coached Wolfe on the harder process of returning home on the zip lines. I spat instructions at him and steamed with frustration. He fumbled in the gloomy darkness on limbs he couldn't see.

The Joyners' property was at the bottom of a four-mile slope from my family's home, so getting here had been as easy as finding a mosquito in June. Gravity had done the work.

But returning home?

The return trip meant a significant amount of vertical tree climbing at each section of line in order to gain enough height for gravity to pull us to the next section. And we would travel on different cables than we'd used to get here—unchecked cables that might be frayed or cut by vandals—cables impossible to see in the dark. The whole thing was impossible tonight. At least it was for the city guy crouching next to me.

We—I—needed to stay here at the Joyners' until morning light, when traveling would be safer. I lifted my head from my worn sleeves.

Wolfe nodded. "God agrees with me? I always knew your God had sense."

Though my mind had peace about the decision to stay here tonight...and had accepted the hope that my family really was just a few miles away...my hands still trembled. Weak. When had I last eaten?

I stood and headed for the acorn-sized kitchen.

Fragrant ropes of drying vegetables hung above the wall shelves. Mrs. Joyner wouldn't mind if I borrowed enough for dinner. Anyway, they were from my family's garden.

I tore off two onions. "You like onion stew?"

"Not really."

"While I make it, you light that lantern and hang it next to the unshuttered window. If the Joyners return tonight, that'll give them warning they've got guests. We don't want to surprise Mr. Joyner when he walks in." I began to slice the onions.

"Is he... like Gilead?"

"He's way smaller."

"Oh good."

"But he's the Ochoco champion for spear throwing. Never misses. He taught Gilead after my dad died, which is half the reason Gil is so good."

Wolfe's footsteps hurried toward the window. "C'mon, c'mon." He fumbled with the lantern. "Ah. There we go."

I glanced up from the onions. A flame throbbed inside the lantern's glass, casting a yellow glow on everything except the orange sunset that filtered through the open window.

I added the vegetables, crushed garlic, and salt to the lump of deer lard sizzling in a pot. A few tendrils of herbs grew from Mrs. Joyner's garden shelf. I threw in some plucked leaves and pushed the mess around with a whittled-out utensil.

"Hey. That actually smells all right."

"Better than all right." It'd been weeks since I'd ingested a hot meal. Gilead, Trinity, Micah and I existed on raw vegetables and fruits from our garden and daily gifts from Wolfe—snacks like doughnuts and canned tuna that we could consume without cooking. A fire in our shelter during the drought would've been suicidal.

Jezebel had once tried to bully me into her home for "a surprise" homecooked meal one afternoon, but I'd fought and won that battle. By choice, I hadn't stepped inside the Picketts' home all month. If fanatic-haters wanted to vandalize my garden...fine. But I wouldn't give anyone reason to destroy the expensive structure my friends called home. The Picketts hadn't had to lie when neighbors asked if radicals lived inside. *No. The radicals did not.*

My ears followed Wolfe's whistling as he moved from the window to the hammock. He stopped at the crib.

With a sigh, he flopped into the bearskin-covered rocker. "Nice place they've got here."

Another understatement. The aroma of caramelized onions, the golden light, the small shelter full of signs of a happy couple's life, complete with a hammock I'd sleep on tonight instead of the ground...this place was a cozy patch of Heaven.

The rocker creaked back and forth. "I could see myself living in a place like this someday. How about you? Would you like a place like this? Someday?"

I stiffened. Then I lifted the water jug and sniffed to determine if its contents had spoiled. I splashed some into the pot. A cloud of steam rose up, blocking Wolfe from sight. I added some more salt, gave another stir...then couldn't find anything more to do with the stew. I set down the stirring stick.

Wolfe quit rocking. "Would you? Would you like a place like this? Someday?"

"Uh..." Why were my knees wobbling again? I

plunked down in the bear-skin rocker opposite Wolfe's before he noticed my weak reaction to a simple question.

Would I like to live in a home like this? Yes, of course I would. I belonged in the treetops. I even preferred the tight quarters of this space to my own family's sprawling tree home. But I sensed an intimacy here that belonged to a married couple—a couple devoted to each other. A couple in love.

The fact was evident from the marriage certificate displayed above the door, to the crib crafted for their baby, to the pair of matching chairs, to—worst of all—the wide hammock woven for two.

My eyes traced a pattern in the bright rug Mrs. Joyner had made, probably to keep Mr. Joyner's feet off the chilly winter floorboards while he soothed their baby. Was Wolfe asking me what I thought? Did I ever wish to live in a place like this...*with him*?

He stood up. With a loud scrape, he repositioned his rocker next to mine even though it was a tight squeeze. He plunked back down. Side by side we gazed out the un-shuttered rectanglar hole at the indigo sky. His fingers twisted around mine.

We held hands sometimes. I also held hands with Jezebel and Trinity...and a hundred years ago, with Melody and Stone. But in this moment, our linked hands seemed to symbolize a hazy future. This could be us, joined together, in our own house in the trees...someday. If I spoke up.

The pot rattled.

"Stew." I tugged out of his handhold and wobbled for the stove.

Wolfe followed and leaned against the wall next to the tiny flame. "I didn't know you could cook."

I let out the breath I'd been holding. "Doesn't every kid try? Even Gilead fried up a mess of earthworms once. But my mom...she cooks for us and so does my aunt."

As I uttered the word *mom,* a whispered warning caught my ear. *Unequally yoked.*

I dropped the stirring stick and frowned up into the tanned, cheerful features that my eyes sought more than anyone else's. I found my words.

"I like this place. I like you. But I can't have a place like this with you. Not ever. I can't be unequally yoked."

Wolfe laughed, the guffaw brittle and forced. "What about unequal yolks?"

"Not egg yolks. Yokes. Those wooden things that oxen wore in the old days to pull loads. The oxen wearing yokes had to be paired right, the strong with the strong. The weak with the weak. Balanced. It means I can't ever end up in a relationship with a non-Christian."

"But what if I'm not a non-Christian?"

"Huh?"

"Listen. I'm not an idiot. I get God is important to you. That you love Him. I've given up on the idea of you ever ditching Him. So, I'm willing to share you. Even if that means me becoming like Stone or Micah in order to share."

The impossible idea of him becoming like either of those serious, bearded Christians made my lips twitch.

"You approve? Just tell me what I need to do—is there a ceremony? Do we find a priest or something and have him say the right religious words? Growing out my chin hair might take a few weeks, but I'm serious. I'll do it. For you, I'll become a fanatic."

For me? My heart lurched. "You can't say magic words. Or decide to become a Christian because you love me. You have to love God. Then tell Him you know you're a sinner. Believe that his son Jesus Christ died for your sins. And invite Jesus to control your life through the Holy Spirit."

"Control my life? Are you sure we can't just find a priest and—ow!"

I tossed my spoon-weapon on the counter and lifted the pot.

Wolfe lurched away.

Instead of throwing its contents at him, I filled two wooden bowls to the brim with the steaming stew. I pushed one at him. "Here. Eat instead of talking."

We carried our bowls to the table and sat down. He waited for me to finish praying and then lifted his eyes to the rafters. "Like she said. Gracias."

I'd expected to drain my bowl of the hot, salty broth in seconds. But because of the knot in my gut, I could only sip at it.

"And I never said I love you." He grinned at my spoon frozen in midair. "You said I couldn't become a Christian only because I love you. I never said I did."

"Oh."

"Although I do."

"Enough, Wolfe! Or I'm zip lining out of here tonight, and you can find your own way to my home tomorrow morning. I've enough problems with my family missing. I don't need you...you—" I tossed my spoon into my unfinished broth and pointed at the Joyners' bed with an unsteady hand. "I'm going to sleep. Do you want the hammock? Or the floor?"

He picked up our unfinished stew and carried the bowls to kitchen. "No, you get a good night sleep for once. Enjoy the hammock. I'm sure the rug and I will be very comfortable together."

I hurled the bearskin onto the rug and then flopped down on the hammock's woven strands. Why did my idiotic heart still gallop in my chest? I forced my mind to the stars instead of following Wolfe's movements around the cozy home.

Keep me strong. Protect Trinity underground. And give me a dream of red, so I know where to go on my journey to find my family. Show me the way.

5

I awoke from a dreamless sleep to a *tap, tap, tap.* Not a knock on the door, only a woodpecker.

My head's jerk had started my bed swaying. I stretched in the giant hammock and relaxed into the familiar, rocking motion. I wasn't curled up on the ground. I was back in the treetops where I belonged. At the Joyners', although they hadn't returned.

I continued to grin at the sloped ceiling boards. God hadn't sent me a dream. No informative dream meant I wouldn't have to go on a long journey to find my family, didn't it? Wolfe was right. They were safe, most likely at the Braes' place with Trinity. If I hurried, I might see them before lunchtime.

As my hammock swung toward the spot where Wolfe sprawled across most of the floor, I jumped over him. *Thud.* He opened his eyes and glanced at the burned-out lantern, at the closed door, and then at me in the kitchen. He shut them again. "Onion stew. For breakfast?"

I gulped another mouthful of my unfinished broth from last night. "Flavor is even better the next day cold. Yours is right here waiting."

"You eat it."

"I plan to. But you better be up and ready to go by the time I'm finished. Getting home isn't going to be as quick—or as fun for you—as yesterday's trip."

~*~

The throbbing sun veered for the western horizon by the time we collapsed back home on my family's deserted platforms. I half-crawled to a bench hewed out of new pine and curled up. My thighs and calves ached from the amount of tree climbing I'd accomplished.

Wolfe flung himself beside me. There was a red burn line across one palm where he'd brainlessly grabbed the cable toward the end of the last line. "Looks like Trinity isn't back with the family yet."

"Nope."

He blew on his wound. "I can't believe Mr. and Mrs. Joyner do that every time they visit."

I reached out and examined his palm. He was lucky it wasn't worse. "Mrs. Joyner stopped visiting after she got pregnant."

"Still. Tough lady. Uh...and why couldn't we have just walked to your home?"

"It takes a lot longer. There's a couple of undercut ledges and sheer drop offs on the way."

"Hmm."

"Also, we'd run the risk of Heathen attacking us."

"Dove, I'm a Heathen. What a dumb reason. You're telling me we could have just hiked?"

I shrugged. "Thought you were pumped about the zip lines."

"I changed my mind. And about that stew, too. I'm ready for some, even cold. I've never been so starved in my entire life. I'm already skinny enough and look like one of those stick bugs—"

"Trinity!" New strength surged through my muscles at the sight of my cousin emerging from behind the rusty camper in the distance. I leaped over Wolfe's legs and flung myself against the rail. My eyes scanned the junk piles and nearby forest. Where were the others she'd found at the Braes?

"Oh." I stumbled back to the bench. "She's alone. You...we were wrong."

Wolfe patted my hair a few times while we waited. "Hey, Trinity. How were the tunnels?"

My cousin stood before us, her usually intricate loops of shining braids were now fuzzy and dull with tunnel grime. Her torn pantleg hung like a flag, and mud streaked her tunic front. Yet her dirt-smeared face pulled into a tight grin.

"Hideous. It doesn't matter because…beautiful news. The lost have been found."

6

I launched myself off the bench as if I had wings and my destination was the moon. "You found Mom? And Saul? And Grandpa? And—"

While I bounced in circles, Wolfe swung Trinity off her feet. "You found them. You found them! I said you would!"

A small potato blurred past my shoulder. It hit Wolfe's ear and burst into pieces.

"What did you not understand about my warning, Heathen? Put my cousin down."

Gilead stood on the ladder's threshold holding three rabbit carcasses. Micah, further down on the rungs, scowled past my brother's hip. The crook of his arm supported a pile of pine cone-sized potatoes.

I scooped up the largest fragment of potato off the floor and chucked it back at my brother. It flew wide. Micah snorted at my aim.

"Let it go, Dove. Don't fight. What does it matter if the jerk throws potatoes at me? Because your family is OK. That's what matters." With a grimace at Micah, Wolfe retreated to stand at the top of the back-entrance ladder.

Trinity stepped over the starchy mess and sank onto the pine bench. She laid her head back as if her hair coils were heavy. "No, no, Dove. You guys don't understand. I found *some* of them. Not everyone."

My glare switched from my brother to my cousin.

"Sky alive, Trinity! You said you found them."

Gilead cleared his throat. "Explain. Where have you been searching, Trinity? And what have you found—or not found? Was it Saul? You girls were supposed to wait for me here."

I summed up the situation for my brother so Trinity could get back to more important explanations. "The whole family has disappeared. I checked the Joyners' place for them, but they're gone, too. Trinity just got back from checking Micah's place and was telling us who she found when you barged in."

Micah trudged past an immobile Gilead to the bench. "Gone? My dad? My...my mom?"

Trinity's grime-covered body shuddered. "Micah? Your home is a terrible place to live. Terrible."

"I know."

"The dirt and complete blackness is like a suffocating tomb. There's no color or sunlight or anything to make you want to live. And the lighting...it's bad."

"I know."

I threw up my hands. "We all know. Rotten place to live. Tell about our family, Trinity. Who'd you find?"

"Jovie—"

"Only Jovie?"

"Let me finish, Dove." She held up a finger of warning, frowned at the ugly, half-moon of dirt around her fingertip, and began to shine it with the bottom of her shirt.

"Trinity! Quick. Tell us."

She sighed. "I found Jovie, Zion, Abel, and Isaac."

"Only your sister and brothers. No one else?" My question came out as a squeak.

"They're living with Micah's mom and sisters. And Millie, the Joyners' baby, was there. Every adult except Mrs. Brae has been taken away."

"Where?" My brother spoke for the first time since threatening Wolfe, his voice now deadly calm. "How could Grandpa have allowed it?"

I settled on the floor next to Wolfe's shoes and rested against the wall planks to listen. I had to know...but my hands itched to cover my ears.

"I asked Zion to tell me what happened," Trinity said. "He and my brothers and Jovie were in the camper fixing up their fort a couple weeks ago when vehicles rolled onto our property. People in uniforms got out. Grandpa let those uniformed people into our home without trying to stop them."

Gilead looked down at his hands, fisted and resting on the tops of his knees. "Because I wasn't there to help him stop them."

Trinity shrugged. "While the trespassers met with Grandpa up here, Jovie discovered the Joyners alone, locked inside one of the strangers' cars."

Wolfe low-whistled next to me and was cut off by a glance from my brother.

"Mrs. Joyner pleaded with Jovie to go hide and take care of Baby Millie once everyone was gone. So the kids hid inside the camper. Zion made them stay under the tarp for a long time in case the people in uniforms searched the place."

Gilead grunted. "Smart kid."

"When they came out of hiding and climbed up here, everyone was gone. Including my dad. And your dad, Micah. He'd been visiting that night and must've been taken by the people in uniforms, too. I think he's been lonely since you and your sister left. Maybe that's why he visited that night."

Micah fiddled with his potatoes.

"After that, you can guess. Jovie ziplined to the Joyner's place, got Millie, and brought her back home. She did her best to feed the baby and the other kids, but after a week, even Zion was worried no one had returned. He decided they should check if Mrs. Brae was still around underground, and she was. Since then, she's been keeping the kids safe and fed, although I think Jovie and Zion are really the ones in charge down there. It's quite...interesting."

Zion and Jovie were in charge? Zion was only fourteen, and Jovie was the youngest of all the children. Nice kids, but both of them were bossy. No doubt they found joy doling out the days' chores to their siblings, despite the darkness and the problem of missing parents.

Micah and Gilead exchanged a long look. My brother nodded. "Who were they, Trinity? The people in the uniforms?"

"Zion didn't know. Mrs. Brae thinks Heathen officials. Possibly cops. Or government workers."

"That makes sense." Gilead rounded on Wolfe. "You, Heathen. Your sister said there have been other Christian disappearances reported around here?"

Wolfe shifted one foot onto the top ladder rung. "Yeah."

Gilead turned to Trinity. "What was Micah's mom's reaction to the news that his dad—her husband—had been taken?"

My brother's question surprised me. What did her reaction matter to him? Gilead never cared about anyone's feelings except his own.

Trinity gazed into Micah's averted face. "A lot of

the time she seemed like she'd given up. But at other moments...she was furious. She wanted me to promise that—never mind."

Micah dropped his vegetables. He took her hand and looked at her in that nonblinking manner he usually saved for me. "What did my mom make you promise, Trinity?"

"She asked me to find your dad and the people who took him. And make them pay."

For the first time ever, smile lines appeared in the corners of Gilead's gray eyes. "Bullseye."

7

Trinity faced Micah another long moment then turned. "What...what do you mean, Gil?"

"Nothing. We'll assume the Uniforms are Heathen, and the Uniforms might come back." My brother approached the wall where I leaned. He waved the rabbit carcasses at the rafters. "Someone should keep watch and give us warning if they do."

His eyes, no longer smiling, drilled into Wolfe.

Wolfe's eyes widened and he pointed a slow thumb at his own chest. "Me?"

Gilead nodded. "You'll do. C'mon."

"Where are we going?"

I gestured at the ceiling. "To Grandpa's lookout tower so you can keep watch?"

Gilead nodded and stepped onto the first maple branch to make the descent to the forest floor. I moved to the rail to watch. Wolfe followed him. The dark-haired figure didn't embarrass himself on the easy climb down—a miracle, with his hurt palm and after all his climbing today.

My brother motioned for Wolfe to lead the way up the sky-reaching ladder to the platform with the bell. When Wolfe made it to the pile of leaves at the top, he turned with a grin of victory. *Clang, clang! Clang, clang!*

Gilead, his head just below the platform's floor, pulled a metal tool from his rope belt. "No more noise, idiot. Only touch the bell when you sight a trespasser.

Got it?"

"Sure. I got it—Hey!" The smile dropped from his lips.

Using his crowbar, Gilead pried the first nailed rung from the tree trunk. Within seconds he'd removed the ladder's first five rungs, letting them freefall to the ground below.

"Stop it, Gil! Don't be a jerk." I dropped from the maple's last handhold and met my sibling on the forest floor. "You've stranded him up there. He can't climb off the platform like we can."

I surveyed the five-foot gap between the plank floor and the nearest high branches—a leap I could make in my sleep. But Wolfe couldn't.

"That's the point. It'll keep him focused on being lookout. Stay off those limbs, Dove. I mean it. If I find you up there with him, well, I won't be responsible for the consequences."

"Don't prisoners at least get meals?" Wolfe's long legs dangled off the edge. The nearest rung was about ten feet below his rubber soles.

Gilead seemed to consider the dead rabbits on the ground. Then he called, "Micah? Food?"

A couple raw potatoes arced from one tree canopy to the next. Micah's aim was lousy. One nicked the platform edge and fell, but Gilead caught it. He tossed it up at Wolfe.

"Ow! Hey! They're not cooked!"

My brother ignored our lookout's complaint and thrust the rabbits at me. "See if you and Trinity can make something worth eating with these and the rest of the vegetables. I'll harvest some honey and help when I can."

Wolfe's muffled voice called down, "These are

bad. So bad. Go make dinner, Dove—and hurry."

A strong hand gripped my shoulder. "Dove. I don't want you up there. For any reason. Promise me."

I shook it off and swung up toward the sound of the radio, which blasted from the living space. "Go get the honey, Gil."

I waited until he was out of sight behind the first garbage pile, then I climbed higher—not to my grandpa's platform, but to a hidden seat, surrounded by leaves. I balanced the floppy meat in a crook and leaned my head back. From the canopy above came the occasional grating of Wolfe's teeth against the raw potato. Was he aware he wouldn't be getting anything else to eat tonight—at least if Gilead had his way? Probably. The guy had a habit of acting more brainless than he was.

I shut my eyes. Why had I tried so hard to keep my brother alive last spring? This whole month while we'd lived as Sent, he'd been pigheaded and full of prejudice and hate. Now the rest of my family was gone, and I was stuck with him.

A hint of smoke wafted to where I sat. Either he was sedating the bees at the hives or Micah and Trinity were charring the potatoes in an attempt to roast them. Probably the latter. Trinity was a terrible cook. I shifted and reached a hand to climb.

The radio voice stuttering in Amhebran halted me. "Mo-more of us taken!"

My brows twitched down. Who was broadcasting? The voice was a male's...but not Danny's warm bass. Yet the broadcast had to be from Rahab's Roof's station since the person spoke in the language only Christians used.

"Oregon's Council hasn't...hasn't told us what to

do. But I expect any day we will hear. You should stay tuned and check in often. Because we must take action. Done for now. This message will be repeated."

I flopped back. The stutterer was the garbage-bagged Christian I'd met twice before. At our last meeting, he'd loomed at the top of Portland's tallest building with the red moonlight splashing over him. He'd called me a Heathen lover. He'd threatened to throw me off the roof because of my message for peace. And now he was telling everyone over the airwaves to expect a call for action from the Council. He was angry about Christians being taken away, like Mrs. Brae was.

None of this was good. My missing family. The other missing Christians. The anger boiling among us Christians left behind. If this continued, peace couldn't. And finally, Reed and Gilead, and all those other pigheaded Christians who panted for war would get their way.

The Reclaim would begin. And what would I do?

I heaved myself up to salvage the dinner I'd eventually sneak to my friend. I paused, halfway off the limb.

Of course. I'd do what I always did—I'd do what was right. Even if "right" meant defying my brother and all the other believers that stood in my way.

8

Gilead ushered Wolfe into our living space with the same air Savannah had used when leading me into the courtroom last spring. Micah switched off the radio, and the ongoing bird chatter suddenly dominated the early morning.

My brother pointed at a chair. Wolfe dropped into it.

I bounced to my feet. "Sky alive! Are you Jezebel's brother or a slug? Have an inch of her backbone."

Wolfe grinned but spoke from the corner of his mouth, as if not sure he should be talking. "No, thanks. I'm choosing to keep all my teeth. And to continue to walk on two, unbroken legs."

A moment later, he relocated to a different chair a foot away and began to whistle an unsteady tune under his breath. My brother allowed this flea's amount of defiance and settled in Gran's rocker. He nodded at Micah, as if finishing an unspoken conversation.

"The Heathen has an idea. Tell everyone, Heathen."

The pitchy whistling warbled off. "Uh, sure. As I lay sleepless last night, alone, on your grandpa's hard floor, under an old blanket that smelled of opossum, an idea occurred to me. I'd say it was about two in the morning—"

A maple seed pod launched from the rocking

chair.

Wolfe rubbed the pink mark it left between his eyes. "To sum it up, today I'll drive to the Christian Terrorist Detention Center and check for your family. I'm the best choice to go since I'm not a fanat—a Christian."

"Brilliant."

"Brilliant," I echoed my cousin. My arms crossed. "Except I'm coming to the CTDC, too."

"We'll all go. We ride together—stay together—this time." Gilead glanced at our neighbor, who nodded.

My mouth flopped open. Gilead agreed to be a passenger in Wolfe's Jeep?

"Gil's right," Micah said. "We need to move fast on this...find out if they've been taken to the CTDC. If they aren't there then..." He shrugged.

My brother headed for the branches that led to the only working vehicle on our property. "If they aren't there, then we find the trail of the uniformed Heathen who hijacked our people, hunt them down, and take back what's ours. Trinity, leave a note under the kettle for Micah's mom in case she sends Zion up for us. Tell her we won't be back until we all come back."

All of us back. For the first time in days, my brother made sense. I grabbed my backpack, added my jar of green pennies, and flung my bulky belongings over my shoulder. I hesitated at the rail to soak in Gran's chair. My hammock. My parents' marriage certificate on the worn tabletop I'd eaten off of since babyhood.

No, I wouldn't give into the lump in my throat and go teary-eyed. Because I'd be back. Like Gilead said, we'd all come home.

~*~

The cop car eased over the pavement and headed toward our parked Jeep. I pulled up my floppy hood, worn ragged by Gil's head years ago. Next to me, Wolfe slid his dark glasses onto his nose and drummed a soft pattern on the wheel in time to my brother's quick respirations. Micah hunkered on the floor behind me, barely breathing, his beard jammed between his knees. Trinity was also silent.

The car came nose to nose with us, slid past, and turned out of the parking lot.

I swallowed when it disappeared down the road. "You'll stay here, Wolfe. I'll go inside and ask instead. Since it's my family."

"Sure...jailbird." With that cryptic warning, Wolfe exited the Jeep.

"I'll be right back." He gave a little wave and sauntered toward the CTDC—the building where I'd spent several weeks last spring.

Wolfe understood my familiarity with the exact shade of pink on the walls, the ripped mattresses, the cardboard-tasting food, the guards. And equally important, he knew that the other occupants of this vehicle were clueless that I'd ever stepped foot inside the CTDC before.

"The slug grew a beautiful spine after all," Trinity commented.

Micah uncurled to sit up straight. Gilead hummed.

I threw a look of question at my brother. *Why are you so cheerful?* I turned back just as Wolfe's black shirt disappeared behind the CTDC's shaded glass door.

My knees jiggled up and down and sweat trickled between my shoulder blades. The sunlight oozed over my skin like molten lava.

The few other vehicles coming and going in the lot lined themselves up in the shade of the bordering, dying pine forest, far away from our chosen spot. We'd parked in a hostile corner next to a garbage bin that reflected the heat. Shards of glass from a broken bottle glinted on the black tar, an excellent buffer between us and shiny cars with fat tires visiting the terrorist center.

Trinity sighed. "This is an ugly spot. Filthy and hot. It looks like someone threw up on that metal bin."

Where was Wolfe? Why didn't he return with an answer? Yes, they were here. No, they weren't. Either way, a ten-second response. What took him so long?

Micah retracted his head back through the Jeep's open side. "It sure does, Trinity. And it smells like someone threw up. You think we should have brought something to drink?"

Wolfe kept water bottles stashed behind the back seat, but I didn't offer up this information. Gilead's hum grated on my nerves.

I kept my squint on the CTDC's front doors. "How come you wanted Wolfe to drive us here?"

The humming stopped. "Mom and Grandpa are missing. It's not just Uncle Saul, who might have forgotten where we were or wandered off again. Knowing the whole family is gone changes our priorities. We've got to find them, even if that means using a Heathen to help us track them down." He continued his tune.

His words made sense...but why was he acting happy?

I clamped my lips together, folded my arms, and willed a figure to step through the door.

"Hey Trinity—isn't that your dad over there?

Between the pine trunks?"

"My dad? Really, Micah? I don't see anyone."

I slid over the seatback, shoving under Gilead's armpit. "Where, Micah?"

"You know, on the other side of the cars. Next to the pines. You don't see him? Keep looking...huh...I thought. Oh well. Never mind."

My eyes narrowed. No human was there. Why had Micah lied?

I swiveled around in time to catch the glint of the CTDC door closing and a gray pantleg disappearing inside. I returned to my chair and readopted my fixed squint.

Micah spoke over my brother's wordless singing. "Even boiled pond water would taste all right about now."

~*~

My brother eased his bulk onto the pavement next to the bin.

My eyes burned from staring at the doors that reflected the setting sun. "Are you going in after Wolfe?"

He stooped to gather a palmful of glass shards. "'Course not. We're hungry and thirsty. Micah and I'll track down something edible. You stay inside this vehicle. Promise me."

Micah bobbed his head and bounced on his heels like his sister used to when excited. Then he bounded after my brother and slipped behind the veil of pine trunks.

I refocused on the CTDC exit.

Trinity leaned forward. Her shudder shook my

chairback. "This is an ugly spot, Dove. Even if a person removed the building, the pavement, and the garbage and tried to replant nature, nothing would grow. It's too—what are you doing?"

"I'm going to find out what happened."

"Find out what happened to our moms? Or to *him*."

I paused in swapping my homemade shirt for the skimpy, cream-colored garment Rebecca had left behind in the glove box. "Him? You mean Wolfe? Our friend who has allowed himself to be beaten and bruised by Gilead in order to help us? The person who delivered food to us every single day we stayed in Sisters? Who—"

"OK, I'm being a jerk. I've been around Gil too much."

"Do you care, Trinity, that Wolfe's stuck inside?"

"I care."

"Do you?"

"Yes!"

"Good. Check behind the backseat."

With a gasp, she surfaced with a water bottle in each hand.

I waved off the one she thrust at me. My thirst had been jolted away by my hammering heart.

I would go inside the CTDC, even though the occupants would recognize me on sight because this factory-made shirt wouldn't be enough to convince them I wasn't the jailbird who'd lived inside a cell last spring. I would never be able to disguise myself enough. Unless...

I gripped my cousin's raised arm. "Trinity? I need your gift. Turn me into a Heathen."

9

I clutched the Jeep's side mirror, whose reflective surface distracted me from finishing my prayer. My blonde hair waved in willow-leaf curls and framed a face that wasn't mine. This couldn't be me.

I brought my face closer. My eyes stared out from the huge, dark smudges, like Diamond wore around her violet eyes. Only my gray irises were still mine. And my scowl.

I smiled—and winced—practicing what I would do when I questioned the guards inside about a missing teenager. Even though it hurt my cheeks and lips that stung from Trinity's brutal pinches to make them pink.

"Hurry," Trinity whispered. "Micah and Gil will be back any minute, and then you won't be able to do this."

I released the mirror and shouldered my heavy pack. I was stupid to wear the recognizable bag, but it'd been with me through so many nail-biting moments of my life. I couldn't not bring it now.

I tried to hurry toward the building, swinging my stiff, tattooed arms like a normal, godless girl, but then I tripped and almost face-planted. Trinity had done too good of a job tightening my pantlegs with borrowed metal car clips. The material gripped my legs in a stranglehold, the way the godless women wore their pants.

"Don't rip them, Dove. And smile!"

At the hissed command, I glued on the fake grin that made me groan. A man exiting the building eyed me a second too long. My reflection glinted in the glass behind him. Too many teeth showing.

I readjusted my lips, stepped through the doors, and stopped. My homemade soles pressed the shiny white squares underfoot. *Go ahead, Dove. Walk. Move forward and ask.*

My feet refused to march toward the lone woman inside behind the desk. I wasn't prepared. My heart hammered against my ribs while an icy sweat broke over me.

I hadn't prayed—hadn't consulted with God about coming inside to ask. Should I hurry back to Trinity and pray? Better yet, I could run into the woods and keeping going until I reached home.

The woman's lazy voice broke through my dizzying panic. "Yes?"

I tugged, but my shoes adhered to the threshold.

"Yes, miss?" The familiar woman in the uniform shuffled papers on her desk. She hadn't looked up. If only she would never look up.

My hands fisted and unfisted. I ripped my unwilling soles off the tiles and approached the desk. "A boy...I mean a man...somebody came in here a long time ago. Today, so not that long ago. He didn't come out. Why? I want to know."

The bear-hipped woman looked up. The black eyes above her snub nose widened and then narrowed.

"His name?"

I moistened my bruised, upturned lips. "Wolfegang."

"His last name?"

Sky alive! His last name was Pickett, the same one I'd borrowed when I'd been arrested last spring. The moment I said his full name, she'd remember and know who I was. I continued to smile into the unsmiling face.

She leaned forward, as if she rooted for something in my features she couldn't quite find. Something familiar she didn't see but guessed was there. "You don't know the full name of the person you're here to find?"

"He wore a black shirt."

Her eyes slid to my arms and lingered on the tattoos.

I tugged at Rebecca's shirt. If only it had long sleeves. If only its owner were here, drilling this guard about Wolfe's whereabouts instead of me.

I squared my shoulders the way Rebecca did. How would she, a gifted speaker, handle this suspicious female? I'd watched her yield her gift enough that I should remember.

She'd be confident. Yes, and she'd flatter this woman, make her think she was her friend. And she'd appeal to the guard's sense of rightness, even if this uniformed human was Satan's.

I envisioned myself four inches taller. My blonde strands were black, and I possessed the power to persuade others with my fantastic words.

I marched forward two paces. "You are a good person because you chose this job to protect and help people. So, you'll help me. Yes or no, did you see the guy in the black shirt come in?"

Why didn't the woman relax her face and cough up the information I wanted? Had I said it wrong? I smiled bigger and shifted back a step.

She rose and pushed a button on the radio that hung from her waist. "What was his last name?"

I retreated another step. My grin stretched wide, the cool air chilling each tooth. *You will tell me where Wolfe is.*

"Let me guess. His last name was...Pickett?"

Even when masquerading as someone who often lied, I couldn't. "Yes."

"Pickett, it's you! I've got Pickett!" She scurried from behind the desk.

The metallic door behind her swung open, and two men in uniforms charged forward. From the fluorescent-lit hall behind them a voice shouted. "Dove...not here! Run!"

10

The guard's rough hand slipped off my sweaty skin. I twisted away and barreled through the glass doors. Wolfe's command rang in my ears.

Run!

The panic in his tone spurred my legs to move faster than my pants allowed. *Rip*. With more looseness around my knees, my strides lengthened. The excited, rasping voices dropped back.

"It's Dove Pickett! Grab her!"

"The fanatic from that show?"

"She came back like the caller said she would. She came to break out the other radicals—"

"Then quit wasting breath and catch her! Don't let her reach the woods! No, don't shoot. Not yet..."

I weaved between two trucks and kept my gaze on the sienna branches at the front of the dying pine forest. The white Jeep in my peripheral vision didn't exist. Trinity didn't exist...because if she did, and I turned my head to check if she was OK, my pursuers would see and guess.

Stay still, Trinity! Don't follow. Don't give yourself away.

The pavement ended at the pines. With a leap, I gained the elevation covered in slippery needles. From habit, my eyes skimmed the trunks as I sprinted past. None of these trees had decent branches, but I didn't need them. The footfall behind me had slowed with the increase in panting, as if my enemies were accepting defeat.

My steps didn't falter as two familiar figures slid out from behind a cluster of tree trunks and joined me. Gilead took his position to run on my left, Micah on my right. The three of us plowed through dry foliage, the Brae feet making more noise than mine or Gilead's.

Keeping half a step ahead, my brother led us into a small clearing where an unexpected, bare-board shelter appeared. An ancient truck, the type that ends up rusting on our property, crouched at its side. I swerved away, but Gilead tugged my elbow to steer me towards the wooden structure.

He wedged his knife blade into the crack of a boarded-up window. I pressed my slick palms against the door next to it, brushing against its solid lock and chain. Ominous. A prickling ran down my spine.

A guard's shout carried up the slope. "This—no, that way!"

"Please, Gil." I gestured at the incline of trees where we could still disappear.

Micah stuck his streaming face close to mine. "No. You'll see Dove. Trust us. We know what we're doing. We found this—"

My brother's hand cut the air in a slashing motion. *Silence*. Then it reached out and hauled me through the window opening.

My hands and knees knocked against the cracked cement floor. I rubbed the sting in my elbow where it'd scraped against a strange, sharp corner. Half a dozen steel, chest-high boxes lined the wall where I crouched.

The guys' silhouettes dropped through the square hole into the stifling smokiness that burned my nose and throat. With a squeak of wood against wood,

Gilead replaced the board over the window. An artificial light chased away the sudden, pitch-blackness.

I blinked at my brother who pointed his flashlight like an accusing finger.

"What—are you doing—in the trees?"

I crossed my arms over my heaving chest. "Since you were too chicken to go into the center after Wolfe, I did it." I left out the part of being recognized as a Christian and escaping into the woods for safety. That part was obvious.

Tap. Tap. Someone was at the door.

Gilead cut off the flashlight beam.

"Let me in," Trinity's voice demanded in Amhebran.

"Could be a trap, Gil."

He disregarded Micah's caution and removed the board to allow Trinity in. He dropped her next to the steel box, being more careful to avoid its sharp corners.

"Anyone see you?" He replaced the window cover and switched on his light.

"Of course not. I'm not d—" My cousin's hand released the capped water bottle she clutched, and her backpack slid unnoticed onto the crook of her arm.

I turned and found myself gazing into the blank eyes of the biggest elk I'd ever seen.

Micah strutted forward and grabbed its antler. "See him? He's dead. Don't worry. You're safe."

I rolled my eyes. The elk's severed head was mounted on the cabin's wall and surrounded by a sea of antlers and a couple of skulls.

Trinity quit hyperventilating and sniffed. "Deer meat?"

"Neat, right? See what me and Gil found!" Micah

moved to one of the six metallic, waist-high boxes that lined two walls. He threw open the door of one as if producing a miracle. *Tada!* Inside, rack after rack of shriveled brown meat dehydrated in its pungent essence.

Creak. A rough rectangle with crude red letters shifted on its hook on the rafters above.

ELK JERKY FOR SALE.

Plastic bags of meat swayed in the blast of warm air from the smoker.

"Eat up, everyone. Dove, what's all that greasy gunk on your eyes for?" Gilead grabbed handfuls of elk strips while Trinity presented a water bottle to Micah.

With my back against the locked door, I slid down it and chugged from my water bottle. I splashed the few drops left over onto my face and rubbed. Soon black grease covered the bottom third of Rebecca's shirt.

With a final swipe, I sat up straighter. "Gilead. You and Micah need to cut out the secrecy. It's obvious you two planned for Wolfe to be arrested because you didn't choose to ride in his Jeep for the pure joy of staying together. You were way too eager to accept his plan that he go inside the CTDC. I know for some reason he's being held there against his will. And you're responsible."

Gilead swallowed the mass in his mouth. "And now he's out of your life. I'm not sorry."

A warmth crept up my neck and then climbed higher. My bruised cheeks and lips throbbed.

He leaned closer. "Now that you're done being distracted with Heathen, we can focus on finding Mom, Grandpa, and Trinity's parents. And Micah's dad." He ripped off more meat and chewed.

Trinity quit tracing the elk's missing body with her finger. "But...aren't they being held in the terrorist center? Like Wolfe is?"

With a clenched jaw, I shook my head. "Wolfe followed through with what he said he'd do. He found out our family isn't there. He shouted, 'Not here!' when he heard the guards run out to arrest me."

"Arrest you? Is that why you were running?" Micah frowned. "They can't arrest you just for being a Christian, can they? Anyway, you don't look like one wearing that."

I fingered Rebecca's ruined shirt, my cheeks aching with another wave of heat.

How dare Micah ask me for answers when he'd been an ally in tricking the rest of us into coming to this place...and in getting my friend arrested. Although I didn't understand the guards' eagerness to arrest me either. They'd recognized me as Dove Pickett, but why were they so fired up to catch me? I'd done nothing wrong lately...or had I? Had I broken any laws?

Before me, Micah's dark head morphed into Lobo's older one. Lobo, nearby in Sisters, searched for me. Fuming over my breach of contract. Calling the local CTDC to find out if I was there?

Even if Lobo had asked them to arrest me, that didn't match up with the guard's words as I sprinted for the woods.

She came back, like the caller said she would. She's here to break out the other radicals...

I removed a clip from my ripped pantleg and pointed it at Gilead. "Someone called the CDTC and told them I was coming. Someone reported I would attempt to break into the center and release the prisoners. No doubt this same someone told the center a lie about Wolfe—the reason he's stuck."

"I'd never hurt you, Dove. Think. Would I ask those Heathen cops to lock up my own sister?"

"You confessed you're responsible for Wolfe being taken."

"That's different." He stood. "Finish eating. We're leaving for the Council."

Micah continued to fidget with his bottlecap. He squinted at the sign overhead.

I leaned forward. "Micah? What did you guys do?"

He started. "I...my family..." He withered under Gilead's menacing scowl.

"Trinity?" I murmured.

She clasped Micah's narrow shoulders. "Tell us. Dove and I need to know. We're worried about our family too. This..." She gestured at the mutilated elk head and beyond. "This whole mess is awful. Ugly. Make it better. Us knowing the truth makes it better."

"Enough!" Gilead plucked bags of jerky from the beams as if harvesting fruit and shoved one at Micah. He threw the rest into his own pack. "We all want to know about our families, and we'll find answers at the Council. Let's head to Mount Jefferson and speak to the leaders about what they know. And we can join in the training camps." He moved toward the boarded-up exit.

I lurched to block him. "How do you know there are training camps there, Gilead? I never told you that. The radio never said anything about training camps."

"I...I..."

I glared at my tongued-tied brother then at Micah, who still fidgeted.

"You two met someone on your hike to Ochoco, didn't you? A Christian who told you about the training camps at Mount Jefferson. Did that same person make the call to the CTDC to set up Wolfe? And me?"

"No!" Micah's fists trembled at his sides. "No, he wouldn't have tried to hurt you."

"Shut up, Micah." Fierce gray irises bore into mine. "You're coming to the Council with us."

I crossed my arms. "I'm staying."

"Mom and Grandpa aren't in that building down there."

"I'm staying."

"Trinity?"

"I'm staying with her. But...Dove, what does God want us to do?"

Did she really expect me to focus on the small voice when my ears thudded with my own angry pulse? I sighed and pushed my attention beyond the scraping sound of a knife blade against the splintered windowframe. Away from my desire to hurl my handful of clips at Gilead.

I reached out and clutched at the easiest truths first. The simple ones that were always close. God is good. God is in control.

More truths flowed. God's message became clearer. I nodded. "He wants us...not to hate. To forgive and...love."

I opened my eyes at Gilead's snort of disgust. "What?"

"Love? Right. Enough stalling, sis. We're going to the Council. All four of us."

My breathing hitched. "You only want to go to the Council so you can play target practice with the other boys. So how do you propose you get me there? You can't carry me the whole way to Mount Jefferson. Unclog your ears. I'm staying here to help Wolfe."

He cracked his knuckles. "Last chance to come with."

"Staying."

"If you don't stay with me, I can't keep you safe."

"What about Wolfe's safety?"

"Fine. When you get tired of waiting for the impossible to happen, head to Micah's home. Wait for us there. And if anything bad happens to you in the meantime, it's not my fault. You're choosing this."

With a shove, he dropped over the window opening. His obedient shadow, Micah, followed.

I leaned out into the warm night air, holding my side. Their jogging figures melted into the trees' shadows.

Trinity jammed herself next to me. "They're...he's...gone?"

My fingers clenched the rotting wood of the sill. "Yeah."

"Fine. Go then, Micah. Go!" She jerked handfuls of the dried flowers from her pack and hurled the fragile stems after our neighbor, who'd left without a backward glance.

I slunk to the far side of the room where it was darkest. Gilead had taken our light source. I placed the jar of pennies from my bag under the elk head, payment for the jerky we'd taken. I wasn't a thief. Only a Christian avoiding arrest and a sister to the most selfish brother in the world.

11

Morning dawned, ending one of the worst nights I'd ever survived. I shifted aside my light blanket and turned my cheek against the rough boulder at the top of the pine slope overlooking the CTDC. With heavy lids, I watched three guards exit their vehicles in the parking lot and wander to the shaded glass entrance. Beyond those doors, Wolfe lay on a plastic mattress with rips.

"If we had uniforms, we could walk in and—" Trinity snapped her fingers.

She'd smudged a picture on the surface of the boulder we hid behind. The black, familiar eye with its spider lashes was a huge contrast to her own red-rimmed, blonde-lashed orbs.

I pretended not to notice. "It's not that easy."

"Fine. Since you're the expert, how do we break him out?"

"No clue."

"At least the guys had a plan."

"Then you should have..." I bit my lip against retorting that she should have gone with Micah and Gilead. That I didn't need her.

Her icy hand clenched mine. A throbbing motor ripped the morning quiet, and a two-wheeled vehicle roared onto the pavement next to our Jeep. In the sudden quiet, both riders dismounted.

Trinity groaned softly. "Don't even breathe, Dove.

It's—"

Forgive.

With a rush of goosebumps, I stood and waved my arms at Diamond.

Jezebel stopped spinning in a circle next to her and pointed. "It's Dove! Over there by the trees—hi, Dove!"

I allowed my cousin to haul me back down behind the boulder. Seconds later, Jezebel catapulted off the top and landed on my legs.

"Oof!"

Diamond's tight face leered down at me from the boulder. "I told you this is where we'd find the Christian terrorists, Jezzy. At the Christian Terrorist Detention Center. Makes sense. Where's the rest of them? Like that big, ugly bro of yours?"

"Gone." Trinity sighed. "Far away by now."

Lines of disappointment gathered between Diamond's brows. She flicked the knife she held shut.

My arms fell from Jezebel. Sky alive! Did Diamond not hate my brother? No. No way. She spewed violence every time he showed up in Wolfe's backyard. Threatened us with a different weapon each time. But, at the same time, wasn't that when she showed up—when Gilead tagged along?

I shook my head.

If she liked him—which couldn't be true—then that was the reason she was here now. Why else would she let Jezebel talk her into tracking me down? She didn't care if I left Sisters forever, but maybe she cared if Gilead disappeared?

Jezebel poked me. "And Woof? Where is he, Dove?"

I motioned at the CTDC.

"You mean...?"

I nodded. "Yep. Arrested as a Christian terrorist."

Diamond yanked me to my feet, dumping the kid off my lap. "You mean Wolfe is in there—behind bars—for being what you actually are?"

I jerked away and dropped behind the boulder before anyone inside spotted me. "I. Am. Not. A terrorist. I've done nothing illegal."

Her purple eyes narrowed. "So, what are you doing hiding out here?"

"Trying to decide how to break him out."

Diamond nodded. "That's illegal."

"And this is dumb." Jezebel jumped off the rock and skittered down the slope. She lifted her arms in a shrugging gesture. *What else can I do?* "I'll go in and tell those dummies he's no Christian."

Diamond carried the squirming kid back up the slope and dumped her at my feet.

"Hold the brat. I'm going to fix this."

~*~

My splayed fingers stretched to cover the sun-seared, red patches on my forearms. The burns would sting worse later, but right now they were nothing compared with my neck. I reached up and rubbed the muscles, stretched and worn from craning around the side of the garbage bin.

"There! There she is! Diamond's come out of the center. Oh. But she's alone. Where's Woof?" Still whispering too loud, Jezebel crawled forward over the littered pavement. "Dove, she can't see us over here. She'll think we ditched her. I'd better shout."

I grabbed her ankle to anchor her. "No. That's the

point. At least stay behind the Jeep another moment until...just until."

"You don't trust her?"

"She's tried to stab, shoot, drown, and crush me this summer."

"Oh, that." She dismissed the attempts on my life with a shrug. "But she's no tattle-taler. She wouldn't have told the guards on you."

Diamond made her solo trek to the group of rocks where she'd left us. She balanced on the highest one and peered around. Still no uniforms emerged through the doors. I relaxed. Jezebel was right. She hadn't given our position away after all.

The kid's whisper started back up. "But even if she did do those things to you, aren't Christians supposed to forgive and—"

I let go of her sock. "Fine, Jezzy. Tell her where we are."

But Diamond had spotted the girl, poking out from behind the vehicle. She wandered over. Instead of joining us in the minefield of broken glass and trash, she settled in the front seat of the Jeep. She stared straight ahead as if ignorant that two fanatics hid behind the garbage bin next to her.

"They won't let him go. The morons are convinced he's part of a Christian cell that's responsible for a majority of the local detention center break outs. Nothing I say will change their minds."

Jezebel rummaged around in the back of the Jeep. "Who ate the rest of my candy bar? I was saving it to give Woof."

I slouched against the warm, rusted metal and massaged my neck. "Did you at least talk with him?"

"Huh! Tried. All he'll say is, 'I know.' Repeats this

brilliant phrase to everything. I asked, 'What happened, Wolfe?' 'I know.' 'How can they think you're a Jesus Fanatic?' 'I know.' Oh, and then he kept whistling some strange tune."

"What tune?"

She whistled a few notes then broke off. "How should I know? I told you it was strange, didn't I?"

I eased my neck around to Trinity, next to me behind the bin. What was my cousin's reaction to why Wolfe—the guy who wouldn't shut up—had suddenly clammed up and would only say two words and whistle?

Her face was super pale under its tan. At my gaze, her eyes flickered up from the greenish brown stain at our feet where flies congregated. "I can't think, Dove. It's too gross here. You figure it out."

I shifted my feet away from the insect larvae. "What else did you find out, Diamond? What did he look like?"

"I swear, radical, I will come over there and beat you if you're imagining his pretty, kissable face—"

"I'm not. I mean, since he was talking weird, did he look weird—do anything else strange?"

"I told you! He just sat there. Except one time he pointed at the wall behind him. But when I asked him why he pointed he said—"

"'I know.'" I rested my chin on my knees. "Maybe someone on the other side of the wall was listening. Someone who..." Who what? What could another prisoner do even if he or she did listen in?

"I'm hot. Are we getting my brother out or not?"

Diamond's voice answered. "Sure, brat." *Click.* "I'll go start the fire in the back. When they bring him out front, we grab him." *Click.*

I lurched in a hurried crawl to the dumpster's corner and peered around. A sharp stab zinged through my kneecap from the broken glass I kneeled on so I could see Diamond. She reclined in the front of the Jeep, flicking a lighter on and off.

I slashed my arms in an X. "No way. No fire."

"You telling me what to do, fanatic? I'm in charge now. I start a little blaze, and I let you use your wind powers to aim it at those morons holding Wolfe. What? I watch TV."

The memory of Satan's wildfire that'd chased me through the Texan desert last spring scorched my skin—although the burning also could've been from the heat reflecting off the garbage bin.

"No fire." An insect clipped my ear on its way to the larvae pile. "No fire. We use bugs instead."

I reached into my backpack for a small, hollow object and held up my bee call.

12

Diamond's elbow smashed my kidney. The bee call I never left home without fumbled and fell from my lips onto the pine needles.

"Save it for later, fanatic. That's enough bees for now."

I picked up my belonging and smirked at Diamond. She hated my bee call as much as she hated me. A year ago, I'd used this tiny object to summon a miraculous horde of bees to my defense when she attacked. And again today, God provided. The amount of bees my call had already drawn to this parking lot made my old enemy edgy.

Diamond turned her back on me. "Jez, you ready for your part?"

"That's as bee-stung looking as I can make her." Trinity scooted back to scrutinize Jezebel's face. She swatted at my hand when I tried to touch the kid's shiny, red cheek. The slit eyes. The lips that appeared bloated, triple their normal size.

I breathed deep. "Uh. Jezzy? You're sure it doesn't hurt?"

The little girl snorted. "It's makeup, dumb-dumb. Or whatever your cousin used to make me look all stung up. Do I look like I'm dying? I want to see."

Diamond grabbed Jezebel's arm, but it slipped out of her grip. Both of them were well coated with bee repellant. "You can see your reflection when you get to the doors. Now tell me again. What do you say when you get inside the center?"

Jezebel spoke in a flat monotone of boredom. "Help. Killer bees. I've been stung. You've got a monster hive out there..." More energy entered her words. "...and my mama's going to sue your pants off for—"

"Stick to what I told you to say." Diamond's hand smacked the girl's backside. "Show them your face, scream something about a huge hive, and then beat it before they catch you."

"They won't catch me. I'm too fast!" She ran in place, her spine curved forward with the speed of her high-pumping knees.

Diamond grabbed the back of the girl's purple shirt and steered her from behind the boulder onto the pavement. She let go when she reached her motorized bicycle and pointed at the CTDC. *Go.*

Wolfe's sister bounced toward the doors alone.

Trinity groaned. "All my work making her look like death, and she's skipping. I'm not watching, Dove."

I thrust the tubular object at her. "Fine. It's your turn anyway to call the bees."

A low car pulled into the lot and traveled in a collision course with the skipping girl. Its fat tires screeched to a stop, the car's thin nose a couple feet from Jezebel. *Honk*! The car reversed and pulled out of the lot.

"No. This part of the plan will work, Trinity. See? She spooked away those guys in the car. You're right, she looks like death. When the guards behind the desk see her...no way they'll risk having that happen to them. The godless don't like to take chances with their lives. Their number one priority is to stay alive since they think they have no better alternative."

The lazy, droning of the bee call petered out. "So, what happens if Diamond realizes the risk is too high for what we're about to do?"

The sun reflecting off the glass door wavered. Jezebel reappeared, burst through, and sprinted for the two-wheeler idling at the edge of the concrete. Diamond hauled her onboard and took off. They roared around a bend in the road, and the kid waved at me.

Seconds later, the only sound interrupting the silence was the frequent whine of an annoyed insect. But those two nonbelievers would be back. I needed them to help me carry out our rescue plan. A plan that included bees, a blackout, and a quick getway.

My breath whooshed out. "God uses Satan's workers for His purpose too. Leave Diamond to Him. As long as we don't forget that though we work together, she's godless. And she hates us."

"Dumb, Dove. As if I could forget."

~*~

Hours later, I eased up on the fragile branch of a half-dead fir. The tree was positioned in the tree line at the edge of the woods next to the CTDC, a stone's throw away from the back of the building. From my position so high I could see my cousin on a safer branch below, the heat shimmering up from the detention center's flat roof and the almost empty parking lot next to the road.

Diamond pedaled across the white-lined pavement on a bicycle. She passed the parked Jeep and stopped at the front corner of the building. Her hand held a bulky object, which she raised to her brow as if searching for us.

Jezebel jumped off the back of the bicycle where she'd been a passenger. She also held something in her hand. Had she and Diamond been successful in gathering the supplies we needed to rescue Wolfe?

I shook my branch for their attention. Why were they being so blind? I shook it again. Finally, I made an owl sound.

Hoot. Hoot.

"There they are, Diamond! Up in that tree behind the building—the big tree in front of the deader ones. See them? Dove! Trinity!" Jezebel dashed down the narrow strip of pavement at the side of the CTDC toward us and beamed up at me, her face no longer swollen.

She clutched the power-killing piece of technology and waved it in the air. "I found it, Dove! Woof's last EMP. You'll never guess where he'd hidden it. Under a drawing of you in his—"

"And I got some bolt cutters. So at least my part of this highly improbable plan will work." Diamond glared up at us from the fir's lengthening shadow. "Why are you freaks messing around in a tree? And give me some more of that repellant, but if you drop that jar on my head, I'll drop you on yours."

I swung down, leaving Trinity above to keep summoning the bees, *if* she remembered. She kept letting the call droop from her lips. Her dreamy eyes focused far away...probably somewhere close to Mount Jefferson by now.

I handed the jar to Diamond. "What took you two so long to get back here? Pest Control showed up forever ago. Actually, they showed up so fast, Trinity and I barely had time to hide."

"Think about it, idiot," Diamond said. "This is a government facility. If they reported a little girl fatally stung on their property, then Pest Control was going to be burning rubber to get here fast. But too bad they didn't arrive five minutes earlier and catch you. Knowing you were locked up where you belong would've made my afternoon more bearable."

I shrugged. "They hunted for the source of the bees but gave up. We kept out of their way in the woods and ended up in this fir. From so high up, we'll have a decent view of people going in and out of the building, and we'll be better hidden than in front. It won't be long now until they relocate prisoners."

"How do you know?" She paused with a golden blob on her fingertips.

A shiver ran through me. From Diamond's presence? From some other evil approaching? I snatched back the jar, grabbed Jezebel around the waist, and heaved her to the lowest limb. I faced Diamond. "You coming up?"

She picked up the bolt cutters and stepped closer with its sharp edges between us. "I'm counting the minutes, radical, until Wolfe is free and I don't need you. But if you let Jez fall...I can help Wolfe without you."

She marched toward the front of the low building to her bicycle. She had returned with a nonmotorized one this time since the EMP would eventually kill all power in this area, including her motorbike's ability to work. She settled closer to the center's front doors.

I climbed up and balanced on a limb above Jezebel's head. "Either keep blowing, Trinity, or hand the call over."

She handed it. We passed around the tubular object every couple of minutes until Jezebel, unable to create a sound, attempted to hurl it into the underbrush. After that I distracted her with elk jerky from Trinity's pack. We shared the last of the water and a can of fizzy juice from Jezebel's pink purse. The bees' buzzing filled my ears while Jezebel's purse whipped back and forth at them.

"Let's quit blowing."

Evening morphed into a night of moving black dots. Finally, three official-looking vehicles with flashing lights lit up the parking lot. Their headlights glanced off Diamond, who still waited at the side of the building nearer the front doors. She eased back into the building's shadows and flicked her lighter once.

The signal.

I secured my pack over both shoulders and placed the compact EMP device in Jezebel's greasy hand. "Hold it tight. Keep your thumb on the trigger. But don't press until I say to."

"I'm not four years old, Dove. I've done this before."

I paused. How many illegal EMPs had this girl activated? I shook my head and scurried up past where Trinity studied the pricks of starlight between branches.

Perched on the high branches yards above her head, I could see the fake light radiating from the building's glass doors and the single light post at its exterior. The far-off Jeep was a white ghost next to a rectangle that was the garbage bin.

Humans in uniforms exited and moved into the building. The net masks they wore over their faces to protect from stings muffled their conversations.

My whole body quivered and pulsed with the need for action.

This would work. So far, each step of my plan had been flawless. The bees had arrived. Jezebel had terrified the CTDC workers into believing the insects to be killer wasps. She'd found a spare EMP. And now...the people in charge had decided the insect threat to be serious enough to shut down the center and relocate their prisoner—Wolfe—to a different facility.

I crouched, locating Jezebel's round head in the tree below. As soon as her brother appeared, I would give the whispered signal, and she would kill the power to the area with her EMP.

In the confusion of bees, darkness, and nonworking vehicles, Diamond would grab Wolfe and race away...or hide if needed. The bolt cutters would free him from his shackles so he could run or share Diamond's bike, whatever they decided.

The getaway was Diamond's part of the plan to figure out. My part was to watch for Wolfe to come out. Positioned higher than the rest, I was the only one with visibility to know the moment for Jezebel to set off the EMP...

"Get ready," I whispered.

Two uniforms came into view, sandwiching a figure in orange that towered over the guards. Too tall to be Wolfe. The captive also had light, frizzy hair.

I bit my lip. It was the prayer warrior I'd knelt next to last autumn at the Council. He was the one who'd cracked up under the strain of a possible attack thousands of miles away and became hysterical.

He disappeared into a car that would transfer him to a new facility. My body leaned forward as if to help him. But no, I couldn't. And Diamond would only have time to free Wolfe.

Another orange-clad figure emerged, also male. But he was way too short as well as having a beard the same shade as Micah's.

I slipped down the limb an inch. "No!"

"Now, Dove? Did you say now?"

"Hang on, Jezebel. She didn't say that," Trinity answered. "Dove, what's wrong?"

"No!" I breathed.

Zechariah Brae—Micah's brother—turned his head in the direction of my denial. The fluorescent light illuminated his wild eyes that seemed to lock onto me. He paused at the opening of the car and lifted his handcuffed hands to mime locking his lips. He tossed away the invisible key. Then, stooping, he climbed into the vehicle.

Blood thundered in my ears. *He* was the prisoner Wolfe had been too afraid to speak in front of, no doubt on the other side of the wall. They'd met before, and Wolfe must've believed Zech to be dangerous, even as a prisoner.

"Now, Dove?" Jezebel asked.

I blinked at the vehicle that held Micah Brae's older brother while something orange moved in my peripheral. Zech's mocking motion proved he didn't mind being locked up as a Christian terrorist. He thought it a joke. Was he here by choice?

"Now?"

Sky alive! It was *Zech's* fault that Wolfe was captive. He'd made contact with my brother and Micah during their journey to Ochoco and set up the traitorous plan. Yes, it made sense!

The third vehicle door slammed, locking its third prisoner inside its depths.

Oh, no!

"Dove! You stop messing around and answer me! Tell me when to activate this dumb EMP!"

Three unformed officials next to the cars turned. One pointed at the group of trees where we hid. "There's someone back there!"

"I heard the shout, too. Let the dog check first."

A canine barked and cut through my shock. A four-legged body bolted down the strip of pavement towards us. Its padded feet thrummed closer, its excited panting louder, following our scent.

I dropped down past Trinity, snapping branches in my hurry. *Jezebel. Jezebel, on the lowest branch.*

Jezebel screamed.

My hands wrapped around her wrist, and I pulled to get her higher.

I couldn't. She was too heavy. The thick-bodied dog had jumped and latched onto Jezebel's leg or shoe. It dangled, its back feet clawing against the fir's trunk.

My branch bucked as Trinity dropped onto it. She reached for the girl...

Pop. Crack. The branch's ominous breaking noises grew worse, but I tightened my hold. There were shouts. Running footsteps. Beams of light.

The skinny, bee repellant-covered wrist slipped from my grip. I held Jezebel's palm. Her fingers. Her fingertips

No! She fell with a nightmarish thud onto the pavement. The dog's shaggy bulk leaped on top of her.

"Hey-o up!"

The canine bounded aside at the approaching official's shout. The wolf-like snout pointed at the girl's still body.

She rolled onto her side.

I breathed again, and Trinity exhaled in a whoosh. She pulled at me, gesturing. *Move to the roof.* I scrambled up a few layers of branches and leaped.

I cleared the gap to the building and rolled to a stop on the flat rooftop next to Trinity. Flashlights lit up the darkness below where the guards had caught up with the dog.

"It's a little kid!"

"Is she alone?"

"I dunno. Seems to be. But I thought I might have seen something in that tree. The branches were moving."

"Wind?"

I squeezed my eyes shut.

"Maybe. There's no one there now." The man's shoe scraped the ground as he knelt. "You hurt, little miss? Who'd you come here with? There's a hornets' nest around, so you shouldn't be here, especially at night."

"I like hornets. And it's a free country. I can be here if I want to be. Go away—you messed everything up. Put me down!" Jezebel's angry demands faded as the cops carried her to the front of the center.

I raised to a crouch. From the corner of the lot, the Jeep's engine revved. Interior lights gleamed. Diamond had ditched her bicycle and was exiting in the Jeep. Alone, since I'd messed up Wolfe's escape.

As the vehicle turned onto the road, the garbage bin in the corner exploded into flames. The brightness reflected off the four vehicles, and for a moment,

Wolfe's profile appeared inside the third one behind glass. His head was bent forward, resting against the seatback. Giving up.

13

Burn down the center? If I had agreed with Diamond's plan, no Picketts would be wearing handcuffs now. So what if a few extra Heathen had gotten hurt in a fire? Satan's side could spare a few casualties. I hugged the pink mouse purse I'd found in the bracken. It was heavy with the dropped EMP I'd shoved inside.

"Trinity, wake up. Look, it's Wolfe's Jeep. His grandma drove it here. She'll be trying to get Jezebel freed."

My cousin dragged herself over to peer off the roof at the pair exiting Wolfe's ride in the early gray dawn. "The grandma's not alone. Diamond again—wait, or is it? The hair's wrong. And the eyes are more almond shaped."

"That's Jessica. Diamond's cousin." I forced myself to keep crouching on the rough roof until Wolfe's grandma entered the CTDC.

I sprang up. "Jessica. Hey, I'm up here. Meet me at the back of the building. I'll come down. Trinity? Some help?"

My cousin grabbed my hands. While she lowered me, she didn't remind me of last night's failure or question my decision to talk with this new godless arrival. All she said was, "Get over more. You're going to electrocute yourself—watch the generator."

I avoided the smooth plastic with fraying cables

attached to the back wall and let go. My drop penetrated through my worn soles. I limped toward Jessica.

Her arms were crossed tight. "Lobo's been looking for you. You're in trouble."

I stopped short. "I'm already in trouble."

"You'll be in worse if certain people catch you here. And where are all the bees Diamond warned were around?"

"They took off. Why are you here?"

"I happened to be in earshot when Diamond broke the news to Mrs. P. about Wolfe and Jezebel—you know that they're now considered terrorists by the government and can't come home. I figured that might be something the missing survivalist Dove Pickett was involved in. So? Are their arrests your fault?

"No. Yes. I don't know. I messed up the plan last night, but—"

"No kidding? And your God didn't fix your mistake for you? Ha!"

I blinked.

When I was nine, I'd made friends with a skunk, the closest thing I'd ever had to a pet. Each day I'd waited for the fearless creature to wander on its route around the garden. Each day, when it reached me on my sitting stump, it'd eat grubs, straight from my hand. Then one afternoon, after four months of this routine, he'd toddled up to my stump, turned, and sprayed me in the face for no reason.

I blinked again at Jessica, recalling the sting of the spray...but worse than the watering eyes and stubborn stench, I remembered the unfairness of that blast.

Jessica had hinted she wanted to know about God. I'd looked forward to her visit for two months, had planned out what I wanted to tell her. And now...

She raised the palm-sized electronic the same way she had the bulky camera a thousand times last spring in Texas. But her sneer was worse than I'd ever seen. "Don't forget to remind me how much He adores you. Really, Dove, can't you fight against your religious brainwashed upbringing a minute and think for yourself? Your god has checked out. He's not even real. I can't believe—"

"Do you really want to know who I blame for the mess I'm in?" I would not stand silent and be unfairly skunked again. My chin lifted, and I pointed a shaking hand at the CTDC building.

"Everything that's awful in this nation is the fault of every so-called human who doesn't have brains to accept the truth, who laughs about God. Do you like being a puppet? Because that's what you are. You're all puppets! Satan uses you godless all the time to do horrible stuff, and you're too brainless to recognize it. I'm done trying to convince you...and everyone. You're evil! And if you want to fight against God, go head. But you fight against me."

My glare flickered between the obtruding camera and Jessica's paling cheeks. I opened my mouth to continue doling out blame, but Jezebel's voice stopped me.

Jessica lowered her electronic and stumbled back.

"Dove! Dove! They lost Woof! Last night when they were driving to the other detention center, something happened to him. All the other prisoners and guards are missing, too. They found the cars on the highway headed south, but—"

"Jezebel, hush up. There's popcorn in the Jeep for breakfast. Go eat it."

"I don't want popcorn, Grandma. I'm telling Dove how they lost Woof. And how even if they find him, you can't do nothing to bring him home since he's in trouble for—"

"Jessica?"

"Sure, Mrs. P. C'mon, you. Popcorn time." As if eager to get away, she pried the clinging kid off my waist and herded her across the pavement.

Jezebel glared around Jessica's arm. "It'd better be the cheddar kind. Dove, I told Grandma not to worry 'cause you'll find Woof."

My eyes fell under the older woman's gaze. "I'm...I'm sorry that—"

"What're you sorry for? Did you convince my grandson to march into that center, demanding the whereabouts of Christians?"

"N...no."

"Did you drag my granddaughter to this place against her will?"

"No, but—"

"Then save your sorrys. You're a radical, which is a jagged enough pill for us normal folks to swallow. But personally, I'd say things have gotten good and interesting since you barged your way into my grandkids' lives. You grow pretty decent salad fixings, too. Not a bad thing with food costs bleeding us all dry. But even so..."

I held my breath and waited.

"I'm taking my yard back. Foreclosing on your garden. But I'll pay you for the strawberries and beans already sprouting." She grabbed my wrist and pressed a wad of green paper into my palm. It was money. Paper money.

Her etched mouth under her Jezebel-like eyes

pulled into a smile. Still holding my wrist, she leaned closer. "I hear what Jezebel says about you. That girl won't give it a rest about what 'my friend Dove' says. You don't whine about being roughed up a bit. You don't hurt people neither. It seems to me, if more fanatics were like you—not going around, pointing their hateful fingers at everybody—let's just say I'd invite them into my yard anytime they liked."

Shame forced my gaze to my shoes. Minutes ago, I'd pointed at Jessica and the godless nation and shouted they were responsible for everything horrible. I'd called them evil puppets. And declared I'd fight against them.

A horn honked. Wolfe's grandma let me go. "Need to bum a ride?"

"You're going to get Wolfe?"

"From where? You know where he's at?"

I shook my head. Zech probably did, but I didn't.

"Then not a lot of reason for me to waste gas money driving around searching. He's alive, though. When one of my own stops being alive, I know. I feel it. Here." She tapped her stomach. "But, all the same, if you see him, have him call me."

I nodded.

"Good enough. Jezebel, touch that horn again and I'm locking you back into that detention center!"

14

Feet planted, arms crossed, my cousin and I stood at the edge of the highway that twisted through the dying pine forest. We could follow the road north toward Mount Jefferson and the Council. Or we could head south in the same direction the CDTC cars had been headed when Wolfe disappeared.

Trinity swiveled to face north where a black mountain peak poked against the blue sky. "You only want to go south to find Wolfe."

"And you just want to go north to rush after Micah."

Her cheeks flushed brighter. "We're supposed to be hunting for our family. Gilead and Micah will have figured out by now where family is."

"Gilead's head's full of moss. And he cares more about revenge on Wolfe and training for an imaginary war than finding our moms."

"I don't think—"

"One of the prisoners I saw last night was Micah's older brother, Zechariah. The guy is supposed to be on Mount Washington, keeping their village safe. Instead he shows up here. Here, Trinity! I'll bet you my last piece of jerky he ran into Gil and Micah when they were hiking home to Ochoco. They complained to him about Wolfe tagging along, and Zech hatched up the plan to get rid of Wolfe and urged them to go train at the Council afterward."

"But if Micah's brother was being transported to a detention center, that means he was captured."

"On purpose."

"Dove. No one gets captured on purpose."

"Except him. Zech was laughing at us last night, glad to be transported. And today, he and Wolfe and the other Christian guy went missing on the way to the other detention center. That's what Jezebel said."

"I know. I heard that part from the roof."

"And remember Diamond told us Wolfe kept answering 'I know' to everything she said? Odd."

"Yeah. But Wolfe's an odd guy. Plus, I wouldn't answer Diamond either. She's liable to knock your teeth out."

"No, Trinity. Wolfe was saying 'I know' because *he knew* something! Maybe something about our missing family. It was like a code."

"Why use code? Why didn't he just tell Diamond what he knew?"

"Because I bet Zech was in the next cell listening. And Wolfe understands that he's a dangerous guy. They met before. He's gotten us both arrested."

Trinity threw up her hands. "Dove, Wolfe is gone. Give up on him. Unless...does God want us hunting for him?"

My shoulders sagged. I couldn't lie. "You're right. Going after Wolfe is my own idea." I stood up straighter. "But He hasn't told me to chase after Gilead and Micah either. Has He told you?"

"You know I don't hear Him like you do. But I've never been on a mountain before, and I'd like to. To stand with the world spread out beneath me. To be so close to the sun and stars."

"And so close to Micah," I muttered.

How could I make her understand the danger that awaited me at Mount Jefferson? That it was home to Melody and Stone who'd betrayed me, trying to poison me in the desert. Not to mention the Warrior, Reed Bender, who'd been responsible for murdering our grandma. I'd explained some of this to her, but she thought I exaggerated about Reed. That no human would sacrifice Gran's life for strategy.

"Trinity, you agree our first priority is to find Grandpa and our moms?"

"What a lame thing to ask. Of course. And my dad. But to discover where they are...our only hope is to find that info from the Council."

I bit my lip. *God? Why do you remain silent?* New beads of sweat trickled down my temples.

I opened my eyes, struck by an idea—my own...but still better than my cousin's. "We go to Portland, to a place called Rahab's Roof. Our people's radio station broadcasts out of there, and they'll know if there's information about missing Christian families. They might communicate with other stations too."

"Go to Portland? The City of Roses?"

"Uh, more like a city of cement. But if my friend Rebecca still lives there, she'll help us."

"And us going there has nothing to do with finding Wolfe?"

I glared at her.

"Fine. Which way to the City of Roses?"

"Portland." I pointed north.

She brightened. "And on the way, we can stop at Mount—"

"No. No stops at the Council. And we can't walk to the city since it's too far. A car is coming now. Hide."

~*~

I tightened my grip on the swaying treetop. The old-fashioned vehicle with the boxy trailer attached snaked around a curve far below. "Another truck coming, Trinity! A good one this time—this is our ride. Let it fall. Now."

Ker-bam!

A blue jay screamed, startled by the heavy limb Trinity, out of sight on the ground, released to fall across the road. I scrambled from my treetop lookout onto the forest floor and sprinted through the underbrush. I stopped once to smash my stomach against the ground when the engine I raced drew level to me on the road. It rolled past.

"Hurry up, Dove!"

Back on my feet, I hurdled a dying larch.

"Faster." Trinity's hushed voice became clearer. I saw her. She was only ten yards away now.

My cousin crouched behind a bush, her back to the driver of the truck who emerged from its interior, grumbling through the *chug, chug* of the engine. He disappeared around the nose of the vehicle. There were some dragging, scraping noises. The roadblock Trinity had created wasn't light.

"Were you napping, Dove?"

I blew past her and leaped onto the back of the wood and metal trailer that hitched to the truck's back. With a dull *thud,* Trinity clung to the trailer's half-wall next to me.

"In you go." She grabbed the top of my pants and shoved me up at the rectangular opening. I swung into the trailer's dim interior and froze. It was full of horse smell...and a horse. Something I hadn't been able to see from the treetop because of the rusted roof.

The animal's mammoth hindquarters hadn't twitched when I dropped inside. With slow and steady movements, I reached up to haul Trinity in. Still no hoof shot out and struck me.

Slam. The driver must have cleared the debris and gotten back in the truck. Trees inched past. The truck and trailer picked up speed.

Trinity dropped over and fell onto the aluminum floor inches from the hooved feet.

"Sky alive!" She scrambled up and hugged the side wall perpendicular to me. "A cramped horse trailer with an actual live horse? This was your 'good one?'"

Two dark, liquid pools gazed at me then blinked. The horse parted its velvety lips and blew its breath out in a slow gush. Besides the rope, he wore a black cap on his head. I'd never been this close to a horse before, but this couldn't be normal.

The horse's lower legs were cocooned in padding.

"Holy Moses, Trinity, look at his socks. The godless do crazy things. But quit complaining. It's not like we're holed up with one of their dogs. Just ignore it."

15

We pulled away from the endless rows of creeping vehicles. Soon they fell out of sight, and the road under the trailer's wheels became a dirt path pocked with gravel patches and potholes.

"Quit messing with that horse, Trinity. We need to jump out. The driver's turned off the main road, but a sign said Portland is only two miles ahead, so we can walk." I pulled my head back through the trailer opening that didn't have bars. "Wh...what have you done?"

The sad-eyed mare blinked. Dazzled by its own transformation. Its mane swooped in a diamond pattern across its glossy neck. The coarse tail hairs clung together in a giant braid and then separated into a hundred twisted wisps. Fancier than a horse in a fairy tale.

I'd been focused on our route...too focused. "You even polished its hooves? Trinity. The driver...he'll know someone was back here."

"I'm not undoing it." She bit her lip. "Does it matter if he knows?"

I turned back to the trailer opening. "Not really. C'mon and climb over. He's slowed for the gravel. I'll go first."

I hit the rocks, skidded forward on the unstable surface, and rolled. *Scraaape.* Trinity touched down on the road. Cupping my forearm that burned like fire ant bites, I skittered off the gravel and down the bank into the ditch.

Trinity swiped a blob of red off her chin and handed me my backpack I'd dropped midroll. Our shoes rustled through the dry weeds toward the dull roar of traffic. Mammoth buildings huddled in the distance.

Portland.

~*~

Shelters lined the pavement where we walked. Heat radiated like the inside walls of a stone oven. I scouted for cover. How could we stay out of sight in such an open, busy mess of people, vehicles, and dwellings?

"This is the City of Roses?" She nudged a dusty grate in the concrete with her toe.

"Trinity, get behind." I shoved her to the back of a plastic sign dominating the sidewalk. A leathery-faced female in faded green was closing in. A predator sniffing out prey. Her zigzagging path was a direct line that ended at us.

She shuffled to a halt, inches away, and aimed an unsteady finger at Trinity. "You...you...freak. Jesus freak. I'll...I'll—"

"Get away from her." I squared my shoulders and gripped my invisible armor. "You have no power over us. Go!"

The woman recoiled as if stabbed. "The army! The army has arrived." She stumbled down the sidewalk in her knee-high boots. "The army. Fight her army..."

When she rounded the side of a nearby building, I

touched Trinity's homemade sleeve. "She's one of the thousands of workers Satan has stationed in this city, and even his weakest will spot you as a Christian from a block away because of how you're dressed. You need camouflage."

"Different clothes? Like what the godless wear?"

"Like I'm wearing."

"How?"

I fingered Rebecca's cream shirt. The greasy repellant spots. Crusty bits of blood from my scratched elbow. Car grime. One ruined shirt was not enough to share. Where did the godless get their factory-made clothes? At factories?

This was the stuff Wolfe knew. Not me. Wolfe, whistling, pedaling away on his bicycle to buy my family a radio...from where? Wolfe, currently missing, possibly with Zechariah Brae...here in Portland? Dead?

No.

As I turned away from my cousin, my blurring vision snagged on a word on a building straight ahead. *Jonah's.*

Jonah? I blinked and took a step toward the tan, peeling paint. *Saint Jonah's Thrift Store.*

What was a thrift store? But my grandpa's name. That was promising. So were the colored articles—clothes—visible beyond the glint of sunshine on the store's glass window.

"Dove? Unclog your ears. I asked you how."

"This way." My feet hurried toward Saint Jonah's Thrift Store but began to drag at the threshold. They stopped.

"We're going in there?"

I nodded.

"Inside there?"

I didn't answer or move.

"You scared?"

Jingle, jingle. I grabbed the tarnished bell rigged to the door I'd opened, no doubt positioned to alert a person inside of our entry. My grandpa used a larger bell back home for a similar reason.

With a small, tense movement, I darted inside a half a step. A jumble of colors and shapes collided before my vision. The odor of a thousand musty objects filled my nose. I swung around to escape, but Trinity stood in my way.

"Incredible. Like the junkpile...but...wow." She slipped past me and moved forward, her arms outstretched to touch every item.

The fake, cool light illuminated a junkpile of electronics and unknown objects. Books and cardboard. Shoes. Then shirts. A million of them, all lined up. Row after row of shirts.

I jogged after and steered her away from a pink jar laced with primroses but no lid—worthless. "Leave that junk. Here. Choose a shirt, and let's go."

The bell jangled. Before it ended, I pulled Trinity down next to me on the scratchy, stained floor.

"What!" One hand clenched mine. Her other hung onto the chestnut-colored sweater on the rack she'd been stroking. "What's wrong, Dove?"

I answered in the softest whisper. "Someone else is here. Stay low. I sense evil. Don't you?"

"No."

Melody would have. If she were here, we would be having an unspoken conversation about danger. Our communication had formed that unbreakable bond between us.

I shivered.

But Reed had broken it. He'd twisted my friend with his persuasive words and strategy, transforming her into my enemy. Now Melody shared his sinful dreams of taking back America, and she'd thrown away our friendship in the process.

"Hurry up and pick one." I crawled down the narrow path between metal racks. I parted the hanging shirts to peer through.

No one was in sight.

I waited another few seconds and then eased back onto my thighs. As I scooted back a few feet, my palm pressed down on…the toe of a shoe?

It was a cloth, machine-made shoe. Above was a too-tight pant leg, followed by a sky-blue shirt with the words *Saint Jonah's Thrift* stitched on the chest.

The baby-faced girl in the blue uniform gazed down at us. My cousin spared a glance before peeking at the rainbow, paint-splatter shirt in her own hand.

"Looking for something?" The stranger's tone expressed no welcome. Yet her round eyes that matched her shirt didn't glare or widen in surprise that we crouched on the floor of her store.

I shifted my hand off her checker-toed shoe. "No."

Trinity squinted up. "That's a vivid shirt you have on. Peacock color."

Vivid. The shirt was the same type of blue that Rebecca had worn the first time I met her.

"Sure." The stranger directed a bored thumb over her shoulder to a limp curtain at a bare patch of wall in the clutter. Still no hint of disgust or welcome appeared in her pale features. "Dressing room's there."

"To camouflage myself?" Trinity held up her handful of bright clothes.

The girl shrugged. "For whatever."

"I'm ready, Dove. Keep up."

We began a fast crawl toward the curtain, leaving the worker behind. I hesitated in the open space where the row of shirts ended and crouched behind a table holding a ratty bear toy. No one was in sight except the worker, who wandered toward the front part of the thrift store.

"Dove. Get in here!"

I obeyed my cousin's whispered command and snapped the privacy curtain shut behind my back. "Make this the fastest change of clothes in your life, Trinity."

She tossed a plain, black top at my head.

Before I finished pulling it on and shoving Rebecca's ruined shirt in my pack, Trinity posed before me. The image of a godless female.

"Sky alive. I...I'm a worldly woman. Mom would kill me. Look at me, Dove. What would Gran say?" She stepped closer to her image in the splotchy mirror. She touched her hair that rested in a long braid over her shoulder, which her new outfit left exposed.

The splattered shirt of neon colors was nothing compared to her tattoos. It'd been over a year since I'd seen her arms uncovered. Her skin represented every color of the rainbow. My name appeared at least four times amidst a jumble of waterfalls, galaxies, and garden plants. But at least Micah's was nowhere.

I frowned. "There's such a thing as too much ink, Trinity. Why so many?"

"You were gone a lot. I had extra free time."

Her thin fingers curled over the leaf-green letters D-O-V-E on her forearm that ended in the scrolling strawberry vine. "I guess I missed you."

I swallowed and rubbed my own inked shield and

sword. "I get it."

"You got lonely too when you were away?"

"You have to be alone to be lonely. That was rare."

"Because God stayed with you?"

"Him...and others. But I understand because your gift," I held up my tattooed shield and sword, "was a part of you I carried the whole time. It helped me."

A bell jingled, and I slashed the air for silence. No time for mushy, cousinly sentiment. Had a new wicked creature entered the building? Or had evil departed? I clenched the dank, orange material I hid behind in concentration. But Trinity's was the only whisper cutting the silence.

"Do we leave the money for the clothes here on the floor and walk out?"

I rummaged in my pack. My fingers closed around the wad of paper Wolfe's grandma had given me for my crops. "I don't know. I think we hand it to the worker."

"Why?"

I shrugged. "We just do."

The wide, cluttered room still appeared empty of humans except for the worker in blue. She leaned behind a flat counter near the bell-rigged door. Keeping close to the room's perimeter and ducking behind larger objects when possible, Trinity and I crept to where she stood.

The worker set aside the flat electronic that was similar to Wolfe's. Her eyes stayed on its bright images.

"Um. Here. Is this enough? For what we're wearing? Take it." I thrust the wad of paper money between her and the screen.

The blue eyes snagged on the money and then

focused on our torsos. "Tags."

"Huh?"

"You still got the tags on."

She raised a sleek, handheld device and aimed it at the white cardboard dangling from Trinity's armpit. She directed it at me. A little light at the end of it flickered red. "And I wouldn't go flashing this sort of cash around. Dangerous."

With one hand, she separated a piece of money from the rest. With her other hand, she pointed the device at the wall behind us in a vague sort of way. The little red light at its end flashed four times. Paused. Then flickered twice. Four flashes. Pause. Two flickers.

Trinity gasped. "What—"

I elbowed her into silence and backed away. Past the electronics. Past a ripped, red chair. At the shoes, we turned and sprinted away from the front of the store where the worker had become engrossed in her flat electronic.

I hurdled a basket of blue plastic ferns and headed for the rectangular patch of bare wall between the shelves at the back of the store.

Trinity and I threw ourselves against the back door, and it squeaked open. We escaped into the blinding sunlight. Columns of stacked crates teetered in the shade. We dropped down behind them.

"Dove. That was Amhebran code. How did she know Amhebran?"

I released the sweaty roll of paper money back into my pack. "I don't know."

"But the red flashes. She told us, 'Escape. Back way.'"

"I'm not blind. I saw."

"Why did she say that?"

Why? I swiped the new, stretchy shirt material across my damp forehead. "She didn't. We made a mistake. There's no way that worker's a believer or part of the Sent...is there? Let me check something. Stay here."

"No, wait—"

Trinity's glare burned between my shoulder blades as I crept to the front of the building. The worker either knew Amhebran, or she didn't. If she did, she had warned us. *Escape.* Fine then. Where was the danger we had to escape from?

With my quick steps forward, the hairs on my arms pricked. I braced myself in the ominous atmosphere. The blood in my ears thrummed while my body begged to retreat. *Other way.*

I eased around the building's corner.

Three people with crossed arms leaned against the peeling paint at the doorway of Saint Jonah's. The leathery female from earlier stared at the scummy glass. Two lanky, sunburned males in various shades of green waited with half-closed eyes.

Less than an hour ago, the woman had shouted something about us being an army. Was this hers—her troops united, here to meet us...to hurt us...to stop us? How long until they found out the Christians they thought they'd cornered in Saint Jonah's had slipped away and wouldn't walk out that door?

I inhaled the thick air and stumbled backward, knocking into a body at my back.

Trinity! We grabbed at each other and sprinted along the back of the building to a nearby road. We turned the corner onto another and slowed.

My breathing quickened at the sheer number of people and vehicles in the sunlight. Evil. Evil everywhere. Evil hunting for us. A whirlwind of it, surrounding and overpowering.

"Dove. Shalom, Dove?" Trinity snapped her fingers in my face. "You brought us here to look for a building. What building?"

The rectangular shelters wavered in the heat, smearing together into solid walls. They formed a box. A trap.

I scrubbed my face. "A...a tall building. The tallest. And keep your eyes open for a tall, dark girl with bushy hair. And W—" I clamped my lips together.

Trinity's dreamy expression sharpened. "And Wolfe?"

"I...quit looking at yourself in every car mirror we pass, Trinity, and pay attention. Find a tall building with windows. Lines of windows."

I grabbed the back of my slick neck and held on. The city pressed closer—too wicked, too huge.

God. This is too hard. I can't do it alone—

Not alone.

My lids fluttered open. The whirlwind of people and cars against the gray background stilled. And in front of me stood Trinity.

Trinity Strong. Uncle Saul's daughter. Uncle Saul, who obeyed God and understood His will so clearly that he'd located Rahab's Roof last spring without a moment of confusion.

How had I never noticed how much Trinity resembled her dad? With the same eyebrow that arched higher than the other. And the storm-gray irises, created to cut through ugliness and spot potential beauty...and truth.

"Dove, why are you grinning like an idiot? What? What do you see?" She swiveled.

I secured her face between my palms. "I see...you."

She batted me away. "You're sun damaged."

"You have a gift, Trinity, the same one your dad always had—seeing more than the rest of the family."

"Seeing beauty and potential for it? A dumb gift."

"You're as hardheaded as Gilead. Don't you see? Your dad never fully recognized what God gifted him until he spent time alone…wandering, really listening to Him. In that time, he changed."

Her nose wrinkled as if her father stood in filthy rags before her. Her body slumped. "You're right. Dad changed."

I fought the urge to shake her. "Yeah. He changed. For the better. He realized his gift was to recognize truth instead of mere beauty. God's truths. His will. Last year, your dad showed up out of the blue to save me from rattlesnakes. He appeared again to drive me to Portland. He was able to locate Rahab's Roof. He discovered his gift wasn't about recognizing God's handiwork. His real gift was recognizing God himself."

She shook her head. "My dad didn't find the Brae boy that he searched for. He searched for seven years. If he understood God's will so well, then why didn't he find Micah's brother right away?"

I shrugged. "It wasn't God's will for him to know. God stayed silent on that. He reveals what He wants to and not everything...and only what's best for us. He also expects us to pay attention to what He does reveal."

"So?"

"So pay attention."

"I'm not my dad, Dove. Or you."

"No. You're you. God hasn't sent me to Portland

by myself. I'm not doing this job alone."

"You have God."

"And I have you."

She blinked a few times. "I can't help. I don't know where to go or what the building even looks like."

"Try asking God."

"Dumb."

"Have you ever tried?"

"Dove—"

"Do it. Now. Don't worry about an attack. I'll keep lookout. And He'll protect us while you talk with Him."

"How do you know?"

I grabbed her pack away and slung it over my own shoulder. "Quit stalling. Now c'mon. Ask Him."

She threw me a dagger look and crossed her inked arms.

"Ask Him, Trinity Strong!"

After one last glare, she bowed her blonde head.

16

I held my clear bottle up to the late afternoon sun. Not a drop left. I pressed the hot plastic to my lips anyway. My parched throat convulsed while my eyes continued to scan the sidewalk and the humans who traveled it.

Trinity stayed motionless, the rays beating off her pale hair. A wrinkled woman with bags jostled her in passing, but my cousin's sunburned lips continued to twitch in her sweat-drenched face.

A man more ancient than my grandpa paused next to us. His twisted mouth released a blast of nonsense words. Then he spat at my shoes and shuffled off, still mumbling. I dropped my bottle into my bag and eased my weight from one aching foot to the other, avoiding the evaporating spit mark on the pavement.

Honk, honk.

A boxy vehicle passed—the same one that had passed us two times before. I reached my hand out to Trinity and then dropped it.

No. No one had exited the vehicle. I would give her a couple more minutes, until the sun touched the highest roof at the horizon, before I interrupted her attempt to hear from God. But she needed to hurry it up. Because when night fell, we couldn't be caught standing on this open piece of asphalt in this wicked city.

As I pivoted in a slow circle scanning the terrain,

green moved into my peripheral vision. I jerked my head around. The green wasn't from nature—no trees or plants grew in this part of the terrible city. It was faded green clothing.

"Trinity!" As I shook her elbow, an enormous white and blue vehicle displaying the sign *Electric Metro Bus* rolled to a halt on the road next to us. Despite its wall of windows, the bus blocked the green-clad, evil trio from my sight.

"Trinity. Enough trying. It's OK, you can give up now. Really."

The bus continued to loiter, but my legs tensed, ready to run. Had our hunters sensed us on the other side of the obstructing vehicle?

My cousin's gray eyes opened. "I'm not you, Dove. Don't expect me to be."

"I don't." I craned my neck. Was that person darting around the back of the bus wearing green? No. Gray. Gray and black with gold. I continued to chew my peeling lip.

"And I'm not my dad."

"I know, I know. Your dad has a beard."

A quick pain seared my scalp. "Ouch! What, Trinity? Why'd you pull my hair?"

She flicked her chin at the orangey sun setting in the opposite direction of the bus and our hunters. "Pay attention, Dove. We go that way."

17

A sharp edge jabbed between my ribs.

"Dove, you awake?"

I batted away the cardboard piece. "Sure."

Even though my eyes were open, I still reclined in total darkness. As I yawned and struggled to sit, a stack of cardboard slithered down with a whisper.

Thunk.

"Ow. Quit moving," my cousin's voice demanded. "You're making a bunch come down on my shoulder."

"It's just cardboard." But I stopped trying to squirm up. "Do you hear any more cars leaving?"

"No. It's been quiet a long time. It'll be middle of the night by now."

"Then it should be safe to enter the building. Let's go. Umm. Which way is the entry chute into the building?"

"Sky alive, Dove! You're the one who's been in this horrible, suffocating bin before. Which way did you and my dad go?"

Which way had Uncle Saul led?

I glanced up, half expecting to see his silhouette appear as it had above that other snake-infected bin. Was he off surviving on his own now? Or with Mom and Grandpa, being held somewhere miserable?

This was the reason I was here now—to find out.

I shoved a stubborn obstacle from my path and plowed through until my palms pressed the warm, metal side of the bin. There was a thin lip, then...the chute entrance.

"Found it, Trinity. And the stack under the opening is high enough so I don't have to lift you." I shifted aside.

She grunted. Cardboard slid. Her shoe clanged against metal, and her voice echoed back from the tunnel above. "You mean *I* don't have to lift *you*."

A muscle in my cheek quivered at the same comeback Jezebel would have flung at me.

Oh, Jezebel. Wolfe...

Alive. He had to be alive. Right God? You won't let him have begun eternity away from me. Away from You.

I heaved myself up onto the slippery metal. Seconds later, I dropped into cooler darkness. The sharp smell of chemicals assaulted my nostrils.

Trinity steadied me. "Now what?"

"Rahab's Roof...well, it's up. On the roof."

I sensed her eyeroll.

Arms outspread, I eased forward around blind obstacles. A bucket. Possibly a ladder. "Last time with your dad, he started to sing. Really belted out a hymn. To offer himself up as a distraction—a sacrifice—so the guards would be drawn to him and leave me so I could make it up to the roof."

She stayed silent a few seconds. "Is God telling you to sing? Or sacrifice yourself?"

"No...you?"

"No."

"Then we make a run for it. And if you see a guard or cop—"

"Keep running."

"Right." I cracked open the door.

Hurry. The moonlight gleamed against the

polished stone and grillwork. We passed the glowing exit sign, and as I jogged up the endless stairs, my burning thigh muscles triggered a memory of urgency. Of being God's messenger, racing to win against Satan and his plans. But this time, I didn't risk delivering a message. Instead, I sought to find one—or at least a clue to where my family had been taken.

"Where—are—the—guards?" Trinity doubled over on the last stair. Her hands braced against her knees.

"Don't question…God's provision." *Let's go.* Still panting, I stumbled through the door into the empty hall.

A third of the way down the dim, less polished corridor, the sounds of my cousin's footfall stopped. I spun around. She clung to a section of grillwork. Her reflection glowed ghostlike in the pane of vertical glass window.

"Admire your outfit later, Cousin. The way to the roof is this way."

She rested her forehead on the bars. "Is this what it's like?"

I skittered back to her side. "What? Is this like *what*?"

"Standing on top of a mountain...like where the guys are right now. Is this what that's like? Seeing the world spread out at your feet. A galaxy of lights below, pricking the earth."

Despite the idiocy of pausing in this hall and my impatience pulling me toward the roof, I joined her at the window.

I bit my lip. Was it?

Rebecca's little brother, Joshua—a music obsessed city rat—had once compared this Portland to the

Council hidden on the top of Oregon's Mount Jefferson. The goofy kid had claimed the two civilizations were identical. Gullible Melody had believed him, and Rebecca had cuffed him for his lie.

I shut my eyes to the warm lights of the city at night. Beautiful, despite the wickedness of the people they represented.

Mount Jefferson's peak was Christian turf. At night, a person at the Council could see snow patches swallowed by shadows. Rows of crooked shelters huddled against towering stone cliffs. There was no light, except for what the moon gave to the people in animal skins who crowded together for warmth. And Warrior Reed, who accused me of belonging to Satan, now lived there.

I opened my eyes. "No. A mountain isn't the same, but it's just as dangerous. Now c'mon before a guard shows up and one of us has to become a singing sacrifice like your dad. Don't forget, I'm tone deaf and don't sing."

~*~

"*That* can't be Rahab."

"No." The male wearing black clothes and a garbage sack wasn't Danny, the other radio guy, either. I eased further behind the concrete blocks.

Trinity thrust her elbow into my side, toppling me into the open. "Well, hurry up and ask him for information. That's why we're here."

"Shish." I regained my hiding place. Silence settled as the alarm we'd triggered below in the stairwell cut off. I put my mouth near her ear. "That so-called-

Christian, well, he and I aren't friends." Last time we'd met, he'd considered throwing me off the roof.

I waited. But I still didn't hear Danny's cheerful "Righto!" No Rahab skittered around the rooftop like a city squirrel. Only the grudge-holding stutterer I'd heard on the radio days ago lurked at this broadcasting station. Was he alone up here?

Trinity got to her knees. "Fine. I'll go ask him."

"No. Wait." I glanced up at the dark sky and nodded. "You'll be safe. He doesn't know you and has no reason to hate you. Just don't tell him you're searching for Wolfe or anyone who's godless."

"I'm not searching for Wolfe."

"And stay away from the roof's edge. In case."

Trinity picked her way toward where the guy worked with his wide back to us. His large hands adjusted something overhead on the metal tower.

"Shalom."

He jumped. "Sh...shal...who are you?"

She answered in Amhebran. "A Christian looking for my family and answers. They've gone missing. And since you're part of our radio station, I figured you could tell me what you've heard about the disappearances."

"A Christian? You look Heathen. And like someone...familiar." He stepped closer to her.

My breathing hitched. But he went past with purposeful strides toward the roof opening that led to the stairwell below.

I crept to the other side of the concrete pile to stay out of sight.

He knelt at the roughhewn board I'd replaced over the rectangular opening. His fingertips skimmed its grain. "You set off the alarm?"

"Yes."

"You're alone?"

A block's edge dug into my palms.

After a three-second delay, Trinity shook her head. "God's with me. You?"

"Yeah. God. Only God. The others got taken. Danny. And Rahab. Ambushed on a supply run. Your family's been taken, too?" He shook his head and stood. "Bad things happening here. And in California. And Washington."

She nodded. "Ugly things. Who's responsible, have you heard?"

"Heathen. Their military. Terrorist hunters. Rounding up our people. Scared of us."

"That's dumb."

"N-not really. They should be scared." A slow smile stretched through the stubble. He swung an invisible sword and pointed it at the block pile. "We'll strike. Soon. Real soon. And get Rahab and Danny back. Your folks t-too."

With a pounding chest, I ditched the blocks and headed for the broadcasting crate's shadows. I eased myself around the metallic power box connected to cables that snaked the rooftop.

"How do you know all this?" Trinity asked.

"I hear things. Messages. From the Council. From the west coast. Believers are angry. Excited to fight. More disappearance means more Christians joining our ar-army."

"So, the more loved ones go missing, the more believers decide to do violence. Gil was right..." Trinity trailed off, no doubt remembering Gilead's satisfaction when he heard how angry Mrs. Brae had become when her husband was taken. "The view and the lights are amazing from up here."

Lights? Was she at the edge? I shifted up, but Trinity was out of my sight line. Her next question came from the other side of the cement blocks. Safe.

"Have you heard if the Heathen military is holding our families around here?"

My sigh of relief froze. This was the answer we'd come for.

His voice rang out louder than before, without its time-consuming stutter. "Trinidad. That's a town in California, near the ocean. The coast."

In a weary movement, I let my head fall back against the broadcasting crate. California. A place I didn't know and had never visited. A place too far to walk.

Clatter. With my slight jostle, an object rolled off and hit the pavement beside me.

"Wh-what was that?"

Trinity's voice was louder now, too. "Oh, uh, something fell? Haven't you noticed all the meteors and comets and the strange things coming out of the sky..."

I scooped up the fallen earpiece and shoved it next to the microphone on top of the mess of yellow plastic strips. Footsteps approached.

He was coming! Run. Hide. But my body stayed rooted in place. Handwritten words in block letters stared up from the strip of thin, yellow, plastic twisting across the broadcasting surface.

FIGHT. WIN RECLAIM.

I untangled the strip that was the replica of the warning barricade I'd slipped past in the stairwell. There was more handwriting. Around the familiar word, *CAUTION*, a message scribbled in black ink filled the spaces. I slipped the ribbon free of the jumbled radio equipment and held it up to the dim moonlight.

Heathen government retreat at Black—an illegible scrawled word—*Hold enemies for ransom. FIGHT. WIN RECLAIM.*

Invisible fingers pressed down against mine. A warning.

I wadded up the yellow plastic and shoved my fist behind my back. A single breath later, a callused grip enclosed my bicep. "It's y-y-you! Heathen Lover. I knew it! Is she your sister?"

At his tug, Trinity winced and stumbled forward.

The vicelike fingers cut into my arm. A cool numbness grew in my hand and up past my elbow. I stomped my foot. "Let go of her."

"So, your sis-sister distracts me while you sabotage my broadcasting equipment. Did you mess with my generator?" His foot nudged the cables. "Or are you here to send out another message on the radio? Was that your smart plan?"

My free hand clenched the balled-up message tighter behind my back.

With an unexpected smile, his grip relaxed. "I might help you broadcast. D-d-depends on what type of message you're sending this time."

With a rush of warmth, my fingertips began to prickle.

Trinity, rubbing her freed wrist, eased toward the roof opening. We'd gotten the information we'd come for. Nonbelievers held our family captive in Trinidad, California, near the ocean. Time to go, Dove.

I hesitated. He'd let me go when he hated me. What other type of message did he think I'd give our people except for peace? I gestured at Trinity—*scram*—and squinted up into the hopeful, thick-lipped smirk. "Explain what you mean."

His arms crossed and pulled the garbage bag tighter across his chest. "I'll help if you're going to give another message like your last. Re-remember? You said, 'Everything that's awful in this nation is the fault of every human who doesn't have the br-brains to accept God.' And they announced your name."

I swallowed twice before my voice rose above a mute whisper. "I never meant...how did you hear that I said that?"

"The radio on the enemies' stations. I patrol their news." He smiled. "You called them brainless puppets. Believers are joining the c-c-cause because you've switched sides."

"What cause?"

"The cause to fight the godless. And take back America."

No. No! How could I have been so stupid to vent my frustration to Jessica when she had a camera pointed at me? All that I'd done before, risking my life and shouting to Oregonian Christians to love the godless...I'd cancelled it all out. It meant nothing now.

God, how could You have let me be so rash?

He scooped up the microphone. "A further call to pre-prepare? For the Reclaim?"

"No." I knocked the electronic offering from his hands. "I was angry. I never meant to say what I did. I never will again."

His grin vanished. His gaze lifted from the microphone on the rooftop to my arm behind my back. It flickered to the top of the broadcasting surface with its lack of yellow. His scribbled message on the yellow plastic was gone.

"Sabotage," he whispered.

A lifetime of living with Gilead sharpened my reflexes. He lunged, and I jumped.

He missed me by inches. "Give it back!"

My descending foot came down on the top of the broadcasting platform—not as efficient as a springy branch...but good enough. I sprang off of it, higher into the air, and reached.

"Oof." My rib knocked against the steel bar while my arm flung over another. I dangled from a section of the metal tower half a second until my feet discovered secure footing on a lower strip of steel. I began to climb.

"Hey! How did you...you—" His grizzled jaw hung slack as he stared at me, at least eight feet higher than the top of his head. He reached for the lowest foothold.

Now I was ten feet higher. I stopped climbing. My eyes measured the distance to the top of the cinderblock pile. A couple yards beyond that, Trinity's colorful upper body hesitated at the uncovered roof entrance. At my nod, she dropped out of sight into the stairwell.

I held my arm out and let the crumpled strip of yellow unfurl from my sweaty palm. Grasping its end, I whipped it in the still night air.

My pursuer halted, his pupils fixed on it. "Mine. That's mine."

"Number one rule of a messenger. Don't leave your message laying around." I whipped the yellow plastic at his upturned face to accentuate my point. "Keep it near. Keep it safe. Or you lose it."

He sprang up for it and missed. "Tr-traitor!"

I shoved the plastic inside my waistband. Judged the distance again. And leaped.

I made a bullseye landing, but the cinderblocks shifted under my weight with a groaning scrape. Pain twisted through my ankle. I tumbled off the pile and limped for the roof's rectangular hole. Footfall thudded behind me, and my pursuer exhaled in grunts, as angry as a half-starved bear.

My escape hatch loomed ten feet away...five feet...two...

I plunged into the void. My fingers slipped off the roof's edge, and I tumbled to the ground, smashing onto a bulk softer than the floor.

"Even Jovie could have landed that better. Get off." Trinity squirmed out from under. "Are you—"

"Fine. I'm fine."

Loud breathing from above brought me to my feet. My ankle could bear my weight without much pain, so I yanked open the door to the stairwell and shot through into the empty hall. The alarm blared—the second time we'd set it off tonight.

We pelted over the dusty tiles toward the closed door to the far stairway.

"Fourth time tonight!" Through the deafening ringing, a booming complaint issued from the other side of the closed door. "Fourth time! The Department of Workers' Compensation better know it's paying for the hearing aids I'm gonna need after..."

I skidded to a halt and grabbed Trinity. Her hands covered her ears.

We backpedaled, whirled around, and sprinted toward the door we'd come through. But those stairs and the roof weren't an option, so we turned the corner to a new hallway. The tawny moon didn't cast its light so directly through the windows we passed. A few paint cans laid scattered near a lumpy, oversized garbage bag in a patch of shadow.

I paused, staggered, and half fell on top of the bag.

"Ow, *ow*," someone under the sturdy plastic mumbled.

"We're Christians, too," I whispered. "We need to hide. The guards are coming. Help us!"

"Go away."

"What do we do?" Trinity swung back and forth between the end of the hall and the bag.

I kicked the solidness inside the black sack. "Do you have more bags? Quick, so we can hide, too."

The trash bag trembled. A muffled voice replied, "More bags would look stupid. Suspicious. Go away."

Trinity gasped. "This door! It's unlocked!" The door she'd touched opened a crack.

I darted after her into the thin slice of black and eased the door shut. "Lean against it."

"I am."

"Oh. Good." I hadn't been able to tell where she was since it was pitch dark inside the space. I wound the plastic with the message around my wrist, using my teeth to tie a hard knot. "How did you know this door was unlocked?"

"I just knew."

The alarm cut off. "Finally!" a distant voice called in the throbbing silence. I quit nodding at Trinity's excellent use of her gift and braced myself against the smooth wood that cooled my cheek.

The guard's voice became louder. "That's the fourth time tonight that alarm has gone off. I tell you, a wire's not right or something. Go call the alarm company and let them figure it out. My legs are tired of looking."

"Shouldn't we try all the doors? Maybe a thief's hiding behind one?"

Trinity's respirations came quicker.

Make the guards go away. Please.

"Go ahead if you like. We've checked a million doors down below. What's up here to steal? Paint cans? That bag of trash? Naw. It's a loose wire misfiring somewhere in the system. This has happened before, but go ahead and check if you want."

"I think we should."

"Go head, I tell you! I'm not stopping anyone."

I locked my elbows to hold the door in place in case someone decided to push the other side. A distant door slammed. I blinked in the darkness. Had the guard found another unlocked door in the hallway to check? Or had he exited to the stairwell? Maybe one guard had left, and the other was trying doors in the hall.

I pressed my ear against the coolness.

Tap, tap tap.

My head jolted back. Someone stood on the other side of the door. Knocking.

18

"Coast is clear. Open up. Hurry. Hurry fast! Are you deaf?" The unfamiliar voice on the other side made its demand in Amhebran. The door handle clicked frantically.

I wedged my shoe tighter against the bottom of the door. With a grunt, my cousin shoved her weight forward.

"I didn't hear a stutter, Dove."

"No."

"It's probably the antisocial garbage bag guy from the hall. He sounds Christian."

"Probably." I shifted for a second to readjust the too-tight plastic tied around my wrist.

The tapping persisted. "Open, open, open."

My forehead bumped against the door. "Trinity, we've got to be clear of this place before morning. The longer we stay in this room—"

"Right. Let's get this over with. We face whoever this is. Now."

"Be ready to run, in case."

"Obviously."

We stepped back from the door, and a gangly, human figure pitched forward into the room. The scant light from the hall's windows illuminated a lanky guy with a wheat-colored beard. He scrambled off the stone floor from among stacks of paint cans and rubbed his elbow that stuck out from his too-small gray shirt.

"Ow, ow—oh, it's you."

"It's you! Trinity, it's him! He's the prayer warrior guy from the Council last September and the prisoner from the CTDC. Remember? He got into the first car during the evacuation before Wolfe did."

"Nope," she said. "I didn't see anyone being evacuated, because you were the only one that night who had a clear view of—"

"Yes, yes, but believe me, he was there! You were." I latched onto the garbage bag that rustled between his long, restless fingers and gave the plastic a shake. "Tell her. Tell her!"

He yanked, and the plastic slipped from my grasp. "What?"

"Tell her that you were at the CTDC."

"OK, fine. I was at the CTDC. But what's your plan? How do we get out of here? Every time I open a door, another alarm goes off."

"Told you so, Trinity." Again, I grabbed and shook the bag. "Where's Wolfe?"

She knocked my shoulder. "She means, why are you in this building?"

I huffed and let go. "Oh, fine. Answer her question first. Then mine."

"I...I..." The bag drifted to the floor. He pivoted, caught himself against the doorframe, and then pointed at the hall's window where the grayness of dawn touched the sky. He raised both knobby-knuckled hands to grip his scalp.

"We need to get out of here." He snatched up his dropped disguise and fumbled to open it. "I've got to get out of this place!"

I nodded. "Of course. You can follow me. Let's—"

"Go!" He yanked the black sack over his head and

charged out the door.

Clatter. An upset paint can in the hall knocked the tiles, and his footsteps ended in a rustle of plastic. Silence fell, interrupted by an occasional sniff.

Trinity held her head in her hand. "That guy's a spaz, Dove. He's going to get caught."

"I know, but...." But what if he could locate Wolfe? He could at least tell us where the guy was last seen and how Zech was involved in his disappearance.

With a cautious glance into the empty hall, I made my way to where the lumpy garbage bag hunkered.

I knelt. "What's your name."

"Chaff."

"Chaff, we'll get you out of this place if you can keep your brain together and not freak out."

Sniff, sniff. "'Kay." The sack sprouted legs, but still no head appeared.

Trinity shook hers. "He's ready, Dove. We're following you."

~*~

The pink flush of early morning filled the horizon and reflected off the hundreds of windows on the tall building we left behind as we followed the sidewalk. The gleam of water in the distance rippled with the dawn's rosy hue.

Trinity massaged her temples and muttered. "Portland. City of Roses. Not named for its gardens but its color. Not that I'd expect Dove to catch on, but me, I should have…"

I jogged to catch up with Chaff's long-legged stride. He was also talking to himself. "Not good. So not good. This is so not good—"

"Slow down, Chaff, and get a grip."

"This is so, so not good. And you—you don't even try to make it better. You, with your neon yellow and her with her rainbow shirt. Calling all sorts of attention to yourselves. Not good."

I reached out my arm that wore the message like a bracelet. "Chaff, stop a second and explain. Why were you in that building back there? And on the roof? I know you got to the roof since you triggered the alarm twice—once going into the stairwell and once coming out. The guard said the alarm had gone off four times. Trinity and I only set it off twice, so it must have been you—"

"Homicidal Christian-haters everywhere, and you're doing math? Four minus two? So not cool. Look around. This is freaking enemy territory."

I looked around. Except for a few cars in the distance, no one was about. No baking sun. No humans spitting at me. The best I'd ever seen Portland.

He continued his hunched-over walking with his bony knuckles clamped under his armpits and his frizzy beard pressed against his chest. "So, shut your lips, and blend in. Don't call attention to yourself. We'll talk once we're on the train."

"Train? Wait, Chaff. You're traveling by train? As in choo choo? Where—"

"Shut up! Everyone'll hear you. This is so not good, not good at all."

I cupped a hand to my lips. "Hey, Trinity! He's heading for a train somewhere."

Both my cousin and Chaff broke off their unnecessary jabbering to stare.

"A train? Really? I've always wanted to—" She

squinted up at his pale blue eyes that were fast becoming as red as the bulbous end of his nose. "Are you crying?"

"No." He rubbed his too-short sleeve across his cheekbones. "Maybe."

His gangly frame stumbled toward a bush that someone had planted next to a low building. He dropped and folded his lanky limbs so that he took up little space behind the scraggly foliage.

I crouched too, avoiding the cigarette litter in the three-foot patch of dirt. "Chaff, the quicker you give us answers, the quicker we part ways. It's obvious our presence is annoying you so—"

"It does." He kept his gaze on a spider spinning a web between leaves. "But I thought we'd all ride the train. Together."

"No. We're heading to California."

"Right, California. Near the coast." He shifted away from the spider. "That's where I'm going—to Trinidad. That's where the train goes."

"What? How...how did you know that we were going to—"

Trinity twisted a stem between her fingers. "Dove, we should go to Mount Jefferson first and let Micah and Gil know about our family's location in Trinidad. They could help."

"And waste days getting to the Council? They made their stubborn choice and left us. Gil told us we were on our own. You want to go running back to them, begging for help? Because if you do, say so."

Trinity touched a spot on her pack, and the leaf she'd twisted into a flower-shape fluttered to the dirt. "No. We won't go running back. You're right. He—they—left us. They didn't want us, and we don't need them. We'll do this on our own."

Chaff unfolded his limbs and stood. "Right. California. The train. Let's go."

I snapped and pointed at the dirt. "Stay put. Why are you going to California, Chaff?"

"I live there."

"You can't. Because you live in Oregon. You were at the Oregon Council last summer."

He rocked as if impatient to get to his feet. "So? The route to your state's mountain is safer than California's. The train line north gets pretty near Jefferson. I can't believe we're sitting in enemy territory while you drill me on my choice of Council locations."

I shrugged. He probably lied, but what did I care which Council he chose to attend? "Where's Wolfe?"

Trinity sighed. "Dove…"

He was fixated on the spider again. "Who's Wolfe?"

"He was a prisoner with you. Dark hair. Tall, but shorter than you. Laughs a lot...but probably wasn't laughing."

"Oh. That guy."

"Well? Where is he?"

"How should I know?"

"You saw him last. Where was that?"

"In Oregon somewhere. I'm not a compass. There were trees and a road that made me sick. He went off with the crazy-eyed guy while I—"

"That'd be Zech. Where'd they go?"

"You keep asking for answers I don't know. Do you hear me? I—don't—know! But I do know one thing. My reason for walking fast five minutes ago."

"Go on."

"The train heading to California passes through Portland this morning. As in...today. As in...when the sun gets to right about there." He jabbed at the pastel sky a sliver higher than the skyline. "The train comes thru at a certain spot under a bridge where we can get on. And I don't know when another is coming ever, so if we miss our ride to California that'll be here anytime...that's it. We might as well stay behind this bush for the rest of our lives."

I rolled my eyes, but Trinity clambered onto her knees. She faced the spot on the horizon where he'd pointed.

Chaff bobbed his long neck and jammed his hands under his arms. "And if we miss the train, it's not my fault."

Ripping himself free of the bush, he speed-walked down the pavement, hunched over to be invisible. Trinity, a streak of rainbow, stayed at his heels. With a sigh, I clamped my hand over my neon bracelet and ran to catch a train.

19

I stood under the double-decker steel bridge. The growling of a thousand vehicles rattled the metal and concrete as cars and trucks bumped along above my head. A few yards ahead, the parallels of railroad track curled around a sharp bend in the garbage-strewn rocks.

Chaff twisted his awkward hands together. "We missed our ride. It's gone. Let's find shelter for the night."

"It's still morning, and the train will be here." Trinity didn't turn to check the empty railroad tracks. "It'll be here."

Hmm. I skittered forward to touch a rail—to try and make out a vibration or rumble through the jumble of traffic, like I did with the zip line back home. Even if a person couldn't see the rider, the cable never lied. A distinct hum revealed the metal trolley was in motion.

Chaff gripped my pack and dragged me backward. "That…is the way…a person dies. Touching things she shouldn't. And not hiding when she should. And making an overall spectacle of herself." His fingers plucked at the bright plastic on my wrist.

I moved back onto dry weeds littered with trash. My nose wrinkled. *Whew,* it stank worse than a compost pile. In the secluded spot near the train crossing sign, Trinity poised at a clump of half-dead ivy. She faced the expanse of gray-blue water below.

As if oblivious to the stench, she filled her lungs and pressed against the wire fence. "In all your travels, Dove, did you ever see the ocean?"

"That's not ocean," Chaff snapped. "That's a river. Useless. It won't take us where we need to go, so get that idea out of your head about any form of water travel. We're not doing it."

"Agreed." I'd half-drowned every time I'd gotten near a large body of water, and Trinity had even less experience with swimming.

Chaff's long fingers flailed at the parallel rails. "And even if the train does come, you're probably going to end up dead anyway. Unless by some miracle you're a strong climber. Because one wrong step...that's it. You hesitate half-on, half-off the train…shalom. You're done. And you two look the opposite of strong."

The growling grumble of metal and concrete multiplied by a hundred. Trinity abandoned the water dotted with boats. "Like I said. We didn't miss the train."

He threw up his hands. "The train...a bad idea. Rotten. Forget it. It's probably not heading south anyway. Let's go."

"Get down and hide." I flung myself onto my belly behind an elevation of broken rock. An ancient orange and black engine rounded the curve and rumbled toward us, heading south.

Hooonk. The horn blasted, and my eardrums seemed to explode. A new rattling, squeaking thunder drowned out the noise of the cars as well as my own thudding heart and hyper breathing.

As we waited for the train's last boxcar, my

cousin's nails became claws and clenched my hand. But I didn't shake her off.

The last car. Try for the last car. Chaff's repeated advice from the last hour now made sense. If one of us fumbled or slipped while climbing on, we wouldn't get mashed under a close-following set of wheels.

Honk. Hoooonk.

Trinity and I scrambled to our feet. The end of the line of boxcars was still out of sight, but we began to jog alongside the tracks. She pointed at the skinny ladder attached to an open-top car. *You first.*

The train traveled slow enough, but even if it'd been rushing by at full speed, I wouldn't have argued.

Figures appeared from the other side of the chain-link fence, past the weeds where Chaff still cowered. Clothed in faded, factory-made green, a woman and two men stalked toward us.

"Christians! This is our territory. Ours. You bring your army into our city, our territory, and you're gonna get—"

Hoooonk.

I grabbed for the ladder rung. With a gasp, a jerk, and a stumble, my feet left the ground. But my body's instinct for climbing took over. I flew up the steel bars without another fumble and made room for my cousin behind me.

She transferred from ground to train smoother than I had. Together we dropped over the unroofed top of the car, landing on the mountain of gravel it held.

I leaned over the open side. "C'mon, Chaff. C'mon. C'mon."

He was galloping in an awkward lope over weeds and rocks, moving in the same southward direction as the train. I'd seen a picture of a giraffe in motion once. Chaff looked the same, with his lanky legs and bobbing neck. I'd never known why the giraffe in the picture ran. Now I knew. The giraffe was being hunted.

Trinity knelt beside me, yelling so hard her voice broke. "Grab on! Grab on! They're right behind! They're going to catch you if you don't—"

Hoooonk. Honk.

A fourth hunter stepped out from a hole in the fence line and swaggered toward the tracks. Chaff, still yards from our ladder, was corralled.

Jump now, Chaff. Jump, jump, jump...

In a flying jumble of limbs, he caught the rungs and held on. Moisture flooded his eyes—super brainless, since it blinded him before coursing down his cheeks.

"Climb, Chaff, climb—No!" I leaned forward, as if to help Chaff.

He was too far below me. I could only watch helplessly as his sunburned enemy followed him onto the ladder.

Trinity squeezed my arm. The woman and her friends jogged alongside. Two reached up to drag the struggling Christian down among them.

The pressure on my arm released, and a shower of pebbles ricocheted off the group of heads below, including Chaff's. Other than the woman pausing a moment to snarl up at us, Trinity's hurled handful of gravel did nothing to help. We needed a better weapon, something heavier to crack a skull on impact.

"Backpack!" I ripped mine off and plunged my hands into its depth.

Let me find a weapon.

My fingers closed around something solid. My bee repellant jar. I began to pull it out but stopped. How idiotic to chuck such a valuable possession away...and pointless. Even Gilead couldn't make one projectile hit four moving targets. My hand released the smooth container and closed over the object rolling around next to it. A wad of folded paper.

I pulled out the clump of money and held it in the light. Again, worthless. Too light.

My pupils fixed on the green...green...the same shade as Satan's minions' clothes. My lip curled in disgust as if my hand cradled something that belonged to the possessed godless below. A stab of revulsion hit me in the gut.

"Take it. It's yours." My hand released the faded green over the edge, and the nausea vanished.

The money, trapped so long in a C-shape, hit Chaff's shoulder and exploded into a dozen individual pieces. The wind of the train's movement wafted the paper in a flickering swirl onto the bodies around him.

Honk, honk.

Open-mouthed, the woman let go of Chaff's legs and snatched a piece fluttering onto the weeds. The others fell too and scrambled for the mess of green. Crows, getting their fair share of a roadkill.

The red-skinned man who'd been shoving Chaff's nose against the train's metal side released him and jumped off. He came out of his roll and raced to where my litter blew over the ground next to the fence.

"Quit bawling and climb, Chaff!"

Below, Chaff's bearded cheek stayed smashed against the gravel car's orange paint. His large-knuckled hands clung on to the ladder's outside rungs. His long feet stumbled across the rocky ground next to the train wheels.

"Climb!" Trinity and I bellowed in unison.

With his eyes shut tight, Chaff jerked one foot up and then the other. By a miracle, they both ended up on a ladder rung. He made his way up to where our arms extended over the side of the car to haul him in. As he collapsed next to us, our train rounded a curve, and his attackers fell out of sight.

Hooonk. We gathered speed and roared away from the steel bridge and deeper into the sunlit concrete city of Portland.

20

I dug another pebble out of my shoe and aimed it at Chaff's hooded head. The liar. *We'll talk once we're on the train.* He'd fallen unconscious before we exited Portland.

The gravel hit the strong wind from the train and fell short of his hood. Not that it mattered much if he slept or not. Between the crash of the train wheels against the tracks and the wind stealing a person's words before they were spoken, for the last ten hours, conversation consisted of gestures and shouting.

I shivered, flicked my last rock at the twilight sky, and pressed my arm against Trinity's. She'd pulled on her long-sleeved, homemade clothes over her thrift-store outfit. The only extra layer I had was Rebecca's sleeveless shirt. I shuddered under the cool blast of train-created breeze and settled my pack against my knees for a shield.

Hunkered in the pocket of protection my bag created, I unwound the yellow plastic from my wrist. My eyes scanned the words I'd memorized hours ago.

Heathen government retreat at Black—something—*Hold enemies for ransom. FIGHT. WIN RECLAIM.*

The message irritated more than the skin of my wrist. I squirmed up, adjusting my torso to rid myself of the flickers of uneasiness inside of me. My head dropped forward into my hand.

Some Christian somewhere had plans to hold

some government people for ransom. The schemer hoped to pick a fight with the godless, which would escalate into the Reclaim.

My hair flew up in gusts. I reached up, grabbed a clump, and tightened my fist around it. Well, so what? What could I do about the plan anyway? I'd removed the message from a Heathen hater's possession, hopefully before he'd broadcasted the plan to all parts of Oregon. That was all I could do. And it was better than any other believer had done to keep the nation's peace.

I nodded, looped my message back around my wrist, and tied the ends.

The uneasiness inside me grew, a noxious weed with thorns that pricked.

I undid the knot, unraveled the plastic, and squinted at the illegible word after *Black*. Black what? The scribbled word seemed to begin with a B, and it would be the name of a place, somewhere government people would go.

Black Boulder? No. The looped-and-lined scrawl was too short for *boulder*. Black...Bat? Was there a town somewhere named Black Bat?

Trinity hunched forward to read the message for the third time. Again, I tapped the unknown word. Her arm moved against mine in a shrug. *No clue.*

Even if I could decipher the word and figure out where the ransoming event would take place, what could I do to prevent it? I'd be busy in California—Trinidad—discovering the facility or camp where captured Christians were held. And after I succeeded and accompanied my family back to Ochoco, I'd return to Sisters to carry out my job of being Sent and begin my serious hunt for Wolfe. Because I would find him.

Even if Lobo interrupted with a brief trip to a Louisiana swamp.

Right. I'd stop obsessing about a stranger's unrealistic scheme to pick a fight that would lead to the Reclaim.

And I also wouldn't worry about details of how I'd accomplish the upcoming rescue in California. God had been faithful so far in my journey. In all my journeys. Why doubt Him now? He'd show me my way.

I retied my message and mashed my eyes shut. No doubt, my uneasiness wasn't from the message at all. It came from riding on a pile of shifting gravel in a jolting train car. I'd eaten a stomachful of nuts from Chaff's pack and shared his water bottle with Trinity while he hibernated, but when had I last slept? Two days ago? More?

I slid down deeper into the dusty gravel that still held some of the sun's warmth. I'd sleep until we reached California. If Trinidad was an early stop in that state, I might not even freeze to death.

Trinidad.

My eyes flew open. Odd. Odd that the stuttering Christian at Rahab's Roof had been so quick and sure with his answer that the missing Christians were being held in Trinidad. If he knew and shared his information so quickly, then other Christians must know the location, too.

Had any rescue attempts been made? Or had knowledgeable believers given up hope because attempts would be too dangerous? Were my cousin and I flying down these rails into a situation that we wouldn't be able to escape?

Had I—*we*—made a mistake?

I nudged Trinity awake and gestured to the train car. "Mistake?"

"What?"

"Forget it." I leaned back and covered my face with my pack. It was too late for a conversation of whether or not we should be going to California—of whether Trinity had paused to ask God when I hadn't. We'd both decided to go along with Chaff's suggestion we travel this route to Trinidad. No turning back.

Even though Chaff had lied. Was it a coincidence that Chaff lived in the same town where our family was being held? No way.

I yawned. No doubt he had missing family members, too. He'd gone up to Rahab's Roof, learned that Christians were being held in Trinidad, and decided to head there for the same reason we did—to scout around and figure out a way to help. He was just too chicken to tell us the truth.

Then how had he known about this train?

I shifted.

God, I'm exhausted. I'm going to sleep now. I'll wait for You to tell me what to do—

Turn back north.

Hooonk. Honk, hooonk.

I lay rigid. My exhaled air, trapped under my pack, created a warmth on my cheeks. Had I heard right? Or had the train's simultaneous blast of horn screwed up my listening?

Turn back and go north? How? Why didn't God want me to continue on to where my family was trapped?

Did He expect me to leap up this instant, grab Trinity's hand, and jump off this moving train into unknown territory? Then what? Walk the thousand miles back?

I strained my ears. There was the metallic roar of wheels against track. The jostling clang of train cars bumping along. Nothing else.

With clenched fists and burning cheeks, I stayed put...and let the train carry me farther south.

21

When I shifted the pack from my damp face, a cloudless morning stretched motionless above. An unmoving sky? No roaring or jostling below me? The train had stopped.

As a bird twittered, I began to sit up, but Trinity rolled and pinned me against the gravel. She smashed a finger to her lips.

Yard bull, she mouthed.

I froze. When we'd been under the steel bridge in Portland, Chaff had warned us about trainyard bulls—railroad cops. Pacing back and forth, he'd flailed his hands in the air to emphasize his words. "Anytime the train halts, a yard bull hunts. When the train doesn't move, you don't either. Don't even breathe. Stay hidden until the train gets going again at full speed. And if a bull catches you..." He'd gulped. "Enjoy Heaven."

Yard bulls were "the most violent cops in the world." They were "cops who'd maim or mangle any human they discovered hitching a ride on a train." And they didn't attack only Christians but godless stowaways, too.

Kids...elderly strays. Any trespassing human could become a victim. Yard bulls lived to spill blood and torture. It was their own form of twisted religion.

I craned up to see the other side of the gravel mound where Chaff slept. If a yard bull prowled below, would the guy spaz out like he had underneath Rahab's Roof and get himself caught? If he did, Trinity and I'd need to create some space between ourselves and him.

His area—the place where I'd spent yesterday tossing rocks at his head—was an empty hollow. Chaff was gone.

With a lurch, the train began to creep along its track. After an endless minute of staying still, I crawled, careful not to sink too far in the loose debris, over to the body-sized, shallow crater where he'd slept. New divots made by his long feet in the gravel led from the hollow to the top of the ladder.

Trinity crouched beside me and mimed chattering teeth. She pointed at the ladder then at the neighboring boxcar. Chaff had gotten cold and found a more protected hiding spot inside that car? We were all cold. But would hunkering inside a gloomy boxcar make so much difference? Probably not. More likely the antisocial guy relocated to avoid us.

I curled up in his abandoned hollow, jostling along with the train while unfamiliar scenes, such as stretches of roads in dying grass, flew by. A glint of water at the western horizon. Mammoth evergreens that touched the sky. Clusters of low, sad buildings—one with a picture of an unrealistic bear eating a sandwich that claimed to be a California eatery. Then more stunted pines.

I twisted the yellow strip in a circle around my wrist. I was unable to obey God. Unable to believe anything I did would help my family. I wasn't supposed to be here...but I was here anyway.

After a long while my skin began to sting and turn pink. I repositioned so that my own shadow could offer protection from the sun and wind. Then my jaw fell open.

Trinity poised upright on the top of the gravel mound with her arms out, as if in flight. She shook back her blonde head with its long braid and turned her sun-stained face up to the blue sky. She laughed, a joyful sound I couldn't hear, and then opened her eyes.

"C'mon up," she mouthed at me. And laughed again.

I refaced the evergreens. A few hundred more bushes flashed by. Then with stiff, slow movements, I uncurled and pushed myself to my feet. With a sigh, I slogged up the gravel pile. Now what?

My cousin grabbed my hand, jerking my arm out straight like hers. She let go and continued to pretend to fly.

Dumb. This is so dumb. But I copied my cousin—feet apart, arms raised, and chin tilted to the clear sky.

Upright like this, the strong wind hit me full force. It tugged my hair at it roots. It pierced through my clothes and rushed to numb my skin, erasing my aches.

My feet sank into the mountain of pebbles, so I shifted and raised onto my toes.

Incredible. Now I was flying. Flying over the earth, my fears blown away. No failures. No heartache. Just speed and wind and sunshine.

Freedom.

A gunshot rang out, and I toppled over.

22

No pain ripped through me. So, I hadn't been shot, only startled into extreme clumsiness. I skittered low to the train's open side.

A thick-faced man in a black uniform darted around a metal container in the tall grass below. Weapon in hand, he charged at our train car. It had entered a manmade clearing and slowed, arriving where other boxcars sat in short, unmoving lines. Chaff had described this as a trainyard.

I ducked low to keep out of another bullet's path. My breath came in gasps.

Trinity. Be OK.

Her body reappeared over the hump of gravel, crawling closer to the opposite side of the car. Apparently uninjured since her movements were quick and strong.

Danger.

I floundered through gravel to join my cousin. My knees and hands sank down in my hurried flight. The pebbles slowed me as I fought against their quicksand-like shifting.

At last I reached the car's opposite orange edge and threw my legs over the top—no ladder on this side. Trinity balanced beside me, impatient. Her braid flicked back and forth as she watched for a yard bull.

The pieces of scattered trash and weeds below continued to slide by. No time to wait and find out if the train would stop. Side by side, we eased off our perch, dangled by our hands from the lip...then let go.

"Uhh!" I landed facedown, my stomach smacking the rocks so hard I couldn't breathe. The train's wheels screeched by within spitting distance.

"Dove! Get up!"

Another shot exploded nearby.

Hoooonk. Honk.

I dragged in a wheezy half-breath and crawled away from the shooter and the train's noise. Everything ached—my ribs, my stomach, the heels of my hands, my cheekbone...

Trinity reeled before me. She reached for my waist. Oozing scratches trailed down her palm. "Get up, Dove. You can do it. You're strong."

"Freeze, trespassers!" Someone bellowed. "You're mine. Do you hear me? You're mine."

With Trinity's help, I gained my feet and limped for a wooden fence ahead.

"Through there." She pointed at a ragged break in the boards where a rusted-out container pressed.

I chanced a look back. The yard bull hadn't climbed the train. He was still trapped on the other side of the tracks while the cars inched by. His red face flickered in the brief spaces between cars. No doubt as soon as the train stopped, he'd dart through one of those spaces, and after that, he would be on us faster than a coyote on a pair of wounded jackrabbits.

My lungs moved air in and out now with less effort. I quit clinging to Trinity. Together we tugged at the broken, rotten board until it gave way.

Dried weeds and bushes stretched on the fence's other side—no pieces of train or lines of track. I sucked in, wriggled behind the rusted container, and slipped through. Trinity copied, and we began to run.

The sound of wood splintered, as if someone had ripped the fence board clear off its post.

"Not good...not good."

Trinity, three strides ahead, glanced back and stumble-stopped. "The spineless...I can't believe it. He made it out, too!"

Chaff loped past us and headed for the scraggly bushes. His sob drifted back. "You girls—conspicuous—blew it."

~*~

I straightened up from the lonely water spigot sticking upright in the baked ground and swiped my dripping face with my shirt. The small clearing—no doubt, once a green wilderness—now existed as a dried-up wasteland. It was empty except for a lone tree cluster, scattered trash, and a rough wooden structure to sit.

"You think the yard bull is hunting for us?"

Chaff sighed. "Does a watchdog leave its post?"

Trinity raised her brow and shook her head. "No clue, Chaff."

"No. It does not. So, no thanks to you two, we are for the moment...safe. Now, if you'll excuse me, my trail mix disappeared from my pack. And I'm hungry." He drifted toward a waist-high metallic can where flies circled.

I flopped down onto the weathered bench that supported an uneven tabletop. A cluster of drooping alders provided shade.

My cousin reclined in the shade on the table's

other side. "I can hear it."

I raised my head. "The angry bull guy?"

"No. The ocean. Just like I always dreamed it would sound. But better. I can smell the...seaweed maybe? Or is it brine?"

My nose wrinkled. That's not what I smelled.

An armful of spoiled food thudded onto the tabletop. Chaff rubbed his hands together. "Score. I claim the apple aaand...the bagel." He plucked those two items up and shoved the fruit into his ragged pack.

I turned my face away while he continued to rummage. "Chaff, how do we find a train going north?"

His bustling broke off. "What? Why? We're a couple miles away from Trinidad, which is south."

"I made a mistake. Trinity and I coming here was a mistake."

"But Dove—"

"No, Trinity, listen. God told me. And now He's provided us with water and food—OK, *water*—so we can begin our return trip north. And I feel it. Where we are...it's not right."

I braced myself for hundreds of questions. Questions my traveling partners in the past—Melody and Jessica—would have asked.

"OK, Dove. Fine. We'll head back north."

I sat up and waited. Still, my cousin didn't accuse me of wasting time when I led us hundreds or thousands of miles too far south. She continued to lay as if sleeping or listening to a distant roar with her arm covering her eyes.

Chaff rotated the stale bagel around and around in his palm. "You're going away?"

I shouldered my pack. "You say this is your home

territory, right? And you've ridden north in the past to get to Oregon's Council? If that's true, where do we catch a northbound train?" I eyed him. *Confession time.*

He opened his sack and swept the remaining items on the tabletop inside. "Fine. I'll show you. But sound carries, so keep your mouths tight shut. And follow me."

~*~

The Pacific Ocean rolled and frothed onto the rocky shore with a noise like I'd never heard—not bees or cars or anything. It was the sound of a billion rocks being mauled by a huge, forever-writhing body of water. The water's vastness flowed out to the horizon where a couple of white, winged specks—seagulls?—wheeled.

I crossed my arms, which were goose bumped despite the warm breeze. "I don't see any train tracks. Where's the train?"

Chaff bobbed his neck in Trinity's direction and raised his voice for the first time in hours above a whisper. "Figured she'd want to see the ocean first. Talked about it enough."

He cupped his hands to his mouth and uttered a shrill seagull cry. A far-off bird echoed.

I scanned our leafy surroundings, a lush wilderness of ferns and chaparral that was clueless as to the rest of the nation's drought. Somewhere beyond the bluff I balanced upon—but close by—had to be the place my mom, aunt, uncle, and grandpa were being held.

But where? No buildings big enough to contain

hundreds of Christians existed between me and any horizon. There were no buildings or shelters anywhere, for that manner. Where was the town? Trinidad?

Not that it mattered since I wasn't supposed to search.

I bit my lip to keep from shouting for my mom. Because what if she was down there? Waiting for someone—for me—to help her?

A sudden wall of pressure nudged me back the way I'd come...away from the edge of the bluff. I tugged Trinity's pack. "Let's go. This isn't right."

But she was scrambling down through the tangled shrubs after Chaff. Both headed to the dark rocks below that made up the beach.

"I've got to touch the waves, Dove. Just once. I know you don't understand but..."

I hesitated. Then my feet shuffled down the trail that wound between rocks. The green fell away until only quarry-gray surrounded me.

I stopped. I didn't need the whisper from Heaven to know. I shouldn't be here.

"Trinity, stop. Now. We have to turn—"

My lips froze and my hand rose to shield my eyes before dropping to clutch my chest.

A familiar figure waded where the breakers crashed against the lumpy beach. With my eyes glued to it, I rammed against Chaff, regained my balance, then barreled past Trinity.

"Wait, Dove—"

I lost the path and took a more direct route down to where he waited. His back was to me. The waves buffeted around his bright shoes and pantlegs.

I grabbed Wolfe's bare elbow, yanking him around. Tape covered his mouth. My fingers flew up and ripped the gray adhesive square off.

"Wolfe. Why—"

"Because I'm bait. Go!"

23

Wolfe shoved me away with bound hands. Then he slumped and held his palms out. Defeated. "Never mind."

The empty strip of beach became crowded with movement. Yet I couldn't unstick my gaze from Wolfe's to discover who else was here.

Reed Bender's voice cut through the rush and roll of the surf. "Well done. Stone? Take control of your Heathen prisoner."

The ashen-haired giant, whose image I pushed from my mind whenever it surfaced, loomed before me. Stone's light irises flickered over me, avoiding my face, and lit on Wolfe. He gestured with the sharp stick he held like a spear. *Come away.*

His prisoner stepped closer to me. Below the tape-shackled wrists, both hands hunted for mine.

I grasped one and glared up at the Bender brother. "You still have your arm, Stone. Is it all healed? No doubt you thanked Wolfe for saving it by hauling you across the country last spring so you could get your mom's medicine?"

"Can you believe it, Dove? He never thanked me."

The tip of the spear lowered. It became a prod that strained against the orange shirt until the tanned fingers around mine clenched.

Wolfe's white teeth flashed at me. "Sorry, Dove. I'd stay to be skewered if it'd do you any good. Ease up, giant. I'm walking. I'm walking."

He retreated toward the foot of the bluff with his guard. A wall of six or seven humans clothed in gray closed around them. The Warrior emerged from their midst.

"You—" I lunged at Reed, but two Christians barred my way. I stumbled back to Trinity, whose arms were crossed.

I copied her ticked-off stance. "What is all this? Why is Wolfe here? Why are *you* here?"

The Warrior's lazy lids drooped another millimeter. Then he blinked. Was it a signal? Someone with large hands captured my wrists and tugged them behind my back.

"Chaff, you traitor. Let her go!" Trinity sprang at him.

Chaff stumbled, knocking me to my knees.

"Enough!"

Within seconds, my cousin and I knelt side by side on the small patch of wet sand and shell fragments. I tugged against the cords of tape that dug into the flesh of my wrists.

"She has your message, Commander Reed," Chaff mumbled. "The one that Zech had me deliver. It's the yellow plastic—that thing around her forearm."

"No matter." Reed pulled out a skinny knife. "You succeeded in your mission. That particular missive was communicated to its proper recipients despite Dove's thievery. You'll be glad to hear I expect an excellent response."

The frog-faced bodyguard held my arms while the blade sliced through the plastic as if it were a blade of grass. Without a glance at the scribbled words, Reed chucked the message over his shoulder into the waves.

Trinity shifted forward. "You're Reed, huh? You must be the disgusting murderer who trapped Gran. Well, murderer? Are you ever going to answer Dove? Why are you here? Why attack us?"

The lines around Reed's eyes smiled. "I've discovered it's wise to keep my enemies together when possible. Contained and safely out of the way of core operations. And it's best that I'm present to ensure that my plan has been carried out properly...at least when Dove is concerned. No more messups. That's why I'm here...*and* why you are here, Dove's cousin? You are Trinity, correct? Trinity who appreciates pretty things? Flowers and sunsets and—"

"Where are my parents? And my grandpa and aunt?"

He tapped his hair in pretend concentration. "Hmm...not here in California I'm thinking, Cousin Strong."

I squinted at a certain Christian standing behind Reed's narrow body. His familiar shoulders were tilted forward, as if the ocean pulled at him. "Trinity, meet Micah's older, more despicable brother. Zechariah Brae."

At his name, the Brae figure shifted sideways. I shivered at his wild animal eyes. They were worse than they had been last spring, opened too wide with an unblinking intensity.

"Yick." Trinity never hid her revulsion well.

The Brae brother slow-clapped. The sharp rhythm echoed off the cliffs. "You showed up on time, Strongs. As I foresaw."

I staggered to my feet, but Frog Face shoved me down.

"Stop pretending, Zech! You chose a path away

from God's when you decided to support the Benders in their plan to force our nation to sin. Which means you're no longer listening to the Spirit. If you ever truly accepted salvation once, you haven't lost it since you can't, but your gift? Your special insight? Pfft! That's gone. So, don't pretend you saw us coming."

Zech pivoted back to the water. His eerie applause continued.

"Is your sister still alive?" My question burst out before I could swallow it.

The clapping stopped, and Reed chuckled. "Ask her yourself. Melody?"

A tiny figure in shaggy clothes stepped out from behind Stone's solid mass. She clung to his healed arm.

"Melody. Please come forward. Your old neighbor wants to say shalom."

She let go and picked her way across the beach until she stood near Reed. "Shalom, Dove. I—" A rogue wave licked the pebbles at her heels, and she skittered forward as if chased by a viper. The surf retreated. "I...I'm glad you finally showed up."

I swallowed again to unstick my heart from my throat. "Why are you even here? You don't believe in the Reclaim. You know Reed would trade you for a truckload of ammunition if he could. And apparently, the ocean freaks you out."

Reed's arm snaked around Melody's furs, tugging her to his side. "People in love stay together. Where I go, she goes. Even if it's somewhere that 'freaks her out.' Which is ridiculous. She knows not to be afraid."

"Huh."

"Warning, Commander." A muscly blonde woman in ragged deer skin pointed up at the line of vegetation where I'd stood minutes before. "A Heathen vehicle is approaching the trailhead."

Reed released Melody and limped to face the Pacific Ocean. "Reunion's over. Let's move."

I dug my knees into the sand while Melody skittered back to the bluff's base. My glare followed. Let the others follow brainlessly after the deluded leader toward whatever destination he planned. Maybe a hidden shelter across the beach. Or a grouping of rocks in the ocean. Or a train.

Something sharp nudged me. Lurching onto my feet, I batted away Chaff's spear tip. "How could you betray us, Chaff? You owe me. I got you out of that building where you were stuck."

"So? I got you to the train and out of Portland. We're equal."

"A train to where? To here? To a trap?"

"Well...you ate my trail mix."

He must have recognized this was weak because he added in a harsh whisper, "And, *and* I didn't know you when I agreed. I was just trying to repay that Zech guy, the one with the crazy eyes. He could have left me locked in that broken patrol car that night of the CTDC transfer. And everyone would have blamed the guards' deaths on me. But he freed me. Now walk. People are looking at us."

With the weapon directed at our vertebrae, Trinity and I trudged after Reed's group. Wolfe moved at the front of the pack with Stone shadowing his defeated steps.

As we walked, the beach narrowed to a lumpy strip of damp, ankle-twisting debris. To the west, larger solid gray chunks rose up from the frothy surf. The greatest of these was an arch of stacked slabs whose left column entirely blocked the beach.

Reed paused at the column. As if waiting for his arrival, the ocean sucked the water out, leaving an unimpeded expanse of sand and rock under the arch. He limped under the curved structure, followed closely by Wolfe and Stone. A cluster of four Christians dashed through.

Crash! A new round of waves attacked the beach. Angry water swirled, filling the walkway under the arch and separating my cousin and I from Reed's strongest soldiers...from Stone.

I bumped Trinity's arm. *Escape?*

Stone Bender reappeared under the water-pummeled arch. He stayed steady as an oak tree as the water splashed against his hips. He assisted the pale, frog-faced guard through the water with his eyes on me.

I released my cousin's shirt. Never mind. A wall of water wouldn't hinder Stone from catching us if we broke away from Chaff.

Melody stepped from a rare patch of sand onto the rock next to me. I sniffed and turned away. Then I surveyed the empty beach.

"Where'd Chaff go, Trinity?"

She spun around on top of a half-buried boulder.

"Maybe the earth opened up and swallowed him." Her eyes flickered to the tiny figure at my side. "Sometimes traitors get what they deserve."

The waves rolled out, and I ducked through the arch. A rock path stretched ahead into the surf—a crazy kind of hopscotch with one simple rule. Step on the rocks to stay above the water.

"I doubt you're supposed to walk with me, Melody. Or talk with me. Reed wouldn't like it."

"No, he wouldn't. But he's busy talking strategy

again." She squinted at the leader surrounded by his followers while wilting like a plucked lettuce leaf left under the July sun. "He won't notice me."

"You made your choice."

I glowered at the Bender giant who lifted and hurled Wolfe onto a small rock island at the end of our hopscotch. The figure in orange sprawled a moment, then began to squirm across the bare stone without the use of his hands. "Nope, Melody. I won't feel bad for you."

"OK. I won't feel bad for you either."

Crash. Chill ocean water from a wave soaked my shoes. Its spray pricked across my hot arms and face. Trinity's angry exhale at Melody's words morphed into a gasp of pleasure.

She stood ankle-deep in the Pacific Ocean. "OK. Now I can die. I've been in the ocean."

"You're not supposed to die." Melody balanced on her dry rock with scrawny arms windmilling. Fear transformed her pinched face into someone about Jezzy's age. "That's not why you're here...not to die."

My bound arms automatically shot out to steady her...though why did I still protect her after all she'd done to me? Betrayal. Poison. More betrayal.

I dropped them. "Then why are we here, Melody? The truth. Why did Reed get Chaff to lure us to such a faraway place?"

"Sorry. I'm not supposed to say."

"Huh." I sighed. "Go ahead. Grab onto my backpack or Trinity's. No point in your breaking your neck and dying, too."

Splash. Trinity was back in the ocean. A waist-high swell collided with her, and she staggered. "No way, Dove! She so much as touches my pack and—"

"Help her, cousin. She's Micah's sister."

"Oh...oh fine. For him...not that he deserves my help either." Still muttering about brown-eyed Judases, she struggled onto the boulder.

I swayed backward and almost toppled. Melody had latched onto me.

"Oops. Sorry, Dove. And thanks. Both of you. I don't swim good. And I promise I'm not lying about the not-killing-you thing. Reed just brought you here to be far out of the way from...well, I can't say. But it's not because he's scared of you, Dove. He just knows you're super powerful. A powerful opponent is what he called you. He said that Satan's power makes you strong in influencing other Christians. The weak ones, obviously. And he doesn't like that you sway the Heathens' thinking, too. He's frustrated. All his hard work, and you go on that Heathen surviving show and...well, it wasn't the best for getting the Reclaim going. Although, your last message...*that* one Reed approved of."

Heat flared in my cheeks. The one where I blamed the world's problems on nonbelievers?

"But he guessed your change of heart wouldn't last. And that your outburst was a mistake."

I shrugged. "Of course. Reed's a jerk. But he's not stupid."

A body-length gap existed between my boulder and the first rock island, shaped like a turtle. Reed's followers had picked their way over to the opposite side in order to reach the second, larger island.

The water in the gap before me gleamed dark and deep. The kind that a person would need to swim. Which explained Stone's catapulting Wolfe through the air at this spot. It was difficult to make the leap with no hands.

Oxygen escaped my lungs in a gush. "OK. We can make this jump, Melody. Trinity, you…"

My cousin was in midair. Her knees and stomach smacked against the island's surface and then began to slide downward. Without the use of her hands, her feet scrambled for purchase on the slick stone.

I leaned forward. Biting my lip. Pain throbbed in my wrists from pulling against the binding.

She found a hold with her toe and shoved up. She rolled over and glared back across the gap. "Brae, I'm not scraping another inch across this rock, breaking another tooth, or giving myself another concussion until you explain what you meant when you said that Dove and I were brought here to be out of the way...if you're all not trying to kill us."

My hips swayed as Melody tugged my pack in front of herself like a shield. "Your tooth? Ooo, ouch. I'm sorry. I...I guess you sort of need your arms free for balance—"

"Answer her, Brae. I want to know, too."

"But I can't. That part I can't tell you, except...you understand that Reed won't have you messing up the great work he's doing for our people. Right? He doesn't want to kill you...or even hurt you. So, if you both just stopped—"

"Mel!" Reed balanced on the edge of the second, larger rock island where Wolfe rocked forward, as if ready to dive into the water despite his tied hands. His gaze stayed clamped on me. His pale lips twitched. *Don't drown.*

Reed pointed. "Mel, why are you touching Enemy Strong? Stone, why aren't you keeping control of this situation? If Mel needs help on the rocks, you or I help her. Don't trust our enemy. Ever."

Stone detached himself from the finger formation of rock to our right. With red-tinged ears, he landed catlike in the few free inches next to us.

I leaned away from his warm bulk and then gasped. Stone had ripped apart the tape that held my hands captive.

"Um. Go ahead first...Strong." Stone continued to hold Melody in place, completing my memory of when I'd last seen them in the MTV cave at Mount Washington. Side by side. Hands clenched. United.

Except now my gut didn't twist. I turned to the second island that rose from the ocean like a giant, lopsided beehive capped with seagulls. Trinity's feet touched down on its rock lip that rose above the green slime. And Wolfe, wearing his idiotic grin, bobbed his head.

Get over here, bird girl.

I held my arms out for balance and leaped.

24

"Where did Chaff disappear to? How can no one know? This is ridiculous, Enemy Strong. He was nearest to you."

Since tape adhered my lips together and trapped my wrists behind my back, I let my blank stare answer him. *Don't know where Chaff went. Don't care.*

Reed began to pace the small bit of gloomy cave. Christians who lined the cavity smashed themselves against the dank walls to give him room.

Limp, step. Limp, step. "Last seen walking with our enemies...but he completed the mission without fail. Which gives me no reason to doubt his loyalty. But his manner of disappearing...strange. We must find him."

At his decision, his posse moved en masse toward the cave's opening. The oldest follower, a man with a torso-length beard, led onto the skinny ledge above the ocean.

"But...but brother. I think...you're mistaken."

Long Beard paused at Stone's outburst. Every other beard also turned toward the giant stooped over in the rear of the cave.

Stone gulped. "I mean, brother—I mean, Commander—wasn't the whole point of us hiding out on this island and in this cave...to stay hidden? Until dark? And then relocate to the camp so the local Heathen don't see? You said it wasn't time for the

Heathen to—"

"Circumstances change. Plans change. Even perfect plans." Reed limped toward the cave's opening, and the Christians melted aside to let him pass.

He eyed the ocean that stretched to the horizon. "Stone, Bethel, and Myrrh. Head to the beach and comb the rocks as well as the bluff. I will join you. Zech, you told me Chaff is a local resident of Trinidad?"

"Aye, aye."

My slumped shoulders jerked up. Chaff hadn't lied. He did live here. Or at least Zech and Reed believed he did.

"Can you locate his home before sundown?"

Zech paused in sniffing the cavern's aroma of ocean creatures and slime-covered rocks. He saluted. "Aye, aye, Commander."

Reed strode over to where I leaned at the back of the cave. His face mirrored Zech's inhuman expression when he checked the strength of my bonds and Trinity's. He gave an order to reinforce Wolfe's mouth.

"Melody, you'll come with me to the beach. Olive, Noah, and Eli, you'll remain to guard the captured. I'll return before high tide tonight to supervise the prisoners' relocation. Until then, keep them in this enclosure. And do not be afraid to use your weapons. Remember, the ocean is your ally. Use it."

The Benders left to hunt for Chaff, accompanied by the Braes and another set of siblings—a sister and brother with snub noses and serious mouths. Which left only three of Reed's posse to stand guard.

They positioned themselves in a half-circle facing us. Each fidgeted a sharp-edged weapon, except for the strong-looking blonde girl. A gun rested in the holster against her hip.

Wolfe winked. He leaned his shoulder over to brush a white-tinged line on the wall next to him. The horizontal-reaching discoloration separated the upper, lighter rock from the darker wall below. Trinity seemed fixated on it.

I puffed my cheeks out. What? What did the line matter?

Ker-splish. Water spilled across the cave floor from an ocean swell taller than the cave's lip. The crouching sentries sprang up as if stung.

"What in the—"

"Hey!"

They clutched their wet backsides and tunic hems.

Wolfe stirred the inch of pooled water with his orange shoe. "Expect more where that came from. Tide's coming in. And just to clarify, your...err...commander said we prisoners had to stay in the cave. Not you."

"Wha—? No talking, Heathen. Olive, where's that tape cylinder? I'll fix him up."

The gray adhesive square flapped against Wolfe's chin. "Go ahead and add more. Add the whole roll, but it won't work. My skinny head won't cooperate. You saw. Ol' Reed couldn't keep a gag on me either."

"Stop talking." The frog-faced guard created a tighter X over the gray patch on Wolfe's mouth. As he secured the loose end around his black, shaggy hair, another wave covered the cave's floor.

Wolfe scrunched his nose. His jaw and cheeks wiggled. He spit the gag out of his way. "Really. It doesn't matter to me whether you get waterlogged undies—"

"Stop talking!"

Our sentries repositioned themselves in a standing half circle. Wolfe's low whistling echoed around the space.

"Stop wh—"

The water rolled in. A rush of iciness covered my knees and hit me in the gut. As I darted upright, Trinity's muffled gasp became lost in the shouts from the guards.

Frog Face hustled after Blonde Girl to the cave's entrance. He paused on the slick stone lip. "We're watching the cave's entrance from our lookout above, so don't even think about escaping. Or talking. Or whistling. We're trained soldiers, and we don't mind using our weapons like Commander Reed said. You coming too, Eli?"

Eli with the long beard slashed the air with the complicated knifework of an amateur. "Don't…make me…use this. Because I will." He backed out of the cave with dripping pants.

Wolfe's shoulders shook. "Some of your people are real nut jobs, Dove."

Trinity's wet fingers fumbled at my chin. They peeled up the lower edge of tape covering my lips.

I gulped in a mouthful of ocean air and returned the favor.

"Thanks, Dove. That's more like it. What about our hands? We could free them. Those white bumpy things on the wall are rough enough to cut with."

"The barnacles? And then what? Once you're free you'll wrestle our guards for their weapons? Or maybe you'll dive into the ocean and swim to freedom? Can you girls swim? Or even dog paddle?" He smirked. "No, didn't think so. Might as well leave your wrists alone. They'll just tape them together again."

"You can swim, Wolfe. Swim us to the beach."

"You mean tow you to the beach, Dove? Both of you? Around the rocks and breakers? No way. One of you'd panic, and we'd all drown together."

"Fine. If you want to stay and be Reed's prisoner." I plopped back down in the eddies of water. I couldn't cross my arms, so I crossed my legs. "We'll give up on everything in life that matters—on our families—and stay here forever. Because you're a spineless slug. A snail who's too afraid to swim."

"Yup."

My body tensed and shivered as the ocean in the cave rose up to my knees and stayed there. Was this Reed's real, unspoken plan? To trap us three in a cave that would fill up with water until we couldn't touch? I'd never been in the ocean before, but it held obvious power, even more than a train. How long until the power swept me off my feet and pulled me into its depths?

Frog Face reappeared to check our bonds. It was good I'd left the tape loose on my mouth instead of removing it. After he beat a hasty retreat to dry rock, Wolfe sloshed over to the cave wall. He chose an area where barnacles clustered thick like a clover patch. The dull sawing of his wrist restraints echoed.

I uncrossed my legs and moved closer. The white bumps looked like tiny, broken mushroom stems. But they made sharp indents against my finger when I pressed. "Wolfe, what was it you knew? In the CTDC?"

The sawing slowed. "Diamond told you, huh?"

I attempted to whistle the seven-note strain of "Jesus Loves Me." He chuckled. "What I knew was that your parents weren't in the CTDC. Don't think they ever had been."

"Already knew that." At least I'd guessed the last part.

"And crazy-eyed Brae set me up. He was the reason I was stuck in there. And he got himself held in the CTDC too…on purpose." He whistled the same seven notes. The song Zechariah Brae had sung with him last spring on Mount Washington.

I lifted one knee from the chill of the water in an attempt to thaw it. Then the other. "Already knew that."

"He was responsible for the car crash the night we transferred...and for the guards with us dying."

"Knew it."

"How?"

"Chaff told us."

"Oh, yeah. Traitorous giraffe."

Trinity snorted. She paused in letting the ocean drip off her downturned fingers like fast-growing nails. "Giraffe."

He grinned. "And I know that Reed's planning something big. An attack on society of some kind."

"A hostage situation, I think."

"You knew because of Chaff again?" He bobbed his neck in an imitation of the long-necked mammal.

"No." Trinity turned her back to a waist-high wave that rolled in. "Dove stole the message from a guy in a garbage bag who wanted to throw her off his roof."

He threw his head back, laughing like an idiot.

"Shish!"

"That's my girl."

"Quit laughing so loud or Frog Face will be back. Or Eli with his knife tricks. And I'm not your…just shut up and tell what else you found out."

"What else you want?"

"Something I don't know." The unsteady movements of the ocean rocked me. Like Trinity, I turned my back to the cave opening. Better not to see the wild ocean, darkening as the sun lowered in the west. "Where is my mom? And Trinity's? Are they in California?"

"I don't know. Except that...I think Reed knows where they are. Because he never talks about the Christians who've gone missing. Never wonders, 'Hmm? Where could they be?' It's suspicious. I'd expect him to be threatening vengeance on all of humanity, but he hasn't uttered one complaint about it in all the time I've been around him. Which, by the way, has been way, way too much."

"Maybe he already knows where they are." Hope made my voice rise. "Did he happen to mention the name of a place in all his talking? A city or town or anywhere?"

He shook his head. "Only here...and Black Butte, but that's—"

I jumped, smacking my head against the low ceiling. "Black Butte. Trinity, that's it."

"You think our moms and my dad are there, Dove?"

"No, not at all! But that was the scribbled word on the message." I thrust out my bound arms to show the one that used to wear the strip of yellow.

Trinity looked at my bare skin. "The message that doesn't matter and Reed threw away?"

I dropped my arms and let the ocean sway me forward and then back. "Yeah. That one, I guess." She was right. What did that message matter when my mom was still missing?

The sawing stopped. Wolfe watched me through lowered lashes. The naturally upturned corners of his mouth now stretched straight. It made him look older and unfamiliar.

I squirmed "What? What, Wolfe? Spit it out."

"Dove...there's something else I know. But I don't know if I should tell you now. Because it'll make you feel rotten. More rotten."

"Rotten? What does that matter? Wolfe, don't you dare not tell me something I—"

"Rebecca's dead. Stone...he killed her."

25

Rebecca. Dead.

His hands, free of their shackle, caught my arms and steadied me against the swell.

"Sorry. I...I know. It's horrible. Big time horrible." His whispers in my ear came to me from far away.

Trinity didn't bother to whisper. "Rebecca's dead? Who's she?"

Wolfe held on to me as if aware I might sink beneath the freezing water if he let go.

"She was Dove's good friend. And mine. A really smart chic who used words like they were a magic wand. Like, if she were here now, she'd go right up to those guards and tell them to put down their weapons and let us go. And they would."

"Oh. She must be the girl I was keeping my eyes peeled for in Portland."

A coldness worse than the ocean's ice numbed me so I struggled to move my lips. "How...how do...you know she's...gone?"

"Reed asked Stone if he'd taken care of Dove's well-spoken city rat for good. Stone looked him in the eyes and answered. He said 'yes,' Dove. And he was pale and shaky when he said it. Sick."

I'd only seen Stone look weak once—when dying from an infected bullet wound. But killing an old friend might also turn his stomach. So then, Wolfe told the truth. Rebecca was gone and had left this earth to join Gran in Heaven.

I pulled away.

I sensed Satan's laughter as water lapped around my chest and attempted to lift me off my feet. My Enemy sent another wave, more powerful. Pulling me westward toward the deep ocean. I began to shake.

Another horrible truth hit me. Reed absolutely wasn't coming back to this cave.

He had said he would return before high tide to transfer us to a new location. Yet Reed was a liar. A killer and a liar. He had lied, and Trinity, Wolfe, and I were going to die. Not from drowning, but from the cold. From hypothermia.

I put my taped wrists against Wolfe's shivering chest and shoved. "You're free. Go! Swim away. Trinity and I can join Rebecca, but you can't. Go home to your grandma and Jezebel."

Trinity plowed forward in a clumsy swish. "You really think the others aren't coming back to relocate us?"

"He killed Rebecca. Why not me? And you? And Wolfe?"

Silence.

Wolfe charged through the swells, dragging me with him. He pressed my hands and forearms against the barnacles, then dragged my wrists against their roughness. Up, down. Up, down. Stings raked across my half-dead skin.

"Hold 'em up." He lifted my arms off the rocks, and his hands enveloped the backs of mine. He yanked. And yanked again, the muscles in his arms flexing as if my wrists were two halves of a stubborn walnut he wanted to force apart.

Rip. The worn area of tape became a separation.

He dropped my free hands and glared down at me. "No one in this cave is hanging out with Rebecca tonight. You understand? Trinity. It's your turn."

Before the water eased my arms' sting, Trinity stood rubbing her wrists next to me.

Wolfe bent over us, his face transformed by the black, downward slash of his brow. "We swim."

I shook my head and fumbled with the side wall at the cave's mouth. "Trinity and I aren't swimmers. We're climbers. Give us a boost up so we can scout a different way out."

~*~

I shivered in the late afternoon sun and pressed my stomach tighter against the island's warm slope. Four figures balanced near its peak with their backs to us, facing the turtle-shaped island beyond. The water had risen to cover the gray, reptilian-shaped head. Waves pummeled the last bit of shell.

The newcomer who'd joined our three guards pointed a tan-clothed arm at the bumpy strip of beach in the distance. A low voice spoke slow and clear.

"Commander Reed sent me with his message. You are to stay here. Don't retreat to the beach or head to the camp without him. He's been delayed by local Heathen, but you're safe if you stay here with his prisoners. The water is already receding, and your path to the beach will be clear by the time he returns."

Blonde Girl nodded and gestured at the waves with the gun. "Yeah, OK, we'll wait for Commander. But if the water rises any higher, the rest of the rocks to the beach will be covered, and we'll be stuck here. In the dark. The sun is going down."

"Shall I report that you're disobeying orders?"

The gun wavered. "No. No, don't tell him that."

"Then you'll be sensible and wait?"

Three heads bobbed.

"Yes, we'll be sensible."

"Sensible. That's what we are."

"Hey, now!" The beard trailed over the man's shoulder as he lurched forward, his knife in his hand. "But where are you going? I thought we were all going to be sensible and stay here? You get to leave?"

The messenger paused on the dry portion of turtle's shell but continued to face the beach. "I'm the commander's messenger and not his guard. He's waiting for my return. What shall I report about his prisoners?"

"They're here," Frog Face croaked. "Secure. But they might drown soon if he doesn't hurry."

"Something he'll be glad to hear, I'm sure."

I tightened my jaw to keep my teeth from chattering. Without a sound, I slid backward with clumsy movements toward the cave opening. Wolfe's chilly hands grabbed me off the rocks. They lowered me into the shocking water and then hauled my cousin and I toward the back of the cave—away from the open ocean and its impatient tug.

"Can you make it? Are they all sleeping so you can get past them to the beach? Or is there a back route you can take?"

"No."

Trinity shuddered in front of me. "G-good news th-though. W-water's going down."

Droplets flew from Wolfe's hair with his shake. His palm splatted against the wall. "That white line means the water's going to rise that high. Another foot at least. When that happens, the current will pull us out. So, we swim. Now."

A giant swell struck and lifted me off my feet.

My arms flailed, and I kicked something solid beneath the surface. A creature. Like a shadow, its long, black body glided next to my legs. I thrashed as it curled around my knees.

Splash! No chance to scream. My limbs froze rigid with shock. Liquid salt filled my mouth.

26

The creature trapped me beneath the water's surface. It latched onto my face and forced something solid between my lips. Hard plastic.

Clean oxygen poured down my raw throat and into my lungs.

I quit clawing. The tentacle appendages against my chin didn't belong to a sea creature. They weren't even tentacles but hands. Human hands I couldn't see through the gloomy murkiness, but I felt them now. Fingers gripped my arm while others fed me oxygen.

The human towed me through the ocean, which tugged over my slack body. My surge of adrenaline ebbed away. I didn't fight whoever held me. If I did I would drown.

I clenched my eyes shut and inhaled easily. The coldness overwhelmed my body until I couldn't feel anything but a heavy blanket of sleepiness.

My head broke the surface to brightness. My lids struggled to open. Salt stung, smudging the ocean before me. The neck and head of a person in odd fitted black, like the rubber of a tire, bobbed into view. A blurry hand waved and held up its thumb.

"Enough! Let go! Get off...I can swim." A fuzzy Wolfe bolted through the water, away from another bobbing, black-covered figure.

I squinted at a blonde, round thing. Trinity's head. Through the haziness I saw her claw at a small, dark blob against a white oval—her face? She flung the donut-sized, black blob away. Her oval and Wolfe's tan one bobbed closer. "D-D-Dove?"

"What's wrong with Dove?"

"I think she's cold," said a familiar voice. No clue whose, though.

"I'll take her to shore. I can swim faster than you even without flippers. You help Trinity." Wolfe's blurry face loomed over me, vibrating like the rest of the world.

"I got you, Dove girl." His voice faded. Snatches of words reached me in the growing darkness. "C'mon...OK...join Rebecca."

27

A persistent rhythmic drumming woke me.

"Stoooop." I tried to cover my ears, but a cocoon kept my arms smashed against the sides of my frozen body. Wolfe's teeth grimaced down at me through the warm gloom, fragrant with oranges.

I struggled to sit up but couldn't. Besides the annoying cocoon, my body shook worse than a bunny's in a thunderstorm. I clenched my jaw so my teeth wouldn't knock together, but the steady beat continued.

"Enough drumming for a second." Wolfe tossed a chunk of citrus peel at the frizzy-haired kid.

The rhythm stopped. Rebecca's kid brother, Joshua, twirled the drumstick in his fingers and waved it at me. "She's awake, Becca."

Becca? As in *Rebecca?* Where was I? I struggled again, fighting the blanket's stranglehold. "Help...me up..."

Wolfe pulled me into a sitting position and kept his arm around my blanketed back. I felt my pupils dilate, taking in my crowded surroundings.

Trinity leaned against a cardboard box across from me and sipped from a flowerpot. Water from her braid dripped down the front of her leopard-print blanket. The worker girl from the store in Portland gazed at the flat electronic in her lap and ignored the guy jostling her. Hunter. He'd grown a beard since I last saw him at the Council. Clothed in a black rubber suit, he twisted a cord around three torpedo-shaped cylinders.

"I need another length to secure them, Becca."

"We've got no more. Better make it work." Rebecca tilted back in a wooden chair and peeled an orange.

In the middle of our cramped circle, a single electric lantern wearing a tasseled hat projected a yellow moon-shape on the low ceiling and illuminated the objects crowding the tight space. Like the stuffed rabbit with antlers that grinned into Trinity's left ear. And the half-towers of books whose other halves appeared to have toppled around Joshua.

I flopped against the nest of sleeping bags behind me. My eyes flickered back to Rebecca. "Not heaven?"

"Nope."

"You're not dead. How?"

She grinned lopsided at Wolfe and sighed. "Didn't you and me just have this conversation?"

"Don't laugh. Stone told Reed he killed you."

Creak, creak. Her chair rocked on its hind legs. "Did it occur to anyone present that Stone didn't tell the truth?"

Stone had lied?

He'd lied. My slow brain struggled to accept the idea. It conjured up a picture of the giant's pale skin tinged with sweat. His unsteady hands—a result of lying to his brother. Not a result of murdering his friend. Of course, Rebecca was right. He'd lied. Warm relief flashed over me, and I shuddered.

"Here. Drink. It helps." Trinity leaned across the space to hand me the navy flowerpot. Its brown contents sloshed in her unsteady grip.

Wolfe rescued the container and tilted its rim

against my chattering teeth. I swallowed pure, sweet warmth. Chocolate.

"Good...good flowerpot. Um. Glad you're...you know. OK. Trinity." My voice cracked on her name.

In a blink, everyone's eyes were riveted on me. Even the round blue ones from Portland. I nodded at Joshua. "What are you waiting for? Drum."

Rat-a-tat-a-tat-a... I gulped chocolate again, waiting for Hunter to finish his imitation of a nosy owl.

"So? Where are we? And you." I untangled and thrust my heavy arm at the blue-eyed, Portland girl. "You definitely should not be here."

"Whatever. It's my van." As if that explained everything, she went back to her electronic.

Rebecca grinned. "Meet Brooke. Portland's Sent. She's my eyes, ears, and mouth in Portland since I was encouraged to relocate. She lets me know when any Christian stumbles through her door...which happens more often than you'd expect. When she called two days ago, I recognized her description of you and figured if you were risking the evils of Oregon's biggest city, you must be in some big trouble—most likely looking for me to help you. She kept tabs on you and saw you hop the train south before I could get to you. Right, Brooke? Is that how it happened?"

She held up her thumb.

I confiscated the orange slice Wolfe tried to feed me. "But how come you're here, Rebecca? In California?"

"Because you are. We followed your train." She gripped an imaginary steering wheel. Driving. "You were easy to follow, lounging in that gravel car like it was a first-class berth on Trains Across America...until you disappeared in that bull's yard. At that point, I had to guess your direction. And since you were with Chaff, I figured he must be leading you to his home at the coast, which seemed odd, but why else would you come south with him? So, we started searching the nearest sections of accessible coast."

Wolfe pulled his arm away. "Yeah! Why did you come south with him, Dove?"

Sky alive, I'd been dumb. The whole time I'd been on the train, Rebecca had been minutes away in a vehicle. I thumped my head against the cushy wall. Then I met Wolfe's scowl. I shrugged. "Maybe we stuck with Chaff because Trinity's got a thing for giraffes."

"Dove!" Trinity growled.

If only I had obeyed God right away and hopped off the train. I would have avoided the stuck-in-the-cave mess. I wouldn't be frozen solid like one of Jezebel's popsicles or have raw, stinging wrists. We probably could have rescued Wolfe in an easier way. And maybe Rebecca would've already helped me search for my family.

He rubbed his stubbled chin. "But...I thought Trinity liked Micah?"

"Wolfe!"

"Don't be insensitive, Pickett." I snatched the chocolate back. "We don't speak of her obsession with that—"

"Both of you shut up. So, everyone is clear. Dove and I went to Rahab's Roof for information, and a guy there told us missing Christians were being held near Trinidad. We found Chaff stuck in the building, and he also just happened to be traveling in the same direction. We *are* near Trinidad, aren't we? Or was he lying about that?"

Rebecca's bushy hair shook. "No lie. We're parked about ten miles north of the town of Trinidad. Six miles north of Martin Creek Beach where Reed held you prisoner—not a bad choice in location on his part since it's probably the most secluded beach in the state. These luxurious quarters you're enjoying are the inside of the Jonah's Thrift Store van. Hence the jackelope and the old lady furnishings—"

"And scuba gear?" Wolfe pointed at the torpedo tanks and pile of black rubber clothing.

"Um, no. Actually, the scuba equipment was a lucky find."

He grinned at her. "I thought Christians weren't supposed to steal. Isn't it a top-ten rule or something?"

Rebecca's nostrils flared. "We don't steal. Hunter won't forget our first stop on the way out of town is that strip of beach with the unlocked cars—to return what we borrowed. You won't forget, will you, Hunter?"

Up, around...Hunter's fingers continued to tie his knot around the scuba tanks—the same type of knot Gilead uses on permanent jobs where ropes stay in place until they snap from old age.

She nodded, satisfied, and tilted back on her chair legs. "The other stuff you see are pick-up collections to bring back to the store. Part of Brooke's job. She takes her job seriously since she's up for manager. Right Brooke?"

Another upturned thumb.

"Right. Dove, you remember Hunter? And my brother Josh?"

"Yeah. I didn't expect to run into them today either."

"They were with me when Brooke called. They

thought they'd come along for the ride and for a place to sleep...which worked out nicely since we're all a bit homeless at the moment."

"And that girl with the messed-up braid and weird blue lips is Trinity. My cousin."

"We met while you were passed out. And Dove, you've still got slime. Right there." Rebecca touched her own sideburn. "Looks like some regurgitated seaweed."

I shoulder-bumped Wolfe and swiped my ear. "Quit laughing."

Trinity reached out and adjusted the antlered rabbit—the jackelope—so it stared in a direction away from her. "Wolfe, you were right about Rebecca. She uses her words beautifully."

Rebecca's chair creaked forward. "Well, it's a useful gift sometimes...like being able to convince your guards on the island this afternoon to stay put when one was about to go ashore for reinforcements."

No wonder that low, calm voice on the island had sounded familiar.

"That extra half hour of rising water made it impossible for them to get to Reed...and for him and his brother to return to you. The ocean cut off communications. Even if the guards discover the three of you gone, we'll have a couple of hours of safety before they sound the alarm and search for survivors. Or escapees."

Wolfe's arm became a band across my back. "Dove thinks Reed planned for us to die in the rising water. Going off to search for the Chaff guy was only an excuse for Reed to get Stone out of there—and to send his strongest swimmers away...possibly the ones with consciences who would have tried to prevent us from drowning."

"Sure. I'll buy that."

I'd quit listening to their back-and-forth since I already knew Reed's intentions. They were bad. I leaned forward. "Is that my pack? And Trinity's? Last I saw them that traitor Chaff had them."

Hunter grabbed both from the top of a box. Mine landed in my lap.

Thump. Rebecca's chair legs hit the van floor. "Show less hate towards Chaff, Dove. It's not his fault Zech and Reed railroaded him into escorting you to California."

She was right...poor Chaff. Wait! I shook my head. "Why should I be nice? And how do you even know him?"

"We spent a few hours together in the Holy Hall at the Council...mostly me talking him out of his conviction to hide under the bench—in case of an aerial attack. But today, Hunter, Brooke, and Josh wouldn't have scubaed you to safety in time if Chaff hadn't come out of hiding and told us about the secret cave you were in."

I snorted into my chocolate. "I bet the giraffe had hidden somewhere lame—like behind a tree trunk—and you saw him poking out. And then he spazzed and blabbed all he knew...or what he pretended he knew. Rebecca, he's a liar. He lied about living here. And he just guessed about the cave."

"No. You're wrong. Chaff has lived here his whole life and knows this coast. The guy's paranoia keeps him and his sister alive. He told me once, he's created an elaborate fake home as a decoy at Trinidad to throw anyone hunting him off his trail. But my guess is he has at least three decoy setups. His real home is probably miles away in some booby trap-rigged wilderness.

"Trust me, Dove. He made a real choice to help you this afternoon. He wanted to help. I would never have discovered him in the foxhole under the bush."

The drumbeat stopped. "Becca screamed like a girl and fell over when he popped out. Then she did this." Joshua lurched in a jerky crabwalk.

Her orange peel bounced off his grin. "Also, Dove, why would Chaff tell me everything, if he'd allied himself with Reed? He said about how Zechariah Brae pumped him for information about his hometown the first time they met...and how Zech made him promise to deliver messages to the radio broadcasting place in Portland. Zech made him swear that when he ran into you, he'd get you to follow him to the coast near his home. He told Chaff you'd come to Trinidad without a fuss because of the fake message he was sending along."

A fake message. The memory of a plastic garbage bag rustled, followed by a declaration about Christians being held in California. In Trinidad.

Apparently, my cousin's mind was working along the same line. "So, my mom and dad...they aren't near Trinidad?"

Rebecca handed her the rest of her orange. "We drove around looking for you when we lost your trail. We didn't see any evidence of other Christians or a shelter large enough to hold more than about ten people. It's a tiny town."

"So, what are we doing still parked here?" Hunter jangled a bunch of keys over Brooke's downturned head.

She swiped them out of his grasp and set down

the electronic.

Disappointment sat heavy on my chest. We might as well go. Reed had told the truth on the beach—our family wasn't close by. Where were they? Were they even still alive?

Trinity's eyes were becoming slick. I fingered my blanket and pulled it up, over my wet hair. My eyeballs began to ache, and my body shook with trembles that had nothing to do with cold.

Wolfe patted my covered head as I sniffed, unable to keep my tears inside.

28

My muscles had once again decomposed to rotten squash. But at least the wintery cold had passed from my body. Unfamiliar music wafted from somewhere close, and I opened my eyes.

The dead-eyed jackelope grinned his buck-tooth smile from the crook of my arm.

"Sky alive!" I released the two-foot long, stiff figure back onto the floor space next to me. One of its antler prongs collided with Wolfe's sleeping back.

Laughter filled the van's gloomy interior. Joshua's guffaws were the loudest. "Your cousin did it! She tucked the big guy between you two last night. Funny, right?"

Super funny. I squinted around and rubbed my skin to erase the feel of the creature's moth-eaten fur.

Midnight-black curtains covered the nearest windows, a contrast to the golden sunshine that blasted through the front glass at Brooke who maneuvered the steering wheel. Pavement lined with moving cars and trucks stretched before her and Hunter. He snored with his scruffy cheek jammed against his fogged windowpane.

Trinity sat on the van's floor, pitying me with her forced smile.

I gazed down at the creepy critter that had prevented me from any unintentional closeness with Wolfe while I slept. My face burned as I picked up my pack and repositioned myself against the tower of boxes next to her.

A fluttering heaviness filled my stomach. I snagged two pieces of cold chicken out of the red and white cardboard bucket.

"Are we in Oregon yet?"

I held out a chicken thigh, and Trinity accepted it. "We crossed the state line an hour ago. I told them they could stay with us in our place in Sisters…hope that's OK."

"All of them live with us? At our place? As in...the small patch of weeds surrounded by arborvitae trees? There's no way we'll all fit—"

"Motel Pickett has plenty of room. You all can stay with me." Wolfe yawned. His eyes bugged a moment when he sighted the jackelope on the blanket I'd abandoned. "Hey, fried chicken—excellent."

Rebecca stretched. "Wolfe, is that smart for you to live at your home address when you're an escaped Christian terrorist?"

He took a bite and laughed. "Exactly the reason you're invited over. Bippity boppity...good-bye charges against me.

I focused on the unnaturally thick poultry skin. "Yeah, uh, I might need you too, Rebecca."

Chicken had a certain funkiness that made it not as tasty as the wild poultry my mom cooked. But it seemed most people in the world liked the tainted flavor. On our drive home last spring, the peeling-paint structures where we bought meals never sold crow or sparrow. Only greasy chicken.

She groaned. "Oh, Dove. Breach of contract with *Fanatic Surviving*. Again? Already?"

"I don't know. Is that what it means if I skipped a

scheduled trip to Louisiana with Lobo?"

"Definitely."

"Then yes. Um. Trinity. You might be wondering about Louisiana and the *Fanatic Surviving* stuff—"

"I'm not blind, Dove. The only wooly sunflower patch in Sisters is right next to the sign showing your gigantic head. Godless strangers jump out of cars to point electronics at you. And more people chuck trash at you than at me or Gilead...or Micah."

"Oh. Uh, good. Glad you understand." I dropped my voice. "Then after we get to Sisters, we keep searching for our moms...after we, you know, pray about it."

She bit into the chicken piece and chewed as if disappointed.

"Or I can search by myself. If you don't want to come."

She turned pale. Sick because of the chicken? Or that we still had no clue about our moms?

I tried again, forcing out my next thought. "Or maybe...I guess it's fair that we try to find Gilead and Micah. At the Council. Since that's what you wanted to do in the beginning."

Hunter awoke with a snort. "The Council? You heading to Mount Jefferson? No point. Your brother won't be there. None of the Sent or Council people will be because—listen, there it is. The message is playing again. Pump up the radio, Brooke."

"Righto. This is Danny D..."

My head jerked around for the invisible speaker. Hadn't he been captured?

"...broadcasting from the sunny slopes of Black Butte—"

"Black Butte again!"

"Shish!"

"...and for all of my sisters and brothers listening, and especially for those whose knees are worn out from praying over missing loved ones, this announcement is for you, delivered straight from your local Council by Rahab Rae and your own Danny D.

"The Council invites you to join us at this secluded spot in the Deschutes National Forest for a feast of prayer and mutual support. Members trained in security will be in the area to provide for your safety and to direct you to a campsite. So, grab your tent, pack your provisions, and come join us at Black Butte for our first prayer rally at sundown on August First. This is Danny D, signing out. Shalom."

Dead air followed. I interrupted Rebecca, who was translating the Amhebran message into English for Wolfe. "Black Butte."

Trinity tossed her chicken piece with one bite missing to Joshua, who caught it with his teeth. "Yeah, but a prayer rally? A support group for Christians with missing loved ones? That wasn't the message about Black Butte you stole. Not even close."

"Stealing—again? You people."

"Not now, Wolfe." Rebecca thrust her palm at his upturned lips. "What message, Dove? I bet you can remember some of it."

I rubbed my barnacle-scratched wrist. "Heathen government retreat at Black Butte. Hold enemies for ransom. Fight. Win Reclaim...that last part was in big capital letters."

Silence stretched, marked by tires rushing over pavement.

"Those two messages are a...a bit different."

I nodded. Danny D had mentioned nothing about

attacking enemies. Or of starting a war. Did his support group and the Reclaim somehow fit together? I had to get to Black Butte and find out what was going on.

I clutched my head. No! No more wild goose chases to places I wasn't supposed to go. Never again would I throw myself into a situation where I wasn't needed. Where God didn't want me.

Lord, I didn't trust You before, and I didn't obey and get off the train when I should have. I trust You now. I'll go where You send me. I won't go where You don't. So send me. Or don't send me.

"...government retreat every year," Wolfe finished.

I sighed. This happened sometimes—I missed others' conversations during my own with God. "Repeat everything, Wolfe. Uh...please."

"I said it'd be easy for us to check up on the real goings-on since Black Butte is right next to Sisters."

"No, it's not. Impossible. I would have seen it."

His hand drew an upside-down smile in the air. "It's that huge slope right next to our town...packed with evergreens."

Oh, then yes, I'd seen Black Butte. The hump on Sister's horizon hadn't seemed impressive enough for a name—there was no rock face or snow. When I noticed it, I just called it 'the hill.'

"Black Butte seems like a bunch of trees, but it really hides a village near its foot where rich people go for vacations—to be in nature. So, it has lots of fancy buildings, spas, swimming pools, tennis courts...plus a couple bike paths to enjoy trees from the comfort of asphalt. And every summer, government officials from Oregon stay in that village for a secret retreat. A retreat, Dove and Trinity, is like a work getaway where the employees sometimes bring their families along. But this one's always hush-hush for safety reasons."

Rebecca leaned forward in her chair. "If the retreat is a secret, how do you know about it?"

"Because every summer when it happens, security around the Butte gets tight. And officials' families end up in Sisters to shop. Our town isn't resort quality, but we have more stores and restaurants. The retreats are part of the reason Sisters has a western theme—it's supposed to give our town charm so more tourists will visit and spend money. But it's embarrassing. As if we should all be galloping down Main street looking for a saloon, tipping our ten-gallon hats at each other."

Did he mean all the wooden building fronts with old wagon wheels and flowers were part of an odd western theme? I shrugged. They seemed more normal than Portland's style, with its crowded, peeling-paint concrete.

Josh shifted in his sleeping bag, scattering chicken bones among books. "So, Dove's message's hostage situation will take place soon during one of those planned retreats?"

Wolfe studied his half-eaten wing. "It's not likely, right? No one would be so dumb or evil to march in and kidnap our state's leaders. Or their families."

"What month do the retreats happen?"

"Um, August? July at the earliest."

"It's July now."

"Well then, August."

Rebecca quit questioning him and must have transmitted a mental vibe to keep quiet while she rocked. Josh and Hunter drifted back to sleep. Wolfe rolled onto his side, possibly reading a book from the scattered piles. Every so often a page rustled.

Brooke continued to drive. She must've been a decent driver since no more boxes or books toppled, but the churning in my middle worsened with each snore and page turn.

Cold chicken. Thick, greasy skin.

I should have stuck to eating leftover oranges.

Trinity looked as horrid as I felt. She focused on the van's lichen-colored ceiling and, after a while, she buried her pale face in her knees. A sheen of sweat plastered her rainbow shirt against her spine.

Hours passed. Nothing changed. We slept. Rocked. Drove. Read. Breathed deep. Until finally the never-ending engine cut off.

I crawled into the van's front and over top of Brooke. "Coming through."

I spilled onto the Pickett's sharp grass. Trinity dropped onto the weeds behind me. There must have been another, secret door at the back of the van because Wolfe already approached his home's front door.

It opened. Jezebel leaped and dangled from her brother's neck like one of those clingy baby animals that are too lazy to walk. She released, pivoted, and chose me as her next human to climb. "What took you so long to get him home, Dove?"

Boom. The home's door flung open again, crashing against the wall's tan paint. Her grandma poised in the doorway. She tugged a fringed, sand-colored towel through a small opening in her fist. *Pull, flick. Pull, flick.*

"Grandma! Wow, do you look great. You'll never guess—"

"No lies, Wolfegang Pickett. Because I know exactly what you've been up to."

His smile faltered. "You do?"

The other passengers had their heads down. Stomachs sucked in. Trying to slink past the angry woman and enter her home without being noticed.

I pointed at the van. "Hey, Jez. Jackelope. In the back."

"Whoa! Freaky." She released her grip on my ribs and raced for the van's open door in her bare feet.

Trinity and I backed toward the sidewalk but not fast enough.

"Hold it, everyone!" The towel continued to snap through the white-knuckled fist. "No one's going anywhere until I ask my grandson one question. Wolfe, did you make your apologies?"

Wolfe relaxed his tanned shoulders. A real grin replaced his tense one. "I'm sorry, Grandma."

"Not to me, you oaf." The beige cloth whipped in my direction. "To her. You owe that nice Christian girl a busload of sorry for all the trouble you caused. You went and got yourself missing—without a word to anyone where you were headed. No doubt she had to locate you without any help from you. Didn't bother to call or send her a message, did you? Hmph! I figured. I swear, grandson, someday every female in your life is going to quit wasting time and breath on you. Now stop trying to hug me and start telling me who these people moving in with us are. And how many frozen pizzas will they want for dinner?"

Trinity tugged, unsticking me from my spot on the sidewalk. Still, my mouth dangled open.

His grandma had called me nice. A nice Christian girl.

29

The swags of old man's beard moss still drooped around the top of our bushy enclosure. Except now the swags were shriveled, like a real old man on his deathbed. Even the branches of our tree ring were brown and brittle. But what did it matter? The earth was firm and motionless against my stomach. And not a hint of chicken for miles.

"She told Wolfe you're nice," said Trinity.

"Mm-hmm."

"Your ribs OK? That kid could out-hug a bear."

I grunted, inhaling the fresh scent of dried grass under my nose. Each of Jezebel's skinny fingers had forged a tiny bruise. I turned my cheek so it rested on the ground's scratchy cover. "His grandma...do you think she'll let the others stay for a while?"

Trinity grunted an affirmative and lifted her face. The queasy pallor had faded. "Not a single thing thrown at you in town this time."

"Mmm."

"And tons of the godless were out. They saw us."

"Mmm. Sisters missed me."

"Or got used to us Sent."

I was too worn to mention the real miracle that happened during our trek from the Pickett household to our tree shelter—that Trinity had forgotten to cringe and stare at the trees for escape. She'd lost her suspicion and fear of all godless people, no doubt a result from embracing her true gift. I closed my eyes to the filtered sunlight.

When I opened them, the sunlight had vanished, but Trinity still sprawled on her stomach next to me. The moon, with its usual red blush, hovered in the chill air near the eastern wall of my shelter.

"Ow! What in the—" The wall shuddered. A few dead evergreen needles trickled onto my arm.

I sighed. No wonder I'd woken before sunrise.

I contorted to get around the intertwined spikes protecting our entrance. On hands and knees, I avoided Gilead's strategic piles of burrs.

The cows weren't out and about in the field yet. Only Wolfe. With crossed arms, he leaned against one of my enclosure's half-dead arborvitae tree, his motionless body between spikes.

He glanced away from the meteor shower above. "Good morning. Lots of stars moving up there."

"You've got burrs on your shirt."

"Do I? Well, I might've stepped on something that made a bunch fly up and get me."

"It's called a booby trap. Gil made it. I can untangle them. I've had practice."

"Leave them. They don't hurt. I'll just throw the shirt away when I get home."

"Wolfe?"

"Yeah?"

"You're stuck to the side of my shelter. Don't lie."

He let his arms drop and shifted. A chunk of his shirt stretched to the tree like a squirrel-sized hammock. "Um. Yeah."

I picked my way over and untangled the white cloth from the barbed end of the spike. Since he was junking the shirt anyway, I didn't mention the rip I made in the process.

"Thanks."

"Right. Now go away. I want to be alone."

"Ha! Then you should've left me stuck to your hideout. Now that I'm free, you can't stop me from coming with you. I know you're dying to find out what's going on at Black Butte. You were planning to slip away by yourself this morning to scout it out. So, I figured I'd meet you before dawn and let you know too bad, I'm coming, too."

I scowled. How had he read my mind and guessed my plans? And worse, why did he continue to show up, eager to help? Scouting out a possible government retreat, looking for signs of other Christians...this stuff affected my world. Not his.

"You're wrong, Wolfe. I was going to pray about going first."

"Then pray. I'll be here when you're done."

The blushing moon still hovered in the same spot when I dusted off my knees at a burr-free section of grass. I strode in the direction of the black hump on the horizon that was Black Butte. God was silent—for now. But I didn't hear Him say no to exploring that village.

"Where'd you park the Jeep?" I squinted through the dim light. "I don't see it on the road."

"It's not. Grandma took out a piece of my engine to make sure I stick around for a few days."

I faltered but continued to plow through the field. A half day's walk to Black Butte—or even a whole day's—was nothing.

"Just joking about no ride. Ta da! And you thought we'd have to walk!"

I blinked at the expanse of weeds with the wire fence border. Beyond these stretched the manicured backyards that ran smack against boxy homes. No white Jeep.

"What are you babbling about?"

He vaulted over the cow barrier and patted the object I'd assumed was backyard junk. He patted its seat again and grinned.

"You stole Diamond's motorized bicycle?"

"Motorcycle. And we're borrowing, not stealing. Christians are allowed to borrow. Remember? Rebecca does it."

"Diamond will murder us. Correction, murder you. Because I'm not touching her motorcycle."

He cocked his head. "You won't ride the transportation I provided us—to save your legs and feet—because you're afraid of Diamond?"

"I'm not scared of her."

"I see. Then it's because you're afraid of motorcycles in general? This one's self balancing. It can't tip."

I squared my shoulders. "No."

"Well it can't be because of my driving skills. Because you know I can drive anything."

My eyes narrowed.

"Fantastic. I risked myself on your zip lines. But you're too chicken to try my way of traveling? Wow. I mean...wow."

"There's only one seat. And I am not riding the handlebars this time."

He laughed and threw a leg over the motorcycle's curved frame. "It's a big seat. Just sit tight, hold onto me, and we'll be at the rich-people village in time for breakfast."

30

Cool gusts of pine air slapped me between waves of heat from Wolfe.

Wolfe, too close.

Wolfe, the only thing I could anchor myself to in a world that tilted and blurred at high speeds.

The forest quit moving around me, and the motorcycle's throbbing engine cut off. We balanced at the edge of a thin, paved road.

"Let's walk the rest of the way. OK, Dove? Dove?"

I forced my stiff arms and hands to unclamp, and then I slid off. A blob of blood oozed from the inside of my healing wrist. No doubt an extra injury from a shirt burr I'd mashed myself against.

Wolfe turned his back to the road. He dropped into a valley of trees that led away from the nearby massive Black Butte.

"I figured we'd explore the village first while people are asleep. We'll scope out the retreat and look for a possible hostage situation. We'll hike Black Butte to check for Christians later."

"Sure."

After a trek that took a few minutes, the rain-starved wilderness ended. At my toes began the smoothest expanse of grass ever. Even in the weak morning light, I could make out its vivid, maple-leaves-in-June color. Emerald green.

The lazy, rolling terrain reached most of the way

to the horizon. Then buildings began. These were larger than Wolfe's and his neighbors' in Sisters and boasted extravagant windows and lanterns. Beyond the structures, the earth stretched in a flat, treeless line. I squinted. A field?

Wolfe readjusted his dark blue backpack and stepped forward. My feet sank into the springy softness, so different than the tough tufts and clumps of the cow pasture. Within seconds, a cold dew drenched the tops of my feet.

"Typical. Even in a severe drought where the rest of us only get one-minute showers, rich people get to water their golf courses."

"Are the government people here, Wolfe? Can you tell?"

"Nah, still too far away to tell. We'll check the vehicles parked in the lot and see if we can get close to the main lodge and villas. If officials in uniforms chase us away, then we'll know the retreat's begun."

We continued over the terrain of manmade perfection. There were no signs of a hostile Christian presence—no bullet-riddled targets or bald patches worn down by Christian soldiers training for battle.

FIGHT. WIN RECLAIM.

Maybe Reed's message I'd taken didn't matter. Maybe all Christians had refused to heed it...or else the Council had vetoed Reed's plan to fight, replacing it with the wiser decision to come together and pray. That made the most sense since Rebecca and Hunter and the rest hadn't heard about ransoming government officials over the radio.

Trees continued to border the grassy clearing, but no one moved between trunks. There were no shelters or tents that meant Danny D, Rahab Rae, or any

Christian travelers headed east to pray on Black Butte.

"Let's go this way first." Wolfe steered us away from the buildings and parking lots I thought we'd headed for. Suddenly, three yards ahead, the grass ended. An expanse of dark water started up.

"I figured you'd want to wash, Dove, and this lake is a good one."

My hands moved to my hips.

He fumbled his pack under my cold stare, picked it up, and began to paw through. An aluminum can and book spilled out. He thrust them back in and continued to root. "I mean the first thing I did when I got home was shower, and you don't have one, so I figured you might want to....um...anyway, here are some clean clothes for you. I'll be over there."

He broke into a jog. "I'll be waiting in the sandpit!"

I let the offered wad of earth-tone garments flop onto the grass. Without removing my thrift store ones, I waded into the water.

My breathing hitched. He was right—this lake was a good one. Better than the ocean at least. Warmer, and it didn't pull me off my feet.

The sky gleamed pastel when I slogged my way back to the empty grass bank. No doubt Wolfe was hunkered in a pit of sand somewhere. I wrung out my hair and held up the new shirt. My dripping arms stayed frozen in place.

"Oh, Mom," I whispered. "Grandma."

The tunic and pants were factory made and soft, but even so they were an echo of the outfit my mom, grandma, and aunt had created for me a year ago—the one I'd worn the first time I'd left home. The one Wolfe had ruined.

Tears welled up. A strange sickness twisted my gut—different from being chicken sick or van sick.

I was family sick.

I buried my damp face in the tunic but still saw my grandma in her willow chair. And my mom stood just behind her, holding her surprise for me. My surprise gift. The clothes with the Armor of God she'd made from the plants grown on our property.

I scrubbed my lids, but my mom's determined smile remained. How long would it be until I saw her smile again in real life?

I bit the inside of my cheek while peeling off wet clothes. I pulled Wolfe's gift over my undergarments.

"Hey, Pickett!"

His tousled head popped up molelike from the first green knoll. "Do they fit? I know the shirt doesn't have a hood. And it's short sleeved instead of the long ones you like to cover your skin—"

"Wolfe, get over here...please."

He jogged toward me. "It looks like they fit. But if they don't—"

"How?"

"How?" He approached slower—prey creeping toward a predator, ready to bolt if sharp teeth appeared.

"How did you get these clothes? Look at the lines." I tugged my tunic front. "That's the shape of a breastplate. And this belt design is exactly like my old belt of truth."

A wide grin threatened to break his face. "You like them? Wait. I forgot your helmet. Warriors wear helmets, right?"

He pulled out a brown, half-brimmed hat. The type Jezebel sometimes wore—baseball caps, she called them.

He fitted the cap on my wet head. "Helmet of salvation."

I swallowed and kept my arms crossed tight. They wanted my mom, but they might fly out and squeeze him instead if I gave permission.

"Hungry? How about breakfast before we scout around?"

Food, too? My fingers gripped the sides of my new tunic, fighting off the impulse that rolled through me, strong as ocean swells.

Since my feet weren't tempted to act stupid, I allowed them free will. They followed Wolfe to the back of the clustered buildings from earlier.

Up close the structures were huge, though not as tall or wide as some in Portland. But Trinity would appreciate their smooth cedar sides and copper lanterns. And she'd bury herself in the thatch of white, trumpet-like flowers that cascaded over a half-wall behind the closest structure.

"All clear. Looks like the restaurant workers aren't here yet." He settled down behind the flowered wall. Yards away, the lake rippled with a warm breeze.

He unearthed twin plastic sleeves with white-sugared contents. "Early bird special."

"Doughnuts!" I fell to my knees and grabbed one.

Ker-click! Ker-click! He opened two juice cans and shoved one into my fingers.

"To onion stew!" His can bumped mine.

I chugged down the lemony sweetness and kept my eyes on my doughnuts. I was being paranoid—onion stew was a joke. It had nothing to do with the loaded conversation about our futures we'd had while eating that certain stew a couple weeks ago.

"Well, Dove, at least this date is going better than most of ours."

I kept my pupils fixed on breakfast and shoved a whole doughnut into my mouth.

"People our age go hiking together. And camping. And they hang out at the beach or go ziplining. But when we do those things, it's not very relaxing. Half the time one of us is bleeding."

I crammed in another doughnut and chewed.

"Wouldn't it be something to stroll into that restaurant behind us with the white tablecloths...and eat breakfast off plates together?"

He gestured at the restaurant that loomed behind me. A white table flanked by two stiff-backed chairs sat on the other side of the window.

I swallowed and inhaled the scent of flowers. The lake glimmered with the sun's first light. A blue jay called from the far-off trees.

"Food tastes better outside."

He grinned. "You know what's best? The trees. And that great setup the Joyners have. I wouldn't mind living—"

I crumpled the empty wrapper and stood up. "The parking lot is northeast. You said we'd check there first, and I don't know what type of vehicles government people own, so come on. Quit stalling and show me."

31

The whisper of approaching bicycle tires warned me to move.

I retreated from the strip of snaking blacktop until the roughness of the horse barn pressed my spine. I stayed at the wall, though still in sight of the path.

Since relocating to Sisters, I'd quit bolting for a hiding spot every time I sighted a nonbeliever. Yet I found it smart to keep a buffer between myself and any potential fists, weapons, or projectiles.

"C'mon, Wolfe. Move away."

He folded his arms, positioned his stubborn self against a pine at the path, and waited. Sunburned legs and dark glasses appeared. The pair of bicyclists were the same type of godless we'd already spied occupying the village's tennis courts, pools, and parking lots.

The man had been pedaling without a single tire wobble, but he now lost control. The orange metal frame skidded across the tar, dumping the rider. He continued to kneel where he landed next to his bicycle, as surprised as a bird who's flown into a screen.

I tensed but didn't gasp in surprise at the badly timed accident. During my stay in Sisters, cars routinely broke down next to the sidewalk I traveled and residents became locked out of homes I passed. These events were Satan's doings, as he hand-selected his worst-tempered puppets and then nudged them into my path.

The female companion, shaped like a butternut squash, abandoned her own mount and searched for scratches on the fallen man's body and then on his bicycle's frame. With a sigh of relief, she thrust a beverage container at his shoulder.

He accepted and pointed the cylinder at me. "Her!"

It would take me three seconds—four tops—to reach the haybale formation stacked to my right. From the top bales, I could reach the barn's roof no problem. Yet I stayed like a paint fleck against the barn wall. For now.

Tell me when to move, Lord.

The woman continued to brush invisible dirt from her companion's too-tight shirt. "What, honey bun?"

"Her. She's the reason I fell." He chucked his plastic bottle. Its pink contents sloshed to a stop at my toes.

Wolfe chuckled.

The bottle's owner took a step toward me. "I've got zero tolerance for fanatics who—"

Wolfe threw his head back and let loose, laughter racking his frame.

The man's head swiveled. His eyebrows shot up. In a hurry, he tripped before he mounted his bicycle and pedaled away.

"Hon!" the woman called after. She glanced at Wolfe, flung herself onto her ride, and sped off. "Hon!"

Wolfe's shoulders quit shaking. He leaned his head back against the pine. "Later, Honey Bun. Trash talkers are such cowards, Dove."

I sank onto a low haybale. "Especially when you turn into a psycho each time one of them doesn't like me."

His eyebrows went up. "Psycho? All I did was stand there—"

"Like a maniac. Your body all angry. Your face lit up like you saw your first zip line." I shrugged. I'd seen his bizarre reaction to keep threatening people away from me a hundred times since I'd become Sent, so I'd gotten used to it.

"My body—and especially my face—do not do what you said. Anyway, since there's no sign of any government visitors or their tightened security, we should start hiking. Or head back to Sisters. Unless..."

My chin raised from my sweaty palm. Unless?

"Unless I get into the main lodge, steal a look at the village's reservation calendar for their rentals, and find out which days they've scheduled extra security. Then we'll know what days there might be trouble."

"That, Wolfe. Let's do exactly that."

32

We squatted at the leafy backside of a horse-shaped bush next to a granite sign. *Village at the Butte*. A family exiting the main building's front doors moved past without noticing us, except for the shirtless toddler on his dad's shoulder. He held up his toy pistol and took aim. Then waved bye-bye.

"I'll be right back, Dove."

I latched onto Wolfe's hem. "Liar."

"Huh?"

"You're a liar. You said 'be right back' when you went into the CTDC, and you never came out. I'm going in with you this time."

He grinned. "Shatters your world, don't it?"

"What?"

"Being separated from me."

I kicked moist village dirt onto his favorite shoes and stepped around the western-themed foliage.

He paused at the glass doors. "Let me do the talking."

"Obviously."

The lone woman behind the long cedar counter wore a warm, wide smile...until she saw us. "Yes...sir?"

Wolfe smoothed his hair but missed dislodging the stray piece of hay. "Good afternoon. My—er...wife—and I were interested in staying in a villa. Not today, of course."

Her cool green eyes rooted me to the stone floor.

"Oh?"

"Tomorrow."

"I'm sorry, sir. Our rooms are full tomorrow.

"The next day?"

"I'm sorry. Full."

"That's OK. I meant next week."

"Still full."

Wolfe drummed his fingers against the countertop. He pointed at the electronic in front of her. "You could, you know, check for reservations on your calendar. It's the professional thing to do."

"I don't need to check. Sir."

"Religious profiler!" He slammed his sunglasses down. "You are religious profiling us! That's illegal."

Her green orbs shrank to the size of spit bugs. "Excuse me?"

"Refusing to help us because you suspect that she—my wife—is—"

"Sir. Lower your voice. I don't need to check because we're booked solid for the next three months—until October."

"Oh. Popular place. Good for you." He stuck his glasses on his hair and readopted his smile. His fingers drummed. "The reason we want a room is because we have a friend, a very well-known friend, and he'll be renting a villa here in the next week...or two...maybe three. I misplaced his number and hoped you could tell me when he'll arrive. We have plans to hit some golf balls around together at your village's superior green."

She made no move toward her electronic. "Your friend?"

"A hint. His name begins with 'Gov.'"

"The governor? You and the governor of Oregon are going to tee off together?" Now her eyes were as round as the oversized buttons on her tight shirt.

"No...of course not. I meant...Assistant Governor."

I mopped my flow of cold sweat with my hat. Was "Assistant Governor" even a thing? The title sounded made up. But this was the stuff Wolfe knew, so I forced a smile onto my lips like an agreeing wife.

"Sir. You have thirty seconds to exit our premises. And then I'm calling the police."

As my mouth fell open, Wolfe backed, his hands up. "Whoa, whoa! No need. We're all friends. All friends...grab it, Dove."

I started at his breathed instruction in my ear. "Wh—?"

He nodded at the electronic.

I gave a miniscule shake. *No. Not stealing her electronic.*

"Borrow."

A man entered, wider than the side doorway he sauntered through. He was, I guessed, a village worker as well as a brother or cousin of the yard bull in Trinidad. Same purple-veined, unsmiling face. Same thick fists.

He tilted his battered leather hat at the green-eyed glarer. "A couple of strays, ma'am? May I assist them out?"

Wolfe quit hissing at me and retreated for real. "No need. Leaving. We're already gone."

The man's boots clumped after us through the glass doors. With a grunt to follow, he led us across the pavement, walking with the swagger Micah sometimes adopts—except this guy wasn't trying to impress me with his toughness. He was tough, the same way deer jerky just was.

He grunted disapproval when Wolfe and I made

to slip away at the green grass. "Nope. You keep moseying along with me...my way."

Did *his way* end in a secluded section of woods where no one could hear our shouts?

"Of course, sir." Wolfe's thoughts must've run a similar course to mine. He mimed hurling his pack at the large head, us sprinting across the grass, a motorcycle—

Not an enemy.

"No straggling. Keep up, girl."

"Dove. I'm Dove. A Christian." I shook off my shock as well as Wolfe's wild jerk on my elbow.

"I know who you are, Dove." Tiny eyes peeped sideways from under the hat's brim. His gravelly voice lowered. "You came here? After you escaped Texas?"

"Eventually."

The guy spat in the grass like my grandpa does and grunted again. This time, it was a signal for us to follow him into the pine-tree wilderness. These woods began at the far edge of the village's grass, an area we hadn't yet explored.

"Never did think the TV execs give you contestants a fair deal. I'd like to see one of them try and survive without their thousand-dollar bags of gear. It takes more than faith to get a human out of one of those hellholes. Like luck." The eyes peeped again. "Or...for it to be the contestant's god's choice, too."

He cleared his throat, and redness fanned across the purple cheeks.

I smiled at the sky overhead. "Not luck. But yeah, God's decision."

The hat bobbed. "And common sense tells me, since your God let you survive through so much—all those episodes of bugs, fire, and flash flooding—well it must be for a reason."

"For a reason," Wolfe agreed.

The slit eyes shifted to him. "You a Christian, too?"

His white teeth flashed. "Sure."

My hands balled into fists. Always joking.

Our guide grunted and led us past a cluster of cedar-paneled homes, no doubt the villas where rich guests slept. "Well, if your God's got a purpose getting you through all that *Fanatic Surviving* mess in Texas, then don't you go wasting yourself getting arrested here at Black Butte. You get my point?"

"You mean, don't come back here. Or I'm going to jail."

"And if I was you, girl, I'd quit that fool show. Or did you already film the next location?"

"Not...not yet." I bit my lip. Swamps. Werewolves. And Lobo and Jessica, who would kill me if they caught up with me. Or most likely have me thrown into a CTDC.

"You remember what I say. You've got a purpose, kid. Don't waste it."

"Are you a Christian, sir?"

"Watch your mouth. A man could lose a decent-paying job because of such a rumor." The small eyes crinkled. "But if a man ever chose to become radical, would he be able to survive like you? Not much flooding in these parts, but we get plenty of wildfires."

I squinted up at the sky. *Would he?*

I shrugged. "If God chose so. Being a Christian isn't about using God for His miracles. It's about being in a relationship—a friendship with Him. You talk to God...and try to recognize what He says back. Sometimes yes. Sometimes no. Sometimes He's silent for a while. No matter what, you stay close and trust Him. Understand?"

He snorted. "Understand? About as much as that boulder does, plus needing answers to a few million more questions that would make a man's head split."

"Hey, I got something that helps." Wolfe dug in his backpack—probably to offer him a plastic-wrapped cheese or can of juice.

I focused on a dip in the terrain ahead where an unexpected cement building appeared among the sparse pines. The structure was twice as big as the main lodge and a hundred times uglier with chipped, beige paint. Graying boards covered each square pane of scummy glass.

Wolfe fell silent, and our guide's boots clumped slower.

The brimmed hat nodded. "Old employee lodgings. Abandoned now. Village hasn't torn it down yet."

My heart thumped. From fear? Or excitement? I squinted at the relic for a clue that would tell me which.

Wolfe whistled. "Creepy. A thousand workers could live in that haunted mansion. But who'd want to?"

"Most we ever had living in there was a-hundred-fifty. Could've housed double, no problem. It's not haunted but not a good place. Village spent their money building the quarters grand-sized, and then they did the rest too cheap. Air conditioner broke most summers. Electrical was wonky, so we lost power every winter. And the backup generator was junk."

He toed a plastic pipe running between a shoulder-high metal box and the concrete wall. "That was mostly the chipmunks' fault, see there? Teeth marks. They mess with the generator's connections. Don't know why they're so eager to chew through the conduit and sever the cords inside. After that the dang power won't work."

Plastic rustled, and a chipmunk scampered around the building's far side. Plastic rustled again.

I froze. Silence fell. An expectant silence...as if something—or someone—waited. Hidden.

I dashed to the end of the building, rounded the corner...and faced garbage.

Bags of it sprawled against a section of the wall mixed with loose food item containers. The pile towered so high that it blocked two bottom windows. I swatted at flies and leaned away, studying the boarded-up state of the windows.

"Someone must live here. Someone who eats..." I nudged an empty box with my toe until it fell over. "Fruity-Funflakes."

"Naw. That's just illegally dumped trash from skinflints too lazy to drive the mile to the transfer station."

"Dove understands about trespassers with trash."

Was that why my throat tightened—because my brain associated this trash-bag mess with home? Then why did my pulse continue to race?

A bullet casing glinted in the sunshine at my feet. I palmed the hot metal and nudged a long, grimy piece of gray duct tape plastered with pine needles. I refaced the building and all of its boarded-up windows. Where was a door?

"Now, I got to get back and saddle some horses up for the next trail ride. You keep walking straight down the slope, and you'll get to the main road."

I followed Wolfe's whistling three strides down a slope with dead ferns that looked like they'd been trampled. I turned.

"Your name? Sir?"

"It's Bull. Remember, don't waste yourselves. I don't wanta see you here again."

Wolfe and I didn't pass any other shelters as we followed his directions to the road. My head kept whipping around toward the village, but my feet continued forward. I would not race back to the abandoned building right now and explore. I would not ask Bull questions about scheduled horse rides that required extra security. Because I would come back for those things tomorrow.

Wolfe, imitating the high buzzing of a sparrow's trill, ended with his seven-note "Jesus Loves Me" song. "You're probably wondering about that thing I gave Bull back there—"

"What thing?"

"You didn't see? Then never mind...hey look. The cowhand's shortcut worked. Up ahead is where we parked."

"But then..." The strip of pavement shimmered empty in the late afternoon heat. I snatched my hat off in case its brim interfered with my ability to see Diamond's motorcycle.

He sighed. "Yep. It's gone. Stolen. Diamond is going to kill me."

33

Wolfe and I trudged through the empty field. The cows must've abandoned it for the barn hours ago. Not a bad idea. My own body moved as if sleepwalking, too worn to notice obstacles or boobytraps.

There was a sting at my ankle—maybe I'd upset a burr pile? No matter.

"Uh, Dove? Does Trinity have a lantern with her?"

"Of course not."

I screwed the heels of my hands into both eye sockets. Chinks of weak light filtered through the cracks between dying foliage of the tree copse where we lived. I sped up until a murmur of Amhebran met me...familiar voices. I exhaled and dropped, crawling through the entrance and scraping against sharp sticks.

"Lamebrain!" Trinity's face loomed out from the half dozen others crowded in the lantern's cool glow. "I woke, and you were gone. Look at how many fingernails I've ruined worrying about you."

Before I glimpsed the bodily damage I'd caused, Jezebel—the one person not glaring—shoved her way through and hugged me. "I told you all she and Woof were together. Dove's always OK. She knows what she's doing. You shouldn't have worried."

The tallest figure drew herself up—either that, or everyone else shrank a few inches. "Wolfe, you do realize you're wanted by the government as an escaped Christian terrorist? Why would you even think about moving around in the open? So close to home?"

"You're right, Rebecca. I didn't think...maybe I can explain—"

"Save it." She pointed an accusatory finger at me. "And you, Dove. Not only have you broken your contract so that Lobo has every right to take legal action against you, but what was the point of getting Reed to believe that you're out of the picture? If word gets out that you're making appearances around Black Butte…"

My head, hanging with exhaustion, jerked up. "How'd you know we were near Black Butte today?"

"Diamond was stomping around town, growling about her wheels getting stolen. Jezebel gave us a description, and Brooke and Hunter located her missing motorcycle at the road next to a certain Cascade land formation." Her brow arched. "Off doing some recreational hiking on Black Butte?"

"Diamond has her bike back." Wolfe let out a shaky note of relief.

"Yeah, but she says she's still going to punch your face." Jezebel unglued herself from me and rummaged through her brother's bag for snacks.

I swayed in the doorway where I kneeled. Somewhere in this crowd of bodies must be a clear patch of weeds where I could curl up.

Rebecca eyed me. "You'll have plenty of time to rest. Because you understand you've got to stay inside your shelter, unseen by anyone but us, until after the first of August?"

I counted on my fingers—twice since they were blurry. "That's more than a week away."

"Eight days. August first is the prayer rally at

Black Butte. Too many Christians will be camping around these parts up until then, which, no doubt, will include Reed and his weapon-yielding groupies. Plus, eight days will give me time to hash out a new deal with our friends at *Fanatic Surviving*."

I nodded my head. Then shook it. "No need to hide. I didn't see a single Christian today."

"Dove, Hunter and Brooke didn't just hunt a missing bike today. They hunted for—and found—believers. Ten groups of Christians spread out and camped nearby in the foothills."

I closed my eyes. "Ten? That's not so many. I can stay away from them. No need—"

"It'll be a hundred groups before the week is out."

I shrugged. No doubt she was right. But believers...nonbelievers...Reed...I was through hiding from any of them.

"Dove? Look at me."

I dragged my lids up.

Her brown eyes were as hard as tree nuts buried in December snow. "Leave the prayer rally—and the possible trouble at Black Butte—for us to figure out. You step out of this pasture again, and I'm calling Lobo myself. I'll tell him where you are, and I won't speak up for you anymore. You'll be on your own from here on out. I promise."

"You'll quit helping me?"

"Yes."

My body slumped. I believed her.

34

I blinked at the red that glistened like dew on my sparse surroundings. Above me, the dove balanced on Gilead's spike, protruding from the dead arborvitae tree. I blinked again, and the bird became a pure speck of white against the murky sun. A wing fluttered. Beckoning.

Wait up. I launched myself off the blood-soaked weeds and up through the shower of crimson rain. I flew toward a sun that blazed the color of old corn. My fingers closed on the bird's silky tailfeathers. A burst of strength jolted through me, and we headed north.

A couple of breaths later, we touched down in a forest of pine trees. But as soon as my feet hit the damp ground, we shot back up into the sky.

Down. Up. Down. We only stayed a few seconds at each location. Each was identical—another patch of tree-filled wilderness surrounding Sisters. Black Butte stayed a constant maroon-covered hump on the horizon until we turned and headed for its base.

From my vantage point, a familiar, lone cement building below came into view. I swooped lower until the metallic odor mixed with garbage gagged me. The red flowed stronger here—thicker than anywhere else I'd flown. Maroony-black waterfalls cascaded from the building's square, boarded-up windows.

I pulled at the dove to force it to hover so I could

search, but it yanked me further on. The garbage scent faded.

I strained against the unusual power of that tiny, feathered body. "No, go back the other way."

The creature dropped, and we landed in a flat clearing. I released it and ran for the dripping tree line that hid the building, but a sudden darkness dropped over me. I stumbled and groped. Blind.

White light flashed, shaking every bone in my body. I fell to my knees. And the piercing blast of brightness ripped me apart.

~*~

I opened my eyes to brightness that scorched my skin. Three feet away Trinity sweated in the tree copse's partial shade and fiddled with her hair. Bored.

Still panting from my dream, I unearthed my pack from under a pile of food wrappers.

She dropped the moss she wove into her strands. "Wait. We're not staying here five more days like Rebecca told us to?"

"Feel free to stay. I'm not."

She scrambled for her own pack and crouched at the doorway, ready. She didn't ask where we were headed. For the past couple days, I'd been hung up on the idea of getting back to that building near the village. She'd shrugged each time I'd shown her the bullet and explained why I needed to be there among the garbage and chipmunk-chewed wires...but even though she didn't agree with me, my cousin was loyal. She wouldn't let me go alone.

The vision of red stayed before me, more real than

the cracker packs, water bottles, and the fire starter I shoved into my bag. My hands fumbled as I added bee repellant and blankets. God's dream made it clear: I needed to quit hiding and get back into the trees. If something bloody was about to happen around Black Butte, it was my job to stop it. To stop red from flowing. Again.

"Do we leave a note?"

"I guess." Wolfe, Jezebel, Rebecca, and Joshua would show up tonight like they did every night. As would Brooke and Hunter, who would share a few words about the results of scouting in the hills. Since Reed would recognize them the least, especially since Hunter had grown a beard, they had the freedom to explore in safety where the rest of us couldn't.

I rummaged through the wooden crate that acted as our storage and our table and sometimes our chair when our backsides got fed up with the scratchy ground. I pulled out the pink pad of paper—a gift from Jezebel—and began to hunt for a square inch of unmarked surface to write a message on. But every miniscule space was crammed with Trinity's overlapping sketches.

I tossed it back in and located our stubby knife instead. With its sharp edge, I gouged my message in the crate's rough top. I kept it short.

Vision. Left. Be back.

Below the words, I scratched a long rectangle with squares for windows. My cousin's feet scuffed as she turned away—no doubt finding it unbearable to watch me carve lopsided, jagged lines. But Wolfe would understand them.

Done.

I stood with the knife handle in my palm. Oddly, it

felt right there. So, I slid this object, one I'd never before carried on a journey, into my pack.

"Now, Trinity. We're ready to go."

35

"Another campsite to our right, Trinity," I breathed. "Veer to the left and up the slope."

A nonbeliever wouldn't haven't recognized the vacant patch of dirt as a campsite since it appeared the same as the rest of the wilderness. But Christians survived by staying out of nonbelievers' sights. My people knew how to make themselves—and their homes—invisible.

These campers betrayed themselves with subtle signs of camp life that were impossible to hide. Such as the unusual bare patches of ground where believers had brushed away footprints. Or the areas without dead bushes or sticks—removed to become fuel for cooking fires. The too-clean spots in nature caught my attention and told me how crowded the woods had really become.

But it didn't tell me how many hidden pairs of eyes watched our steps.

Here was another trunk with four gouge marks. More evidence of a knife thrower in these parts. Sweat trickled down my spine.

Trinity's head swiveled. She was eager, expectant.

I figured it was more likely we would stumble across the Benders' camp—or one of their supporter's—rather than one belonging to my brother and Micah, like she hoped. Especially since I'd sighted huge cat prints twice today. Yet I kept this stressful thought to myself and continued in the direction where the village and abandoned building waited.

"Dove, it's getting dark."

"Only another hundred yards or so. Keep going."

"Someone's up there. Should we—"

My jaw clenched. "Keep going."

I saw the figure now too—a large bulk with a brimmed hat leaning against a boulder at the top of a shelf of dirt. I veered to the left, staying behind the ground's natural rise. "Keep going. This way around."

My heart hammered and weakness loosened my knees. I could not give up and turn back. The building's crooked chimneys would come into view at any moment. And then the top floor windows. My eyes were eager to locate a crack in the boards and peer through the ruined glass panes.

My dream back in Sisters had revealed waterfalls of blood pouring from those windows, which meant there was someone in there. Maybe lots of someones. Maybe...could it be my family and the lost Christians?

Crackle-thud. A large person dropped down the overhang. His boots hit the dry sticks before us. Trinity gasped.

"Bull! What are you...why are you—"

"You shouldn't be here, Dove. Not with the rest of them around. I knew you was a mule-headed girl, but I didn't take you for a stupid one." His low voice dropped. "It's not too late. Go. Hightail it back to where you came from before the others see you. And here, take this back to your guy. I don't want it on me."

He thrust a book at me, and he whispered, "I got my own now. Smaller version. Can hide it in my boot."

Trinity accepted the book.

I stepped closer. "Who else is around, Bull? You

said others. What others are here?"

Feet sounded in the bushes—more than one pair—moving over the ground behind Bull. Were people at the building? Or further back, nearer the village?

Crack!

We froze at the gunshot. With a grunt, Bull's thick arm shot out and shoved me square in the chest.

36

I tumbled down the incline. Sharpness stung and scratched my flailing hands and arms. By the time I jammed to a stop inside a prickly juniper laced with nettles, Bull's wide bulk had disappeared over the boulder on the hill's crest.

Trinity skidded to a halt and reached around the nettles, searching for me.

I stood and began to move back up the incline, but her hands locked around my arms. "Sky alive, Dove. Did you knock your head and become braindead? You can't go up there. Someone's got a gun—you heard the shot." Her strained voice became a hiss in my ear.

I twisted against her restraint. "But—"

"Stop. Think. Who has guns?"

I quit struggling.

In the distance, Bull bellowed. "Whoa, now!"

A different voice murmured an abrupt reply. In English? Or Amhebran? I leaned toward the slope. If only I could see past the earth in my way. Who spoke? Who else was up there?

A throb started in my wrist, worse than the nettle stings. It was Trinity death-gripping my healing arm and trying to get my attention.

"What, Trinity? What?"

"I said think. Who has guns? That Commander Reed guy does. And idiot Christians like him. And the Heathen—fine, nonbelievers, who hunt believers. In other words, murderous humans have guns. So why would we go racing up there to our suicides?"

"Because our moms are there. Stuck in that building."

Trinity blinked and released my arms. The sun's light had faded and her gray irises appeared charcoal. I dropped my gaze first. Of course, she didn't believe me. She'd heard my theory about that building a hundred times the last few days, and she didn't agree. No one did...except Jezebel.

She nodded. "OK."

My lungs released air in a gush. *She believes me*. But when I tried to move past and up the incline, she immobilized me with her words. "God doesn't want us up there now."

Trinity never lied. Which meant...with her newly recognized gift, I had to believe that God didn't want us at that building tonight. I closed my eyes and swallowed hard.

The messy sounds up the slope had stopped. The way could be safe now. And I could sneak up there and find out if my conviction was correct.

"OK, Trinity. You lead...wherever you think."

"We go back. To Sisters."

It took all my strength not to stomp my feet into the bracken as we backtracked. The darkness grew, making it impossible to tell if the trees were familiar. Smoke tainted the air. Christians were nearby—believers bold enough to announce their presence with campfires. Other Sent?

"What do you think, Dove. Stop here for tonight?"

I peered into the shadows, trying to make out signs of other campers. The earth rose between the trees in a natural mound, good protection at our backs.

Plenty of untouched forest debris covered the ground.

I flopped down and chugged water. It was better to hunker down between earth and bushes than risk tromping blindly into a group of—possibly unfriendly—knife-throwers in an attempt to reach Sisters tonight.

A wisp of laughter reached us. And a faded "*Arookhaw*"—the Amhebran word for dinner.

I nibbled a peanut butter cracker. Trinity's white shirt with rainbow splotches seemed to glow in the darkness. Why hadn't she accepted Brooke and Rebecca's offer of earth-tone garments? There was a pile of them in a box in the van. At least one shirt must have fit.

I pulled my brown cap lower over my blonde strands and hugged my tunic from Wolfe.

Was it only a few days ago we'd hiked these same woods? With Wolfe at my side, the forest had been sunlight and whistling. Doughnuts and laughter. Safety. A warm sensation in my gut.

But no, it was good Wolfe wasn't here now. Because with a knife-thrower camping nearby, it wasn't safe for a nonbeliever in these hills tonight. It wasn't even safe for Christians who wore nonbelievers' clothes.

More snatches of Amhebran echoed...then began to rise and fall. Singing. I strained my ears. The same song I'd heard long ago on the side of Mount Jefferson hovered in the night.

No. Nonbelievers like Wolfe shouldn't be in these woods tonight.

I sat up straight. What about Bull? He hadn't been shot...but he'd shouted at someone. Who had been nearby? Someone with a gun? Someone who'd hurt him?

Goosebumps pricked my arms, and I curled up with my chin on my knees. Despite Trinity's warning, I'd assumed the shooter was an armed, jumpy city dweller who'd been startled by a raccoon or chipmunk.

But what if the trigger-happy human was a nonbeliever who held Christians against their will in that cement building? And Bull had confronted the person?

Or the gunman was a Christian—a believer like my brother or the unknown knife thrower—who'd taken possession of a gun. The shooter could be someone who acted out in hate, who clung to Reed's lies that God wanted us to take back our country by violence.

If Bull had run into that sort of Christian, he might be wounded now. Or...

I hugged my knees tighter. It was good Wolfe wasn't here.

"Here. It'll make a decent pillow." Trinity handed me the book from Bull and curled up on her side to sleep.

A Bible. My fingers traced the large letters engraved on its floppy cover.

I shook my head. Bull had given me a Bible. Correction, he'd returned the Bible that Wolfe had given him the other day when I thought he'd been handing out packaged cheese.

The van...Wolfe turning pages during that long ride. Reading God's Word.

A joyful geyser bubbled up inside of me, but I stamped it down like a gopher hole in the garden. Just because Wolfe looked at a Bible once didn't make him a Christian.

I rolled on my back and talked to God about it for a while. I must have fallen asleep, because suddenly the blushing moon shone overhead. An animal snuffled a few yards to the south of where Trinity continued to breathe softly.

I eased the floppy binding off my stomach and located my knife.

When the coolness of morning broke, the handle's outline left a red indent in my palm. The first sunbeams illuminated a large paw mark in the loose dirt next to our packs.

A cat's? I moved toward it and froze.

"Shalom."

I whipped up my knife and pointed it. The speaker—a stranger in rags— balanced on the mound of dirt next to where Trinity slept.

37

My toe nicked Trinity awake. I withdrew from the spot where three other ragged figures had appeared. Their pale faces peered at me, squinting as if the soft morning light stung.

My cousin found her feet and skittered away from them.

"They're Christian moles, Trinity." Even if they hadn't just emerged from a dugout on the edge of my campsite, I would have recognized them as humans who lived under the earth's crust. Believers in burrows, who possessed waxy skin that'd never seen sunlight. Plus, their clothes were caked with soil, and they sniffed the air as if its freshness was foreign to them.

I held my weapon high. With my other hand, I groped for my pack and fallen hat.

My downward glance fell on my outstretched arms with my inked sword and shield, to my tunic and the breastplate outline and woven belt.

The object I scooped up wasn't a hat but a helmet. Because I wore armor. God's armor.

I lowered my weapon. I wouldn't fight. I wouldn't run and hide.

God, You want me here in the trees? Fine, here I am.

I nodded. "Uh...hi. Shalom."

The woman in the far back gripped the pronged branch.

Plastic rustled. Trinity's hands emerged from her pack holding cellophane-covered packets. "Crackers, anyone?"

The oldest male who'd greeted me now nodded. He didn't smile, but at least his hands unfisted. "Yes. Please. The berries and insects in this region are very limited. Is this where we were meant to make camp for the prayer rally?"

"I couldn't tell you."

The crackers went around. The six of us settled on the pine needles, and the moles studied their squares as if they'd never seen crackers before.

I bumped my cousin. "Just so you know, we're not running away anymore."

She grinned up at the orange sunrise filtering through the branches and tapped the lion's profile decorating her shoulder. "We'll be lions."

"Lions? What—"

"You remember. Those who don't know God run. But those who do right by Him are brave—have no fear...are as bold as lions. Maybe you should read some of that Bible yourself before returning it to your guy."

I swallowed my retort that she was becoming her dad, spouting Bible verses. I bent to pick up the book but straightened.

Stone Bender clutched a nearby pine trunk and stared at me.

My remaining cracker hit the dirt. The blood drained from my head while my mouth opened to squeak, *run*. But I'd promised Trinity we wouldn't run.

He stepped forward. "Dove? You're...you're alive. Melody said you would be. But I didn't think you'd...made it."

I stood. "And you didn't kill Rebecca."

His beard jerked up at the unexpected words I'd blurted. "No, but how...how do you know about her? Did God—"

"It's not too late, Stone. Leave your brother and be your own person. You hate his plans, so why not make a better choice?"

"Can't."

His hand rested on my shoulder, though I hadn't noticed him moving toward me. I squinted up at him and recognized something. Something that made me breathe faster.

A year ago, I'd wondered if he was the person I would someday marry. I'd thought, at the time, I was drawn to him because he was a male from the Christian mold I was familiar with—strong, serious, bearded.

But then he had betrayed me.

Yet now...

I held my fist over my thumping heart as if to keep it in place. Because I recognized the truth. It wasn't just his strength that once drew me. It was his good heart. Sure, he had tried to follow his brother's sinful orders and hurt me. But his goodness kept him from being successful, the proof being I still lived.

Yep. Stone was a good person. Despite following the wrong leader.

I stepped closer. "I need your help."

He closed his eyes as if my words hurt. Then they opened, and the mask was back. "Dove, I can't let you go free."

I waved this away. "No, no. I need your help on something more important. You've got to help free the missing Christians."

His fingers tightened. "What?"

I shifted under their bruising force. "There's a cement building at the edge of the village—a big one, real ugly...with square windows. I need you to ask God about going there, and if He says you're allowed, then you get inside. Locate our people. And free them."

"But, how did you know—"

"Oh, and there might be others with guns near it. But you can find a way around them. It'll be easy for you." Yes, this was the reason God had shut me and Trinity down last night. Because Stone was on his way to me. He alone had the strength and slipperiness to be successful.

Silence descended. The cracker gnawing behind me had quit. Trinity's frown burned into my back, probably because the last time she'd met Stone, he'd acted as our enemy. She didn't understand he wasn't. He was good.

Stone's beard swayed. "Sorry, Dove. Really. And now that you know about that building...I really can't let you go. You'll stay with me, both of you will...until—"

"Release my sister."

Gilead glowered from the top of the earth mound. His leap down dislodged the giant's grip from my shoulder.

I picked myself up and ran to stand with Trinity.

"Is this the other boyfriend, Dove? The bigger one that the Jezebel kid hit with a slug?" He circled Stone. The tendons and muscles stood out in his hands and neck. "Continue speaking, loser. What were you saying about making my sister stay with you? And my cousin?"

The giant's feet mirrored my brother's in reverse. His sun-bleached eyebrows furrowed low in concentration. But even though he loomed over my brother, I didn't bite my lip for my sibling. The Strong fierceness gave Gilead the upper hand...like a third fist in a fistfight.

Gilead made a swift kick to the back of his opponent's knee.

Stone sidestepped in a blur. "I...I don't want to hurt you. I don't like to hurt anybody."

My brother hummed something that could've been a laugh. "Perfect. Because I do."

His fist flew out. The larger figure ducked and countered with a lightening punch to my brother's chin. It grazed the blonde hairs there, but the following punch met air.

Their feet sidestepped faster now. Feinted and fell back.

Gilead lunged at Stone and caught his wider shoulders. The two became clenched in a wild, rib-cracking hug. My brother's commands escaped his clenched teeth.

"Trinity. Dove. And you...whoever you people are. I'm on patrol...security for the Council. I'm here to relocate you to your new campsites...near Camp Sherman."

He rolled out of a neck hold and threw the giant off. "Start walking south. I'll catch up in a few minutes. When I finish."

My spine pressed up harder against the mound of crumbling dirt. Trinity stayed rooted with her nose wrinkled. The moles chewed their crackers like cows do cud, their unblinking eyes fastened on the fighters as though unable to understand such violence after a sheltered lifetime of peace underground.

"Excuse me, security sir? I find a brisk smack to

the cerebellum is an effective stunning technique for most creatures. May I assist?" The fatherly looking figure accepted the branch from the woman and darted a quick step forward. "My family is eager to reach that campsite you've offered."

The woman's elbow nudged my side. "The knife. If you're not going to use it..." She held out her palm.

Gilead rocketed two feet through sunlit air and landed in a sticker bush. Stone whirled around, his cheeks and ears flushed crimson. "You're trying to make me...but I won't hurt you."

He hurdled some bushes. There were a couple muffled footsteps, then silence.

My brother stirred and rubbed his scalp. He leaped to his feet and moved to race after, but the branch-holder placed one grungy palm on his heaving shoulder.

"Ah well, security sir. You can't beat every giant every time. Now, about that campsite. You say we follow you, yes? We are grateful you located us during your patrol."

"Yes...sir."

My brother's bearded jaw stayed clenched while he led us at a jogging pace through the foothills. My brain churned, moving faster than my legs.

Stone was here, near the village. He knew about the building. Did he know if anyone lived inside—or possibly about a future hostage situation?

Gilead spoke only when Black Butte was a hump on the horizon. "That guy didn't beat me. He ran away. Afraid. You're my witness, Dove."

"Sure. He ran away..." *To keep from hurting us.* I swallowed the last bit. Because if I didn't argue, maybe he'd be ready to hear the important information I'd kept bottled inside the last couple hours. "Hey, Gil, listen. Once we deliver this family to their campsite, you and I need to hurry back. There's a cement building near the village on Black Butte. I'm pretty sure Mom is being held there."

His fist jabbed at an invisible opponent, reliving his fight with Stone. I thumped his shoulder. "Gil—listen to me. Mom and Grandpa—"

"Are in California. That's what Commander Reed last reported. They're being held near a town called—"

"Trinidad. But they're not there. He's lying."

My sibling knew about Reed Bender. He'd called him Commander and believed his lies. But he hadn't recognized Stone Bender by sight. I pressed my lips together. I'd be wasting breath to mention that Stone might be in the area to take part in a plan to capture government people. Gilead didn't care about helping nonbelievers. Or about keeping peace.

In front of me, Trinity stumbled under Gilead's sudden glare. "What? Spit it out, Cousin."

"Fine. What would Gran say? You dressed like that?"

Her cheeks flooded.

The straggling footsteps of the mole family quickened until the woman's hand-stitched shoe caught my heel.

"Ignore him, Trinity. He's just in a rotten mood because he lost his fight. Just like he lost his shadow."

"I did not." My brother marched ahead. "And my shadow—I mean Micah—is safe at camp."

Trinity hugged her pack. But she didn't comment as we continued to hike.

When the blazing sun hovered above the treetops, another bearded figure appeared ahead in the crook of a tree. No doubt he was a tree-dwelling Christian since he appeared so at home in the branches. A bird, Rebecca would call him. Like me.

Gilead lifted his arm. "To God's glory."

The tree dweller raised his gray sleeve that matched my brother's. "God's glory forever."

The figure stayed seated while his half-mast eyes followed our trek until we dropped over a crumbling, natural ridge edged with disintegrating ferns. I hurried around a mound of car-sized boulders.

I cleared the last rock and blinked. Christians everywhere. Christians, who had lost their minds. Was this the same camp at Camp Sherman that Brooke and Hunter had described a few days ago? Impossible. Yet it had to be. The unmistakable rush of the Metolius River sounded from close by.

A dozen campfires burned openly even though the chill of night was hours away. Torches pricked among a sea of tents. The homemade shelters crowded together like the buildings of Portland, leaving no room to walk between.

A mammoth, tent-free, clearing of trampled bracken stretched to the west, and people in earth-tone clothes stood in a line among the tree stumps. Their arms supported long-barreled weapons.

"Ready!"

Each body in line dropped to one knee.

"Aim. Fire!"

I flinched, but no gunfire sounded. There was only a murmur of human voices imitating the shots, not wasting whatever precious bullets they had on practice. But they had guns...so no doubt they possessed bullets, too.

"Wait here, girls," Gilead said, "while I show this

family an open campsite. Then I'll take you to our tent."

Trinity moved after him. "No, Gil. I'll come with you and...poke around a bit."

"Shalom, Dove Strong. May God bless you."

My hand, which had begun to shake, twitched up in farewell at the mole family. Anger coursed through me, blurring the scene before me. Yet I saw it too clearly.

These believers practiced for battle, but they'd been invited here to pray and comfort each other over their losses.

I walked to the clearing. In the far corner near a group of torches, children practiced slinging. Their targets were rough-hewn wood, human-shaped cutouts.

I veered toward a cluster of these but stopped short at someone's shout.

More voices called from the trees further along, past the city of tents. A hollow echo rang out—wood clunked together, the sounds of Christians grappling.

I swirled back around. A sign with an arrow poked up from the ground a stone's throw away. It pointed toward a section of forest.

Explosive Testing Area. Stay Away.

Explosives? Bombs? No. These people—my people—could not be creating bombs that ripped humans apart.

I gripped my hair and dropped to my knees.

"Hey, look. It's that Heathen-lover from the Council."

I raised my pounding head. City rats. Their dark clothes were as machine-made as my own. Rubber-soled shoes encased their feet.

"She doesn't love Heathen. Not anymore. She's on our side now. I heard her on the radio. Called them Satan's puppets."

Another city rat with a beard clipped short like Lobo used to wear rounded the side of a tent. "It's Dove. You know, from Texas. Her head is on a big sign down the road that way. You're Dove, aren't you?"

He strode over and presented me with a pointed stick. "Yours now. To mount the heads of those Heathen who tortured you in the desert."

My trembling fingers closed around the weapon's shaft. I licked my lips. Stood. And strode to the tallest stump in the clearing where a target balanced.

I whirled around and knocked the object to the ground. Ignoring the shouts directed at me, I climbed to balance on the axe-hewn stump. I glared around at the humans and met the eyes of those who'd paused.

"Have you all gone crazy?" I swung my outstretched stick and made contact with the nearest target. *Crack*. Wood splintered.

"Your hate makes me sick!" I stamped my foot and jabbed at the only other target within reach. "Sick! People we love are gone, but instead of doing something useful like praying about it, you waste your time preparing for pointless murders and following the path that Satan wants. Come on—all of you! Quit being fools!"

I leaped down and charged the warning sign for explosive testing. As I raised my spear to bash its center, my weapon slid out of my grip. An arm came across my torso and lifted me.

"Shut up and cool it, Dove," Gilead said in my ear. "You're embarrassing me. And yourself."

My legs wind milled. "If I do, then there won't be

anybody to tell these ignorants they're sinning." I raised my voice. "Anyone who wants to actually help our families, follow me—"

"Ignore her," Gilead said to the believers who appeared at tent openings and doorways of branch-made shelters we passed. "Ignore her."

He stopped at the mouth of a low tent speckled with mold. "You want to pray? Fine. Do it in here, the designated spot for praying." He released me into its gloomy depths.

Whump. My backpack landed beside me. His face appeared. "Do not move from this place until I come for you."

I shifted off the lumpy remains of a tree root and massaged a bruised kneecap. My nose cringed in the strong atmosphere of mildew and old canvas.

"Oh, it's you."

I jerked around and squinted. Chaff slumped on his knees in a corner.

"It's you! Chaff! What are you doing here? Rebecca said you were heading home and that you told her you'd never leave your property again."

"Obviously, that was before I got home and found my sister gone. Taken. No doubt caught while wandering the beach. She's always taking risks like that. Being conspicuous. I wasn't there to keep her hidden."

My hot anger melted away, replaced by a chilly heaviness. More loss. I curled up cross-legged next to him. "That...stinks. Poor kid didn't know better."

"My sister's thirty-seven."

"Oh."

He clambered off his shins and began to rock back and forth. "I came for the prayer rally. But it's a joke. I don't think it's going to happen. All anyone here wants to do is sword fight and pretend to shoot. Dumb stuff I could do at home if I wanted to."

"Uh-huh."

"I don't want to."

I nodded. Chaff twirling around with a sword? Nope.

"And my sister's not being held in Trinidad, so don't believe what you hear."

"I know."

"Well you used to think so. And that's what everyone here thinks—the taken are being held down south. It's stupid. Why would I ride a train all the way north if my sister was in California? How about a little common sense?"

"According to my brother, they all listen to and believe Reed Bender. And he lies. A lot."

"And his right-hand man, Zech." Chaff rocked faster. "That liar's creepier than a hobo spider nest."

Spiders weren't creepy. I shrugged. "The taken Christians are prisoners near Black Butte. In a building, next to a village there. I'm pretty sure."

"Wouldn't be surprised."

He believed me. Some of my heaviness lifted. "Stone Bender said something suspicious to me about the building this morning, so I think he and Reed know."

His neck bobbed. "Again. Not surprised."

"I couldn't get there yesterday to free our people. Or help them. I tried."

He shook his head. "Too rash. Did you consider their guards would've caught you if you'd made it there? No, I didn't think you did."

"You're wrong, I did think of that. And I was

careful a few days ago when I explored the village. Reed's message I wore around my wrist in Portland—the one you helped deliver—said Christians would be taking nonbelievers as hostages there. But I can't figure out when that will happen, or if it will ever happen. Did Zech tell you Reed's plans?"

Chaff shook his head. "I didn't bother to ask. Why worry about what might happen to Heathen? I'll save my energy, thanks. We've got our own problems to worry about."

Silence fell.

"I helped save you, Dove. At the ocean. In California."

"Uh. OK."

There wasn't a lot to say after that. While he rocked and wrung his hands, I slid onto my knees.

Fix these stupid people, God. And give me back my mom.

I tried to articulate more, but a baby somewhere began to cry. Rocks thunked targets. Gruff voices corrected trajectories and traded root-based soup recipes. Kids whined.

"Shalom, Chaff."

I opened my eyes.

Trinity crouched at the tent opening. "Ready to go, Dove?"

I scrambled up. "Yeah...what's wrong with your face? Your eyes are red. Did you fall into some poison oak?"

She lifted them to the ceiling that was speckled like a sparrow's egg. "I saw Micah. He saw me. He turned and ran away. The end. Let's get out of here."

I stabbed a small twig into the dirt, imagining a blue-tinged lizard. "Forget about that skink boy,

Trinity. Chaff, tell my brother that I left."

"He'll probably notice without my help."

I tucked my blonde strands into my cap, ducked my chin, and darted out from under the rotting canvas. I kept my eyes on Trinity's feet, following them past some boulders. Up a slope.

"Shalom," she muttered. A good-bye to the guard in the tree?

We entered untouched forest, and the camp noises faded. I unhunched, drawing the pine air into my lungs. The way ahead appeared to be mostly downhill. I plunged forward, letting my body's momentum carry me along. Glimpses of pavement appeared between the branches ahead of us.

"Whoa, whoa, whoa!"

My feet wouldn't slow. I stumbled onto the road and into the glow of headlights.

The car didn't hit me since it was parked. People stood near it—familiar people.

Savannah glanced at Lobo then sashayed forward. "Hello, Dove. Jessica mentioned you were back in town. Oh, and I caught your radio broadcast...calling us evil puppets, responsible for all the horrible goings-on in the world. Brilliant stuff."

She pointed at the parked car whose sleek curves glistened like water in a creek. "Get in."

38

Jessica leaned through the car's open doorway. Her camera lens glinted in the deepening gloom.

Trinity stepped around me. "Who are you?"

Lobo quit stroking the scruff on his chin and strode forward with one hand out. "Valentino Vargas. Lobo for short. You are terrorista Dove's sister? Or another cousin? May I?" He raised a bulkier electronic lens than Jessica's and directed it at Trinity.

The bushes behind us rustled as if something shifted among its dry branches.

Savannah inhaled. She strode toward the vehicle. "Yes, yes. We'll continue this fascinating conversation inside the CTDC. Dove, in the back. Try not to get dirt on the upholstery. Your cousin can—"

*Grrrr…*I spun to face the predatory growling. The high brambles at the road shook as though a three-hundred-pound beast ripped at them, clawing its way through.

Grrrr...

Savannah's high heels skittered over the remaining pavement to the vehicle's door. She dove in behind the steering wheel. "Lobo! What are you doing? It'll be a grizzly."

The cameraman drifted toward the bushes that continued to grunt. A confused expression replaced his smirk. "A black bear maybe. But no grizzlies here. Not for a hundred years."

He parted the trembling foliage and stuck his head inside.

Then he shouted—a gurgling burst of sound. His legs churned, and he disappeared headfirst inside the bush, as if something stronger pulled him in.

Savannah and Jessica began to scream. Car doors slammed. The engine hummed and faded into the distance.

The bear's grunting stopped. Lobo quit yelling.

Trinity raised a slow finger at the now motionless foliage next to the road where Lobo had vanished. "That bear sounded...different."

Lobo's laughter shook the brambles. He stood. An even slighter figure rose up beside him.

"Micah." Trinity lost her grin.

"Trinity." Micah appeared just as miserable.

I moved in front of my cousin. "Savannah left. You missed your ride, Lobo, and stayed behind with us. Why?"

He picked his way onto the asphalt, smile lines etched around his eyes. "Curiosity, Dove. Where did you come from in the middle of nowhere? Not a drop of sweat on you, which means you traveled from a location close by. And why does someone else pretend to be a grizzly in the bushes? I think you might share those answers with me better if we get rid of the person who threatens you with the CTDC. Am I right?"

"You thought wrong." I turned my glare onto my neighbor. "Your black bear impression needs work. Why did you follow us, Micah?"

"You left camp too soon."

"Too soon?" But he wasn't speaking to me. He spoke around me, to my cousin.

His arm swung up. A skimpy bouquet of limp flowers dangled from his fist. "I saw that you lost the roses from your pack, the ones I gave you last month. So here. I brought you these. They're better than the last ones. They'll make your pack smell nicer."

"Why?" Trinity asked. "Why would I want more roses from you?"

He rocked back on his heels. His Brae eyes widened. Afraid.

I crossed my arms. Now he'd bolt back to my brother.

His chin came up and his scrawny chest puffed out like a proud robin's. "You should take them because I like you, Trinity. Each time I saw a wild strawberry plant growing, or some bright leaf or flower, I hoped you'd end up coming to the Council too."

Her colorful arm lifted and accepted the dead roses.

Lobo hustled me a few yards down the white painted line.

I shook him off. "What are you doing?"

"Giving them privacy."

"Privacy? What for?"

"Because when two people love each other, privacy is necessary."

"Ridiculous." I turned. They were hugging. My nose wrinkled.

"Also, we need to talk."

"You got your answer. Micah was a bear to stop my cousin from getting in Savannah's car because he had to give her roses." Roses! Now I understood her obsession with that flower talk in Portland.

"And your location in the woods where Micah

came from also?"

I recrossed my arms.

"I see." He balanced his camera on his shoes and pulled a smaller electronic from his pocket.

"What are you doing, Lobo?"

He held up the small rectangle. "This? It's to call Savannah for a ride. For both of us."

My arms uncrossed and dangled. "Fine. I'll go to that Louisiana swamp with you and Jessica if you leave me alone. No detention center. Please."

"We fly south in two days."

"Five days?"

"Three. And you explain what's located in that patch of trees." He repocketed his electronic.

Kaboom.

A flock of startled sparrows rose from their evening roosts in the treetops.

Micah released my cousin. "Uh-oh. I better get back to camp since I'm the weapon detonation expert. Sounds like someone started testing without me."

"You're the expert?" Trinity wound her fingers through his as if she would return with him.

"Yep. Because I've got the most experience. I've been blowing up things all my life. Tunnels...underground rooms...they don't create themselves. A homemade device can save you a week's digging, if you know how to use it. And I do." He swaggered for the bushes with a beaming Trinity in tow.

Lobo's teeth gleamed. "Homemade explosive devices, huh? Final deal, Dove. We leave for the swamp in five days...no CTDC...and I get a peek at the camp your friend is heading to. Right now."

"Could I stop you from following him if I tried?"

"No, terrorista. Not even a grizzly could."

Bears might not stop Lobo. But Christians with weapons might.

"I think you're being suicidal. But deal. You get two minutes inside the camp, Lobo. And that's it."

39

Trinity smeared another handful of dirt on the knees of Lobo's pantlegs. "You might pass as a Christian in the dark, Lobo. The beard helps. But your hair's too pretty. Too perfect."

Lobo grinned. "Gracias."

Her head tilted. "I need scissors."

I handed her my knife.

She sawed off a few chunks of black hair and ripped his pantleg. "Now lose the electronics and the smile. Pretend your family is missing...or dead."

"They are dead."

"Well, act less happy about it."

He rearranged his expression and stashed his camera under the foliage. "OK. I'm ready. Oh, one second." He fiddled with the smaller electronic from his pocket then concealed it under more pine needles and sticks. "Now I'm ready."

Spending time with Wolfe taught me some basics about electronics. Like the ability to send messages without having to speak. "Lobo, you just communicated with someone. Who?"

He followed the other two deeper into the woods. "Savannah. Letting her know I survived the attack with no loss of limb, so no reason to send authorities into the forest after my body. I also told her I was helping locals trap the bear, which she's knows is something I'd do. I'm never one to turn down any challenge that nature throws at me. And the news of a rogue bear will keep her away from these woods tonight. She's no animal lover, that one. City tough but afraid of anything wearing fur."

Wooden clunks echoed louder than the sound of flowing river water. It was the noise of Christians at camp grappling with weapons. His steps quickened.

I plucked the back of his stained shirt. "How were you waiting for me at that spot on the road. How'd you know I'd show up there?"

"Know? How would I know? I arrived back in town today with Jess and Savannah to discuss tracking you down. We went for a drive, got turned around, and tempers flared—mostly Savannah's. I suggested we pause to figure out our coordinates and cool off."

I sucked in my breath and backhanded his head.

He clapped his scalp and swung around. "Do I annoy you?"

"Yes. Very much. How many miracles does God have to do for you...in front of your eyes...before you believe in Him?"

"Who says I don't believe?" He winked and jogged to catch up with the others.

A wheezy snoring issued from a branch where the tree-dweller acted as guard. We continued on then halted.

The camp appeared a hundred times more horrible in the darkness than it had in daylight.

I blinked at the blanket of smoke that covered the clearing. Campfires and torches cast a flickering, orange glow on the tents while figures with weapons wove around them in a chaotic mess. And that baby still cried. Its distressed wail matched the stomach-knotting scene.

A fire-lit arrow whooshed past. I jumped away from the arc of flames, my nerves pulling tauter. I stepped sideways and extinguished the fire with my sole.

A girl Jovie's age trudged over with a bow and yanked the smoking arrow out from under my foot. She didn't seem to recognize me or care about us strangers loitering at the edge of the camp. Her shoulders sagged as if heavy with the burden of mastering her weapon. She shuffled back to the archers.

Lobo whimpered in the back of his throat.

"Scared? I told you not to come."

The back of his hand swiped at his beads of forehead sweat. "This is a nightmare. Here before me lays the ultimate example of Christian vehemence. A scene of such violence and passion, such as has never been sighted before in my lifetime. Until now. Here it is. And I don't have my camera."

He grabbed my shoulder. "I'll get my camera equipment, Dove. And you don't have to go to Louisiana or anywhere ever again. Just help me film this. We'll need a microphone, lights, and..."

My stomach lurched. Film this? Show every television-owning nonbeliever just how correct they were to be afraid of Christians? No doubt the viewers would react by punishing any Sent who remained in their towns, which was the reaction Reed wanted in order to get his Reclaim started. It was what Satan wanted.

"No, Lobo. Never. I'll smash your camera first."

His voice shook. "I can't...not film this. You don't understand. This is it. My moment to capture the reality of what no other person has before. I can't walk away tonight emptyhanded. Not without revealing the truth to the world."

I'd already spewed poison calling nonbelievers Satan's puppets on the radio. No way could I let Lobo spread more hate through the television.

Another flaming arrow sailed past with a whoosh and a whisper. But the whisper didn't belong to any weapon.

I squeezed my eyes shut and focused. I heard past my thundering pulse and the baby's cries. Beyond the small explosion in the trees, the swords knocking together, and the twangs of bows.

I nodded and opened my eyes. "Lobo, the moment you bring your camera into the open, these people will stop you. Or I will stop you. Or my brother will."

My shout would bring Gilead or some other fighter who would ensure Lobo never used his camera tonight...or maybe ever again.

I swallowed. "You can't film this. But you won't leave these woods emptyhanded of truth. Instead of recording this...record me. I'll let you into my head, and whatever you want to ask me—insider Christian stuff, personal details—I'll tell you. Broadcast it. I don't care. And I'll fly to Louisiana with you. But tonight, your two minutes at this camp are up. We need to leave before someone puts an arrow through you on purpose."

I turned my back to his sputter. Trinity leaned against a far boulder. Alone. Focused on the tree line past the clearing where Micah must've gone to work on his explosive devices.

I picked up a piece of litter—an empty wedge of honeycomb that someone had discarded—and lobbed it at her.

A hit. Rubbing her arm, she moved closer.

"You're staying here, Trinity?"

"Of course not. I'm not ditching and letting you deal with that Lobo guy yourself."

"But if I was...maybe dead...you'd stay?"

"Probably. So what?"

"Pretend I'm dead." I dropped my voice. "Stay. Convince Micah to destroy those bombs. And try to get campers to talk to God. And to hear Him, even if just a little."

"I'm not Rebecca."

Rebecca—a genius idea! If she showed up, these people would listen and quit all this. I spoke faster. "Try anyway. And don't get in the way of the arrows."

"Obviously."

"And be, I guess...happy? Despite this huge mess."

"Lame, Dove." She grinned. "I am."

We gripped each other. Then I released her and dragged Lobo with me into a less lethal piece of forest.

~*~

A second tear rolled down my cheek. Surrounded by forest and half blinded by Jessica's artificial light so the camera would see me better, I blubbered like a two-year-old.

"Explain to us your tears, Dove Strong." Lobo, acting as my interviewer, gave me a thumbs-up as if approving of my dramatic display of emotional weakness. "Do you cry because you miss your mother, who you claim has disappeared? Or because someone murdered your father?"

"No."

He gestured for me to continue. "The truth? You promised."

I wasn't a liar—I had told him I'd answer any question he asked. So, with a runny nose and pathetic, leaky eyes, I described Satan. Powerful and evil. Laughing. Snatching up humans and trapping them forever in his terrible abyss.

"What humans, Dove?"

"You."

His eyes widened.

"Her."

Jessica drew her breath in a hiss.

I squinted at my fingers clenching the hat in my lap. "There was this lady once in Sisters. I was walking past her fence, and a fast car with an open door swerved alongside me. I was hit by the open door. And this lady ran out of her home and chased the car away. She put ice on my bruises, gave me water, hugged me. She...she got mad when she saw my legs."

I scrubbed at my damp face. Then I glared up. "And she's going to Hell."

"But maybe not. You only guess so."

"I know so."

"But your tears and your anguish over non-fanatics and their eternal fates...this does not match up with an eye-witness account from today." He winked. "An account that multitudes of Christians like you have gathered in secret to train in combat techniques."

I held my breath and waited to hear if he'd say the name of our location. But he also kept his promise and didn't.

"OK." My eyeballs were beginning to dry. "So?"

"So why do your people, these fanatical Christians, appear not to share your concern?"

I shrugged. "Because of fear. Lies. Bad leaders." Reed Bender's name teetered on the tip of my tongue. Then I swallowed it. To make his name known among nonbelievers would give him fame and increase his power.

It was the same reason I didn't voice my suspicion at what the building held at the outskirts of the Black Butte village. Or about the possible government hostage situation that might occur soon. Or about the Reclaim that seemed destined to happen despite the Councils' rulings for peace.

Lobo didn't know to ask direct questions about any of these things, so I kept the terrible truths locked inside. Why would I blab about unasked issues that would increase the hate between Christians and non-Christians? It already bubbled like a stew about to boil over.

"And now, Dove. Tell us about your home life. We want details. And secrets you've been keeping to yourself about growing up Christian."

40

I groped for the car's seat and collapsed onto it. On the black stretch of asphalt, Lobo and Jessica continued to load their equipment. The vehicle jostled with each addition—the portable lights. The power-supplying plasma generator. The cables and camera stands.

I pressed my forehead against the cool glass as the two climbed into the front. Doors slammed. The engine started.

During the drive to Sisters to take me home, Lobo gushed to Jessica about the Christian camp he hadn't filmed.

"Fire being used everywhere, Jess. And the bloodlust...even the children training, as if to kill—"

"That's it, Lobo. Turn us around. Take me back. I'm going in to get footage."

My muscles tensed, but he continued to drive us straight.

A new worry struck. Would these two sneak back tomorrow or the next day with their cameras? Why should I trust Lobo's word? All those answers I'd given to keep my end of the bargain...I shuddered. Could my sacrifice be for nothing? I bit my lip, unable to shake off the nausea at what I'd revealed during my interview.

Now everyone knew the exact location of my tree home in Ochoco and that my last name was Strong and not Pickett.

I'd shared the details of my dad's arrest and his murder. Viewers would chuckle over my fear of bicycles, dogs, and Dead Nights. They'd laugh at my answers about God. About why I still clung to my belief of His love during the times when I lay broken and starving. And why I was convinced of a place called Hell.

I pressed my face against the curved window as if to pass through it, outside to where the car's breeze could blow away my new memory of this horrible interview.

"A fire," Jessica pointed out Lobo's window. "Look."

I raised my head from the glass. It disappeared, leaving an open hole. Smoky night air rushed in as Lobo maneuvered us to an open spot of pavement between familiar houses. Men in uniforms were extinguishing my shelter's last glowing embers. They sprayed water, scattering the charred remains of arborvitae trees.

"Luckily, the fire only burned a small bunch of trees in a cow field. Not a house." Lobo shrugged. "Not your home."

He continued through the neighborhoods and stopped in front of Wolfe's house. I got out, since it was the address I'd given him. He called something about meeting in five days and drove away.

I wasn't surprised that Satan had led someone to discover my tree shelter and destroy it. With all the evening visitors the last few days, as well as Brooke's and Rebecca's determination to use a lantern in the field, more than one person would have noticed our presence. No, I wasn't mad. Just tired. And now I didn't have a place to sleep.

A faint sob sounded from close by. I approached the boxy Saint Jonah's Thrift Store van, which had become a permanent fixture in Wolfe's driveway.

Knock, knock. The door under my knuckles opened with a click. Joshua hunkered next to the tassled lantern, his cheeks swollen and tear streaked. Wolfe closed the door behind me and resettled, patting his curly head.

My queasiness, created by my interview, intensified to stomach-heaving panic. Why did Joshua cry? Who'd died? "Sky alive! Well? What's wrong?"

Joshua smeared his tears. "My sister...she's been taken. Brooke and Hunter too."

"Tell me what happened. Exactly."

Joshua shook his head.

"Wolfe? Spit it out...even if it's bad news."

He hesitated a moment. "We...we all saw the drawing you left, Dove, the one you carved on that crate...of the abandoned employees building. I explained it to Rebecca. But I didn't find out that she and the others had decided to head to the village to check it out until Josh showed up at the van this afternoon. Alone and upset. Apparently the four of them made the hike to the village early this morning. Josh played lookout while Hunter, Rebecca, and Brooke took a stab at removing a board from one of the building's lower, busted-out windows."

I leaned forward. "Did they find anything? Anyone?"

"Only trouble. Guys in uniforms appeared and grabbed all three of them. They put a gag on Rebecca before she could talk them into letting her, Brooke, and Hunter go."

"I gave the warning..." Joshua's voice broke. "I

drummed the single buzz roll against the boulder like they said I should do if I saw anyone. But—"

Wolfe wrapped his arm around the boy's thin shoulders and squeezed. "Don't beat yourself up. I'm sure your drummed warning was fine. So was your running. Good thing you've got fast legs and were able to get away. Did you sprint the whole eight miles back to this van?"

Joshua leaned away and picked up a nearby drumstick. He hurled it into the darkness of the van's front seat. "Stupid drumming. I should've whistled. Or shouted. It's my fault Becca's gone."

Wolfe glanced at me, and I focused on the van's worn floor.

No. It wasn't Joshua's fault. I'd made the carving. I'd put the idea about exploring that building in the others' heads.

Brooke's capture. Hunter's capture. Rebecca's. They were my fault.

41

I awoke to find Jezebel's arm flopped over my waist. The morning sun streamed in through the front windows, one of its beams illuminating Joshua. He lay in a ball next to Wolfe's sprawled and snoring frame. A dozen bright food packages surrounded them—offerings from Jezebel to cheer up the devastated kid.

It'd been a tough night with Joshua snuffling through most of it. We'd all taken turns trying to comfort him. My turn was the shortest. I was incompetent at doling out false hope.

I slid out from Jezebel's arm and dug out the Bible I needed to return. "Wake up, Wolfe."

The Bible thudded onto his chest. He grunted and pushed it off.

"We need to find Rebecca. Fast. We could...uh...borrow Diamond's motorcycle and drive to the village this morning to check."

"A bit desperate?" His grin vanished in a yawn. "I am, too. But no need. I found my engine's missing piece in my grandma's lucky casino bag, and I drove my Jeep to the village last night. I couldn't get close though. Too many security patrols now blocking the roads."

"Security patrols?"

"Yep. The government retreat has begun."

Stone's remark yesterday about not letting me go since I knew about that building had convinced me that he and his brother were responsible for Rebecca's capture there. But maybe the Benders weren't guilty.

"So, you think it was those security guys protecting the officials that got Rebecca? Not Christians?"

He shrugged. "Unfortunately, the kid can't tell by the abductors' uniforms or facial hair which side they're on—Christian or non-Christian. They spoke English."

Joshua's back continued to rise and fall as if he were comatose.

I rested my chin in my palm. First my family went missing. Then my friends. And now, the remaining Christians from Washington State to California honed their combat skills in the surrounding wilderness while unsuspecting government officials settled in for a fun-filled retreat.

The retreat goers might as well *ask* to be taken hostage by their stupid choice of location and bad timing.

"I've already hounded Grandma to call the village with an anonymous tip about a potential hostage threat." He shook his head. "For the first time ever, she's denying my request. She says Homeland Security would track her call, and the last thing our family needs is to be mixed up in more terrorist scandals. She threatened to sell my ride if she hears anyone in our family has called in the tip. Just so you know, 'family' includes you, too."

Bam, bam, bam.

Jezebel and Joshua jerked upright at the violent knocking.

Wolfe cracked open the door. "Hey, Diamond. Uh. What brings you here? To my driveway? Super early in the morning?"

"I'm protecting the neighborhood." Her purple eyes scanned the van's interior, moving past me. "Jessica said the loser was back. Where is he?"

Wolfe ran a hand through his sleep-rumpled hair. "Who? What loser in particular are you looking for?"

I sighed. "My brother. She likes him."

42

The cool morning air flowed through the Jeep's open window and eased my throbbing headache, which had begun when Diamond knocked me to the van's floor. My punishment for insulting her. We drove past the cow field, and I faced away from the charred remains, wincing at the acrid tang of smoke.

Wolfe slow whistled and pointed. "I'm never one to volunteer rotten news, but, uh—"

"My place burned down. Yeah. I know."

"Why didn't you say something last night?"

"I forgot."

"The van is a better place to live anyway, Dove." Jezebel—uninvited on our search for our missing friends, yet in the seat behind me anyway—patted my blonde braids. "I'll keep you company every night, so you don't get lonely."

"I don't think Dove gets lonely much, brat. Since she rarely gets a moment alone. Speaking of too much company..." He gestured to the road behind us.

The Jeep's mirror showed Diamond riding behind on her motorcycle. But at least Wolfe and Jezebel's grandma had given up chasing us. She probably stopped when she lost her shoe at the corner.

"Grandma's so funny." Jezebel giggled.

I frowned. "Not funny. Worried. That you'll end up in another CTDC. Or lost like Wolfe."

At the word "lost," Joshua buried his fingers in his

hair.

"Jez, you should've stayed home," I said.

She clapped Joshua's back. "Don't cry, Josh. Becca won't stay lost. Dove found my brother, so she'll find your sister. If she's being held in a fanatic camp around here like Dove thinks, then we'll have her free by lunchtime. Right, Woof?

"Maybe give us until dinnertime, Jezzy. Locating these Christian camps in the wilderness could take a while. And if Reed's soldiers are holding them in a tent somewhere, we might have to wait until dark to use our ninja stealth to sneak them out. Dove, you said Brooke and Hunter reported there are three main areas around here where Christians are camping. Which one do we check out first?"

We? Nope. *I* was the only one in this Jeep entering Christian camps today. I pointed north anyway. "Camp Sherman."

I'd planned to search this site last after I'd explored the other two. I wasn't eager to experience my brother's anger. He'd told me to stay. But with the motorcyclist on our tail...

Wolfe's head bobbed. "Smart. Give Diamond what she wants fast so she'll go away. Even though I still can't believe...you think your brother likes her back?"

"No."

"But if he doesn't, he probably won't stop others from using her as target practice."

I nodded.

We stopped next to the weeds crushed by Jessica's tires last night. Wolfe considered his bicep for a moment and sighed. "Right. I guess it'll be up to me to keep Diamond safe from everyone."

"Wrong. You're staying at the road with these two.

Drive away if you need."

Jezebel put her arms around my chairback, locking them around my shoulders. "I want to go with you to see your brother. And Trinity."

"No way. Too dangerous."

She squeezed me harder. "Dove, are your people going to hurt Diamond?"

I disentangled myself and exited into the weeds. "Maybe."

"But not really hurt her, right? You won't let that happen."

Why was I leading Diamond into a Christian camp? I didn't do it because I was angry at her...or because I needed revenge for a throbbing head. I wasn't afraid of her tantrum if I didn't obey her request. And I definitely wasn't bringing her to Gilead for his sake.

I focused on the hard, blue sky. *Yes, Lord.*

For some reason, God approved of me guiding Diamond. If only He'd be so clear about how I could help Rebecca, Hunter, and Brooke. And my mom and family.

The motorcycle pulled up next to me, and I sidestepped a kidney jab. "Diamond, I don't know what'll happen to you—or me—past those trees."

She snorted. "I can handle myself. And I'm not afraid of a little pain. But you're going to be suffering a whole lot of pain if you don't move it."

~*~

I raised my arm at the lookout, copying my brother's greeting from yesterday. "Um. To God's glory?"

The tree dweller lifted his arm. "God's glory forever."

Whump. He landed on the pine needle carpet behind Diamond and followed us. Suspicious, despite my correct wordage.

"Dove!" Gilead catapulted from the highest boulder into our path, as if he'd been keeping watch, too. "Are you that dumb? You came back and brought this Heathen with you?" His dagger-like eyes slashed across me to Diamond.

The other tree-dweller nodded and headed back to his post. Gilead grabbed my wrist and jerked me behind his body. "I'll deal with you in a minute, sister. But you, Heathen, go home."

I shifted to see around his flexed triceps.

Diamond advanced and poked his chest. "Don't act like you own this land, radical. You and your deluded terrorist buddies are the ones trespassing and are going to clear off."

He froze for a millisecond and then knocked her hand away. In a whirlwind of movement, she jumped, propelling her compact frame into the air. Her right foot kicked at his chest.

Gilead caught her bare knee between both hands and twisted. Diamond landed on her hip in the dirt.

"I don't fight girls. And I told you to leave."

She scrambled to her feet with a smirk. "Make me. Make me, without weapons or bees or fire."

No one paid attention to me, and my time was limited. Stay or search?

I backed around the boulders then dashed toward the sea of tents. I passed a couple campfires issuing lazy trickles of smoke, but no one tended these. No one threw knives or spears. A sleepy peacefulness pervaded the camp.

My heart sped up. *Rebecca...Hunter...Brooke...*were they here? And what about the Benders? The dirt held hundreds of footprints, all made by humans. At least no sign of cat feet.

An aroma of mildew hooked my nostrils. I halted and threw back the tent flap speckled with brown and black rot.

"Chaff, wake up. Rebecca's been taken. And Brooke and—"

"Shh." Chaff waved me silent. "You're being rude, Dove, interrupting us."

I swiped a hand over my eyes. Was this real? Did yesterday's empty tent now burst with strangers on bent knees whose lips moved in prayer? I eased further inside and pressed against the rough cloth. My palm traced the twelve-inch high, green letters next to me. A painted message.

Pray!–Dove

Smaller words formed more thoughts on the shelter's canvas walls.

Time not spent talking with God is wasted time—Ben

Hate makes Satan happy—Gracie

Sword fighting is stupid—Chaff

The author of this last one threw up his bony hands. "Oh fine, fine. What do you want?"

"Dove Strong. Shalom." A familiar member of the mole family waved. "We are praying instead of being fools like the others. Are you joining us?"

I swallowed until I found my voice. "Uh. No. Sorry. I'm looking for some old friends." I turned back to Chaff. "Have you seen Josh's sister? Or Brooke and Hunter? They got snatched while breaking into that building I told you about."

"See what happened? Exploring there wasn't safe, like I said. And no, I haven't seen or heard about them being in this camp. But Ben over there is a leader of security. He'd know."

Ben, a red-headed guy with a redder complexion, shook his head at my description before reclosing his sunburnt eyelids. No trespassers. No prisoners brought in. He was positive.

Chaff bowed his long neck again. One eye cracked open. "You probably won't find them because they're holed up in that building. That's what I'd guess."

"No." But I bit my lip. I'd chased away that shadowy suspicion all morning...that my friends were captive inside the one place I couldn't easily go. Hearing him say it out loud made the suspicion solidify to fact. I eased toward the tent opening.

"Hey, Dove. Do you have any more words for us?" Both of Chaff's eyes opened.

"Huh?"

"You screamed at everyone yesterday to pray—I didn't hear, but a lot of the believers did, and a few have been trickling in ever since to do it. So apparently, something worth saying came out of your mouth."

"Oh." My gaze dropped, but I could feel the others watching me. How could I encourage them when discouragement crowded my brain? My three friends might be holed up in the gloomy cement fortress where I'd accidentally sent them with my drawing. A place possibly guarded by Christians or nonbelievers—or both—and at least one gun owner.

I looked up. "Be...strong. Keep, you know, praying."

My body shuddered with a sudden, excited chill. I

untensed, smiled at the spotty ceiling, and let the words from God flow through me to His people.

"What you prayer warriors are doing on your knees is way more crucial than what any other believer does out there. So don't give up. Ask for truth to be revealed and for love for the lost. For the truly lost—the ones who don't know Jesus yet. God loves lost people."

Chaff's slow clap echoed as I exited the tent.

I didn't spy Gilead or anyone else threatening on my way out of camp. I didn't even remember Trinity until I reached the Jeep. I hadn't remembered Diamond either.

Her motorcycle was gone, and no crimson stained the pavement. It seemed that Gilead had let her walk away. Maybe he did have less hate for Wolfe's neighbor. Or maybe he truly wouldn't fight a girl, as he claimed.

"Bummer." Josh quit craning for a glimpse of his sister and fell back against his seat.

I climbed in. "Don't worry, Josh. I think I know where they are."

Jezebel bounced. "She did it. She found them. Which camp, Dove?"

"Oh, they're not at any camp, I don't think. Or at any place we can get to right now, but we're not supposed to worry about it today. Trust me. Wolfe, the next camp we're heading for is northwest. Drive...please." I leaned forward in my seat, impatient to be at the next campsite.

In my dream, I'd visited three places in the tree-filled wilderness before I'd flown to the rectangular shelter with square windows. Three Christian camps.

43

I opened my eyes and blinked the dizziness away. I lulled against the hot, cracked seatback next to Wolfe. Shadows stretched across the empty pavement as the blurry sun poised behind the wall of pines lining the road.

I ran my fingers over my scalp. No lumps. No blood. How long had I been unconscious?

Wolfe beamed at me. The memory of worry marks was still etched between his eyebrows. "So, Dove? How did it go in that last camp?"

"It depends. How did I get back here?"

"A snarling female built like a refrigerator carried you from those woods and dumped you on this seat. She wasn't much of a talker."

"Oh." I nodded, beginning to remember. I'd picked up a barrel of unloaded guns and lobbed it into a blazing campfire. Then someone had yelled, "Traitor! Guards, stop her. Alert the Commander...it's the dove!" Then...I couldn't remember anything more.

I sucked in my breath. Alert the Commander? If the Benders stayed at that camp, I'd been close to being captured by them again. I owed the Christian, whoever she was and for whatever reason she did it, for carrying me out before Stone or Reed or...

I shut my eyes again. "My visit was a success, Wolfe. I made it out. I did what I needed to do."

"You located Rebecca, Hunter, and Brooke?"

"Of course not. They weren't at that third camp, just like they weren't at the second. Although, I poked around and asked some kids just in case. No one is gagged or tied up, and no tents are off limits."

"So…not successful."

I glared. "Successful."

I'd marched through the smoke and faced another horde of shooters, slingers, grapplers, and throwers, and I'd...well...*encouraged* them to stop wasting time. I'd also located the prayer warriors in a tent among tree roots and anthills and spent some time on my knees. Then I'd found those guns...

Wolfe handed me a lemonade can. "Well, I guess compared with your second camp visit today, you could call this third one a success. At least you didn't have to crawl into a gap under another rock ledge and hide for hours until the people you riled gave up on hunting you."

I pressed the can to my forehead. "It was a decent crawl space."

But the waiting would have been easier if I hadn't had to spend those hours staring at a palm-sized bobcat print next to my nose while I was facedown in the dirt...dreading that its owner might return and sniff me out.

A shiver ran down my spine. I glanced over my shoulder for yellow eyes and unsheathed claws, but Darcy wasn't there. Only Jezebel and Josh, asleep in the backseat.

Yet Darcy lurked. Somewhere close by. I shuddered again.

"Wolfe. I'm done. Finished with the camps. Let's go home."

~*~

"What a boring day." Jezebel kicked the van's wall to emphasize each word. "Boring. Boring. Boring. I didn't find Rebecca or Brooke. I was stuck in the boring backseat all day. I didn't even get to stick bandages on Diamond because she didn't bleed. And now no TV 'cause Grandma's mad and won't let me watch. What a rotten, boring day."

Wolfe flung open the van door, and brightness flooded the mess inside. "Dove, you've got to come in and see something on TV!"

His sister jetted up. "Something good's on?" She rocketed past, into the evening sunshine. A second later, her front door slammed.

I shuffled my feet back and forth against the van's worn floor. I hadn't gone into his house since a year ago with Melody.

"I promise, Dove. This is worth breaking your do-not-enter rule. Grandma says for you to come. She's done being mad at us."

I entered the crazy, cluttered room from my memory. Jezebel sprawled on the fuzzy floor in front of the lit-up screen as if she'd collapsed.

Her grandma chucked a square red pillow at her bare legs. "Get up, girl. You run away from me in the morning, then you don't get TV in the evening."

"But...I'm so tired." The girl slowly raised an arm and massaged the scar peeking from the neck of her shirt. "My chest feels...I don't know. Funny. I'll just lie here. And rest."

"Wolfe, go get your sister some juice."

"But, Grandma! She's faking."

"Are you arguing with me?" The woman raised

another red pillow in a threat.

He dashed from the room but returned in ten seconds with a cup of something pink. "Here, faker. Now shut up about your heart so we can hear. It'll be on any sec—"

"It's Dove! Dove, you're on TV again!" Jezebel bounced up and motioned at the screen with her cup. The beverage inside sloshed over the sides.

I swallowed and closed my eyes. Even so, I could still hear what was happening on the TV. Lobo asked a question in that deep voice of his. I heard my own voice answer again, saying too much about my dad. This interview was worse than I remembered. Tears gushed like a waterfall down my on-screen face. I couldn't take it anymore. I slipped out the front exit.

Wolfe joined me on the concrete steps. He patted my head. "You really get worked up about that stuff, don't you? About people's souls...and hell."

I shrugged. A year and a half ago, living at home and having never spoken with a nonbeliever, I hadn't cared. But now...

"I've got a secret to tell you."

I clenched my hands between my knees. *He's accepted Christ.*

"My grandma has become fanatical. Get it? She's a Christian." His shoulders shook.

Mine fell. Then I opened my mouth and forced words from my throat. "How...how do you know?"

He grinned. "She stole the Bible I bought a couple months back—the reason I held onto that other one I found in the van. I thought Jezzy had taken mine, but I found my stolen property in Grandma's lucky bag with the pieces to my Jeep. And this afternoon, I caught her on her knees, talking to Jesus. She said she was looking for a poker chip she'd dropped, but I heard her."

"Uh...wow."

"Hey, look at me, Dove."

I did. His face was close to mine. His dark brows were raised, laugh lines gone. "Those answers you gave on TV tonight are going to make a lot of people think about Christians in a totally different way—in the way my grandma thinks about you."

I shrugged. "Then it was worth it, I guess. But it was weird how they showed my interview so fast. In the spring if took weeks for Lobo's people to show my first *Fanatic Surviving* episode on TV—except for those first few clips."

He shuffled his feet.

"Spit it out, Wolfe. What?"

"They broadcast your interview tonight on a different station. On *Terrorist Watch*. It's this twenty-four-hour news station that reveals up-to-date footage and alerts on fanatical sightings and attacks."

"Oh. Did *Terrorist Watch* mention the three camps...or Black Butte?"

He shook his head. "Only reported sightings of Christian terrorists from Washington, California, and Idaho. Your people have been spotted traveling to Oregon. But that's it. Nothing specific about where they're settling or why they're here."

"Good."

His hands, resting on his kneecaps, balled into fists. "But you're not a terrorist. They shouldn't have put your interview on that station."

"I'm not mad." I stood. On the horizon, the midnight mass of Black Butte blended in with the darkening sky. Toward its bottom, a spot of light appeared. And another.

It's time. Have faith.

Relief and excitement rippled over me. With a vision of the long cement building before my eyes, I sprang up and jogged to the van. My hurrying feet picked through the Saint Jonah's clutter and then dropped onto the driveway.

"Whoa, why are you wearing your pack? You can't leave, Dove. Your place in the cow field is gone."

I blinked, and my mom's imagined face faded, replaced by Wolfe's real-life frown. A knot twisted my gut, and I reached my arms out. Then I wrapped them around my torso.

"Bye, Wolfegang. I don't know when I'll get back." *If ever. But I'll try to get back. I will.*

A door creaked and slammed. Jezebel wandered down the front steps. "Oh—Dove's going? Where are we taking her this time?"

She skipped to the Jeep and flopped in the back next to a sleeping Joshua.

Wolfe gripped my hand. "That's right. Wherever you're going, we're driving you. So, it's not good-bye. Ha!"

I glanced at the hill's silhouette on the horizon where more lights pricked. At least a two-hour journey there...if I walked.

Without breaking his grasp, I climbed inside the Jeep.

44

Wolfe stopped his whistling but continued to drive. "You promise you'll stay inside on the seat once we get wherever we're going. Right, brat? Brat?"

"She's asleep." I aimed my thumb to the right. "Turn here and follow the highway."

"Sure. So, let my inferior brain catch up. Your Rahab radio station announced a prayer rally on Black Butte at sundown on August first...and you think instead of a prayer rally, these visiting Christians are going to meet to do something more, uh, active?"

"Like create a hostage situation or attack nonbelievers. Yes."

"OK. But your math is off. August First is still two days away. Couldn't you wait to join them?"

"No. I'm leaving with Lobo to survive again."

"What? You're letting him take you to a snake-filled—"

"Don't worry about it. Anyway, the main reason I'm not waiting is because God wants me at this certain place tonight. And when He says for me to go—"

"You go. Fine, I understand. But you do realize the engine you hear behind us is Diamond's? She's trailing us again."

I squinted at the golden circle of light ten yards back. "Why is she following? She knows how to find my brother without my help."

"And the vehicle behind her is Lobo's."

"No." I craned around. "No way."

He laughed at my reaction to this rotten news. "I'm guessing that Diamond called Jessica, who told Lobo—"

"Jessica's back there, too?"

"Yep. Probably hitching a ride with Lobo."

My eyes narrowed. "How do you know this—that he's driving behind Diamond?"

"I recognize their vehicles. Paying attention is part of being an expert driver."

I slumped. "Is your grandma chasing us again, too? If she is, I think we'd better pull over and let her ride this time."

He let out a nicer laugh. "No angry senior citizen...at least not yet."

I let my head fall back against the seat.

"Want me to turn us around and go back?" Hope energized his voice. "You'll wait until tomorrow morning?"

I sat up straighter. "No. You can drop me in the woods as soon as we get into a dark stretch. I'll slip out, you head home, and everybody will follow you back to Sisters."

"No. I'm coming with you...to that abandoned employees' building where Rebecca got snatched. That's where you're headed, isn't it?"

I met his eyes and nodded.

"You know, when you told me your missing family—that all the missing believers in our area—were stuck in there, I laughed. But now, I think you're right."

He steered into the ditch and killed the Jeep's power. "That flashing light up ahead means a road block. The block's a usual precaution the government takes each year during their retreat. But we're still about three miles from the village. You're sure you don't want to wait until morning?"

I stepped onto the asphalt then darted out of the way. Diamond roared to a stop.

"Get yourselves back on that ripped seat and drive home. Now."

I stepped closer to her raised fists. "Why?"

"Just do it!"

Another engine purred to a stop. I squinted into the blinding glare of headlights. Doors slammed.

"Oh, let her go hike in the fresh night air, Cousin Diamond." Lobo emerged dressed in the dirt-stained outfit from our last hike. "Myself, I'm eager to meet this dangerous commander in the hills that Dove's brother says she must be kept away from. I say we continue our journey with our terrorista and see him for ourselves. And this time, I bring my camera. Just in case."

Diamond scowled into the car's lights. "Jessica, you big-mouthed traitor! You told Lobo about him? You blabbed about why I'm here?"

Wolfe threw his hands up. "Will someone please explain—"

"Diamond's here to stop me from hiking near Black Butte tonight. My brother must've asked her to keep me away." I squinted at her. "Gilead asked you to do this thing to keep me safe...and you're doing it. Wow."

"Wow," Wolfe echoed. "Diamond, you must really like Gilead after all."

"Keep talking, and you'll find out what a coma feels like—hey, who's there?"

The upper half of a girl's body in a shaggy animal

skin tunic poked through the shaking foliage next to the road. Her hair coils were lopsided and littered with forest debris. "Yikes. Wrong way."

"Wait," I called in Amhebran. "There are others in the woods tonight, too. I saw their torches and flashlights a couple minutes ago. Where are you all going?"

Her pale face reappeared, and her scrunched eyes flickered around the group until they rested on me. She replied in English, "You're Dove."

"And you're a believer," I said in the same language. "Are you lost, looking for a campsite?"

"No, I'm lost, trying to find the meeting spot. A messenger arrived at camp tonight and said our commander has news about our missing families. He has a plan for their return, which he'll tell us at midnight when we all meet together. A lady in the next tent said she knew how to find the place he described, but I lost her and the rest of my group. It's really dark tonight."

It was as though my mouth was full of dust, and my tongue clung to the roof of it. Tonight, Reed Bender was uniting Christians from the local camps, no doubt to carry out a plan that would put into use all the combat training of the past week.

Is that why God directed me into these hills? To stop him...somehow?

Wolfe ripped his shirt out of Diamond's grasp and approached the bushes. "Did the messenger mention a lake or golf course? Or a building?"

"He spoke of a grassy clearing next to a lake. A spot wide enough for all of us to gather."

Wolfe jerked his thumb. "Head west. That way."

"Shalom." The foliage rustled back together.

I unstuck my tongue. "Diamond, Gilead doesn't want you to cripple me. And he knows unless you do, you can't stop me from meeting with the other believers tonight."

My eyes narrowed at the familiar silhouettes in the bright lights. "All of you leave. You heard that girl—hundreds of Christians are meeting at midnight. These are the same people who've been holding target practices all week. And their leader, Reed, is most likely planning some sort of terrorist attack that you can't stop. Maybe I can't either, but since these are my people, I'm going to try."

Wolfe grinned down at me. "Well, then I get to come with you."

"Unclog your ears. It's not safe for you."

He gripped my shoulders and bent his forehead to mine. "No, Dove. You're the one not listening. I'll tag along with you because these are my people, too. Don't you get it? I'm a Christian."

45

He pulled back as if to better see my expression. Then he chuckled and hugged my stiff frame to his chest. "I made the decision in Brooke's van, on the way home from California. I accepted Jesus as my Savior then, which means tonight I get to come with you. But the rest of you...scram. Only us radicals are allowed in these woods right now."

"Then I get to go too!" Jezebel popped up from the backseat. "I became a Christian before you did, Woof. So I get to walk next to Dove on our hike. You can follow behind us."

Wolfe's torso quivered with laughter. I moved to rest against the dented door, a more solid support, and watched Jezebel climb onto the pavement.

Lobo chuckled. "Looks like we're all hiking these woods tonight."

"Don't tell me," Wolfe said. "You've gone radical too?"

Lobo winked. "What do you think about that, terrorista?"

I lifted my hand and pressed it against my throat where the ache nearly choked me. "I think you don't understand that to become a Christian—"

"Dove," Wolfe said, "do you really think anybody who spends more than a day with you can possibly not understand salvation? Are you that brainless?"

I bit the inside of my cheek to keep control. Wolfe,

Jezebel, and Lobo—the three lost souls I'd prayed for most—chose an eternity with God...and to spend forever with me?

Ridiculous, unwanted tears spilled onto my cheeks. "But...you sin...and then—"

"I know about Jesus Christ, Dove," Lobo interrupted my excited stammer with his calm voice. "And I choose Him."

Wolfe extended a fist. "Does that mean Dove doesn't have to do anymore *Fanatic Surviving* stuff? Since you're a fanatic now?"

Lobo accepted the knuckle bump. "Oh no, she still gets to battle werewolves and leeches...and no, you cannot take her place. The world wants to watch a fierce, fanatical blonde struggle. Not a skinny, love-sick muchacho who laughs too much."

Jezebel let go of my hand and elbowed them both aside. "OK people. Head count. Who else has joined Jesus's team and is coming with us tonight? Jessica? Diamond, what about you?"

"C'mon, Jesse." Diamond straddled her motorcycle. "It's time for us to leave."

"No. I'm staying."

Jezebel clapped her hands. "Yay! Another one has joined Jesus's team."

Diamond gestured at her motorcycle. "Like I said. Let's go."

Jessica shook her head. "No, Diamond. I'm staying."

"Fine. Join the freaks." Diamond kicked on her engine and sped away.

Lobo murmured something to Jessica I couldn't hear, and then he began strapping clumsy bags of gear over their dark clothes.

Jezebel tugged the hem of her brother's shirt. "Diamond was crying, Woof. I saw. It was weird."

"Yeah, she made a dumb choice, brat. Speaking of, we shouldn't have brought Josh along. He'll panic if he wakes up alone next to the road. You'll have to stay with him."

She stamped her foot.

Josh answered sleepily from the backseat. "No need. I'm awake. And I'm already a Jesus freak so...guess I'm coming too."

Lobo switched off his car's lights. "Shh."

Firelight flickered on the other side of the road's bushes.

"Not enough bullets..." The Amhebran comment faded as the torch-bearing Christians hiked away from the road.

I leaped into the ditch to begin my hike toward Black Butte, the meeting spot, and quite possibly Commander Reed, who was in charge of bullets and wished me dead. And who, no doubt, would be expecting me.

46

A ripple of laughter drifted to me from somewhere up ahead in the trees. I lifted my arm for silence, but the night was too thick for hand signals.

"Shut up," I whispered.

My request put an end to the conversation about a new smell-producing camera. Jezebel and Josh quit humming "Jesus Loves Me" through their noses.

The chortle echoed again, louder now.

"Creepy," Wolfe whispered.

I frowned. "You all stay here while I go on ahead."

Someone in our group grabbed my shirttail—probably Jessica since she tended to cling—and the muffled footfall of everyone's shoes sounded behind me as we made our way over the pine needles. I halted in what seemed to be a small clearing. An indistinct figure crouched in the darkness.

A sudden shaft of light flashed on and revealed Chaff. He knelt, a wide grin peeping through his head-to-toe wilderness camouflage—a layer of dirt, dead evergreen needles, and twigs. A stunted bush perched on top of his wheat-color hair.

I swung around, bumping into Jessica at my back. "Turn the flashlight off."

"Sensible, but she should keep it on." Chaff aimed a dirt-stained finger at a hole in the ground. "You don't want to fall into my boobytrap...like he did."

My feet edged closer to Chaff and the crumbling

ground surrounding a man-sized hole. I craned around the brambles poking up from his shoulder. In the faint light, Zechariah Brae's wild eyes stared up from the bottom of the deep pit.

"Zech! Chaff, why is Zech in a hole?"

"Because he's a liar, and I'm fed up with it. I want the truth."

I shook my head. "You can't go around putting people in pits just to find out—"

"Wrong, wrong, wrong, Dove. Since catching him in this trap, I've discovered my sister's real location. I've gotten him to tell me the truth—that Commander Reed Bender and a group of his followers are behind all the Christians' disappearances. Can you believe that Reed obtained Heathen uniforms and vehicles, and his followers used them to round up the Sents' families? From all over the Pacific Coast?"

"Yes."

"Good. Believe it. He's done fooling us all into believing that others are behind their disappearances. This whole time he and his group have been holding them captive."

I leaned closer to the pit's edge. "Where are they, Zech?"

Melody's brother mimed locking his lips and throwing away the key.

"Not smart." Chaff unfurled a woven blanket reminiscent of fallen pine needles over the hole.

"No! Nooo! Don't bury me. Not again…" Zech's sob cut off, and he began to croon a song about a clock, one his dad had once sung.

Chaff settled back and folded his long fingers together. "He doesn't like being underground without light."

Jezebel crawled over Chaff's fern-wrapped shoes. "I'm taking the cover off and letting him out." She lifted the edge of the blanket.

Wolfe shrugged. "Fine. But he's the one who got me locked in the CTDC. And he took me away to California where he wouldn't let me come home. Oh, and he helped try to drown Dove and Trinity."

Jezebel dropped the blanket's edge, calling down to Zechariah through the covering. "You sit in there in the dark and think about what you did!"

I took a deep breath. "Uncover him, Chaff."

"But...oh, fine."

Zechariah stopped singing. His eyes rose to the stars overhead. A gentle smile appeared. "The captives are close...being held in a building at the edge of that Heathen village. Close but you can't get to them. Because we will stop you...yes, we will stop you."

I leaned closer. "Reed will try to stop me? And is Reed planning to take the government officials hostage tonight?" Behind me, someone inhaled as if surprised.

Zech chuckled. "The commander calls that our bargaining tool."

"Bargaining? How is it bargaining if Reed is the one holding both groups captive?"

"Oh, Dove...naïve Dove. That's the beautiful point." He rapped on his skull. "Think. Reed knows this. You and I know this...but no one else does. What will happen when Reed gathers the unhappy Sent, as well as the remaining non-Sent, at the village where important officials are staying? Once there, he'll announce that the Heathen are holding our kidnapped families close by...and that these Heathen refuse to release them. Then he'll suggest a brilliant idea. We take their nearby officials captive. Because, of course, then the Heathen will trade and let our people go. Plus, it'll give them a taste of their own poison."

I slammed my fist against the ground. "Their own poison? This is crazy! The nonbelievers aren't responsible for anyone being kidnapped. They won't even understand what's going on. All that will happen is...is..."

Chaff nodded, rustling the bush on his head. "Exactly. All that will happen is that our people will attack non-Christians, who'll defend themselves. And the war will begin."

Lobo crept next to me, his night-vision glasses raised onto his chopped hair. "But I'm wondering, how can your leader think a small attack like this will matter so much? Violence happens every day. Why will this one cause a war?"

"Answer, Zech." Chaff fluttered the blanket in a threat near the pit's edge.

Melody's brother reclined with his arms behind his head, smiling at the stars. "You all have no vision. Obviously, ours is only the first wave. Other groups in other places are waiting for us to start. Then they'll attack, too. Like a game of Follow the Leader. That's a fun game..."

"The radio," I muttered. "Danny D and Rahab...they'll be broadcasting Reed's movements to others who'll begin the second wave of attacks in their own states."

"Ding, ding, ding!" Zech lurched up, his eyes wide. "You are correct."

47

My fingers tightened around Jezebel's sweaty hand. "Slow down and let that group ahead go on. Their torchlight is too bright."

I kept my voice soft and my face parallel to the ground until the Christians we'd been trailing trudged out of sight. Jezebel's neon shirt glowed another second, and then the night enveloped us.

I wiped my streaming face. The closer we got to the meeting spot, the better chance that Reed's followers were on the lookout for me.

"Are we there yet? My feet hurt."

"Toughen up, brat," Wolfe whispered. "Do you hear Josh whining?"

I pulled her through the darkness to where I could feel a steep wall of dirt rise. A smooth boulder rested above my head.

I was close. This was the spot where'd I'd last met Bull. Someone had fired the gunshot just beyond the slope.

My pulse thrummed in my ears. "Rest here. The building I need to scout for the captive Christians is up ahead. Wolfe, you coming?" I began to scale the crumbling dirt wall, but someone yanked me off.

"Sky alive, Lobo!" I exhaled. "Let me go."

Light flashed, and I bit my tongue. A piece of the tree-filled terrain ahead lit up, and a trio in deerskins approached. Bows and sheaths protruded from their backs.

"It's just more believers heading to the meeting spot." I patted the wall to find my handhold.

"Stone's up there," Wolfe breathed and pointed to a different spot on the wooded slope—to an ominous figure Lobo must've sighted with his see-in-the-dark technology.

The Bender brother stayed still as a tree trunk, letting the lantern-light slide over him, the cowboy hat dangling from his motionless fingers. The group of three trudged past without seeming to notice him.

A circle of light flickered in the opposite direction. It bobbed closer until a beardless, uniformed body with a dim headlamp stopped in front of Stone. "How much longer until we release our captives, Warrior Stone?"

"My brother said to let them go at midnight." Stone's voice rasped as if he'd used it up. "That's fifty-three more minutes. Can't you hold them? Most are old or weak."

"We've held them for a month, sir, so we'll try one more hour. The problem is, a few have begun to suspect who we are."

He rotated the hat in his oversized hands. "Our people guess their guards are Christian and not Heathen? That's...unfortunate."

"Yeah, but I don't know how they've guessed, sir. We wear our uniforms every second. And we haven't slipped and spoken our language around them. I swear."

He shrugged his wide shoulders. "Just...just do what my brother would do."

"Which is?"

"Keep the suspicious ones separate from the

others." His voice dropped an octave. "And...keep holding them."

"You—your brother—doesn't want us to release them when we let the others go free? So they don't fight against us?"

Stone sighed and tossed the brimmed hat into the shadows. "I guess that's what I mean. I'll come with you, in case there's trouble. But I'm not in uniform, so I can't let them see me."

"Of course, sir. Thank you."

The headlamp faded up the slope. I wedged my foot in the crumbling dirt and began to heave up to follow. An urgent tug brought me back down.

"Ouch! Quit pulling on me, Lobo!"

"Except I can see what you can't. Look." He clamped his thick glasses down over my eyes before I could duck away. "See? We still are not alone."

Through his lenses, the woods became darkness and daylight at the same time. I gasped. A human wearing western-style boots was at the bottom of the slope. Bull lay sprawled in a patch of nettles.

48

Bull wasn't dead. But Wolfe's keychain flashlight revealed he wasn't about to stand up and stride off whistling either.

"Help me get him flat on his back. Watch the nettles."

Jessica and Lobo heaved him over, and a small book slipped from his limp fingers.

Itchy hotness stung my wrist as I rescued the palm-sized Bible. I tucked it into his boot. "Sorry, Bull. I'm so sorry." Why hadn't I warned him of the possible danger gathering here? That he should stick to the horse barn and stay away from these woods?

"Lobo, call the police."

I jerked up. "No, Jessica, he can't! That's exactly what Reed Bender would want. You want to make everything worse by bringing more people with weapons to this area? Don't force a fight!"

"Calm yourself, Dove. Jesse, she's right." Lobo pulled up the man's lids, then applied a brisk knuckle-rub to his sternum.

Bull groaned and raised a trembling hand in defense.

Lobo rose. "He's only stunned. Concussed. He'll live. No need to call in the police...not yet."

I exhaled and faced the slope.

"Don't go up there searching for your mom, Dove." Wolfe grabbed my shoulders. "Please. We both know what happened to Bull wasn't an accident. Stone did this. And Stone's at that building."

"But—"

"Please wait. Just a little. Let's go spy out the meeting spot then circle back. We'll approach it from a different direction that's safer. Plus, you heard...Stone's guards are going to release your family soon. So maybe we don't need to do anything except wait and see. Don't...force a fight."

Don't force a fight. I grimaced at Wolfe's use of my own words.

I glanced again at the unconscious figure, strained to hear over the breathing and forest noises then handed Lobo his glasses.

"Stone said suspicious prisoners won't be released. If I don't see my family in one hour, I'll break into their prison myself. I'm not afraid of any Bender."

I pulled my cap's brim lower to hide my face and let Wolfe steer me in a new direction, away from the cement prison and the slope Stone guarded. The place where for sure—in one hour— I'd visit.

The guards wouldn't release my grandpa. Jonah Strong would be a suspicious one, watching his captors with hawk eyes...noticing inconsistencies and seeing through their lies.

Before Jezebel could whine again, we broke out of the trees. Our shoes sunk into the spongy grass. On the horizon to our right, lit-up village buildings cast their glow onto the hills ahead where groups of Christians emerged from the forest's edges. We all seemed to be traveling in the same direction—toward the lake.

"So, Dove Strong, what's your plan?" Lobo's wide lenses swiveled side to side. "Because of course, you have one to foil the evil schemes of this bad dude

Commander Reed?"

Uh, Lord, what is Your plan? Are You ready to tell me what You want me to do?

Silence stretched.

Lobo chuckled. "We'll wing it. My favorite kind of plan."

Jezebel reached down from riding piggyback on Wolfe and patted me. "Dove always knows. Trust her."

Joshua glanced up, his eyebrows at his frizzy hairline in disbelief.

Jessica's strides kept pace with mine. "We shouldn't have to have a plan. What happened to all the security around here? All week they've been blocking the road and snarling up traffic. And tonight, they're what...taking the night off? Why aren't they here, seeing this and stopping everyone?"

Bull...sprawled in the nettles...I bit my lip. Had Reed and Stone used similar tactics against the security people? Were they scattered in unconscious heaps around the village?

The bright lights seemed to blaze brighter on the horizon. I shook my head. "I think they're all...contained somewhere. Focused on something going on, maybe inside those buildings."

"Yeah, they wouldn't be scattered around the golf course at night. They're probably positioned around tables at a team-building dinner." Wolfe, bent over by the weight of his sister, sighed. "Eating rich people's leftover steak and lobster."

I rubbed my damp temples. Strategy. This was Reed's plan. How did Reed think?

I lifted my eyes to the lit rooftops disappearing behind the golf course's swells. "Reed likes his enemies contained in one spot—he told me so at the beach. I think he decided to act tonight because he knows the government officials are joined together with security tightened around them. Probably gathered in one of those buildings for a meal like Wolfe said. It makes sense."

"Fine. Lobo and I'll go interrupt their dessert and tell them to come do their jobs."

"Not yet, Jesse."

She threw off Lobo's restraining hand. "Why not? We'll get them to meet this Reed guy and head him off. The security people are trained. They can force the radicals to stop whatever it is the lunatic has got planned.

I sucked in my breath, my eyes on the place where the rooftop had disappeared behind a hill. "And you'll begin a bloody battle that will excite Christians in other places to start their pieces of the war. Didn't you hear Zech? Why can't you understand? It's too late for nonbelievers to step in and use force to stop what's building. It'd be like adding a smoldering ember to a bucket of tree sap. Or a spark to gasoline. Any fighting here will trigger a nationwide war."

"Kaboom!" Jezebel threw out her arms.

Jessica gripped my sore wrist and pointed. A new source of light had appeared over the slope ahead. The harsh glare came from powerful lightbulbs strung up on poles near the black stretch of lake.

We halted outside the circle of light that bathed the tremendous mass of Christians in its glow. I squinted into the tight-packed crowd of believers who seemed to crawl over each other like bees on honeycomb, flattening the uneven expanse of grass and dirt that ended at the water.

"Whoa," Joshua whispered.

Jezebel shook her head. "Awesome!"

While Lobo muttered in a language I didn't understand, Wolfe reached for my hand. "I didn't realize...so many of them...this is bad, Dove."

I nodded. Except for Lobo, the others hadn't seen the camps, so they weren't prepared for the sheer number of humans carrying bows and spears.

I wasn't either.

A looseness flowed through my knees. My eyes couldn't penetrate past the crowd's outer edges, except for a small section near the lights where the ground rose up. At the tree line to the left, Christians hurled knives at tree trunks. But nowhere did I see fire...or familiar faces.

"I'm going to look for Becca." Josh ducked and disappeared behind a group of girls distributing what looked like bullets to bearded youths with long-barreled weapons.

"Brothers and Sisters. Honored Sent. Welcome!" Reed's familiar voice drowned out every other sound. "Prepare yourselves. Gather stragglers and unite. In ten minutes, we'll begin our rally."

I rose onto my tiptoes, straining to catch sight of the speaker. Ten minutes. That's all the time I had until Reed began something that would lead this crowd down a path that required the use of knives and guns.

"Hold still, Dove."

I started at Trinity's unexpected voice. A rough cloth covered my head, and the scent of home filled my nostrils.

"Quit fighting...or hugging me or whatever you're doing. Keep covered. They're looking for you." Trinity tugged again, and the cloth became a hooded cloak. I could now see my cousin with Micah standing behind her. Neither smiled.

I held the scratchiness in place under my chin. "Who's looking for me?"

"Half of those assembled here. I was clueless before about the number of believers who recognize you...and who wouldn't mind putting a spear through you. Maybe we should've stayed in California. Micah and Gil have been busier than mosquitoes in June keeping me alive since I look like you. What's with all the friends you brought?"

Jezebel sat up straighter and adjusted her purse. "We're radicals now, too. So, we're allowed to come."

Micah snorted, but my cousin eyed Wolfe. "About time. But Dove, bringing them wasn't your most brilliant idea."

"I couldn't stop them. Speaking of stopping people, were you able to—"

She nodded and raised Micah's clasped hand into the air in a symbol of victory. "Yeah. I did it."

Micah puffed out his thin chest. "You mean I did it."

At his overzealous brag, some city rats squinted in our direction.

I pulled my hood tighter and lowered my voice. "Micah, the explosives you're in charge of, Trinity explained about deactivating them? Were you able to—"

"They're duds now, the whole lot of them. It was super easy for me because I knew that by removing a small piece from each, I could kill them. Although of course, no one else knows but Trinity. But see?" He pulled out a metallic disc from his sleeve and offered it.

Wolfe and Lobo jumped backward. Jessica used me as her shield.

I shook her off. "No. We believe you, Micah. Put away the dud. And, um, good job."

He returned it to his sleeve and shifted away from the two women smearing black stripes across their cheekbones. As they painted, their eyes stayed on us.

Micah fiddled with his beard. "Just don't tell Gil, yeah? He and I spent an hour planting the duds between here and the village on routes Heathen might take if they notice us. He'd get mad if he knew."

My eyes narrowed in sudden suspicion. Was Micah lying? It seemed impossible he'd be so eager to sabotage his own handiwork. And disappoint Gilead.

Trinity reached to adjust my blanket and whispered, "He never liked the idea of using them on people. It gave him nightmares. He's really not bad, Dove." She gave the cloth a tug so I stumbled forward a step. "Listen to me. He's not like his brother...or sister."

Melody. My attention darted past the war-painted women, now glaring at Trinity's blonde head, to the bodies milling between groups sitting. Some tapped their sharp-edged weapons against their knees. Others rolled their shoulders and stretched, as if warming up for a training session.

I knew Micah's brother was trapped back in the woods and guarded by Chaff. But Melody had to be somewhere close, probably in this mess of Christians.

"Those must be the radio folks, yes?" Lobo pointed. "Next to the generator on that little hill?"

Distracted, I followed his finger to the blinding bulbs at the top of tall poles. Underneath them, on an elevation near the tree line, Danny D and Rahab Rae stooped, doing something I couldn't see with cables and a plasma generator, a technology I recognized from my own interview. Other indistinct electronics littered the grass at the base of the poles.

Lobo rubbed his palms together. "Let's see...transmitter. Receiver. Antenna. Speakers. We heard a microphone. Ah, yes, they're setting up for a remote radio broadcast.

"Don't worry, Dove. They may have the radio on their side...but what is radio compared to the almighty television broadcast that we can provide? Jesse and I'll slip over and see if we can borrow some power without them getting wise. Here, you wear this until we're ready for you." He reached into the hood of my cloak and fitted a small wire around my ear.

I abandoned my hunt for Melody and blinked at him. TV? "But...no, Lobo—"

"C'mon, Jesse." They jogged into the crowd with their bulky bags of cameras and equipment.

"Dove's going to be on TV again. Lucky." Jezebel banged her knees against Wolfe in excitement.

"Quit it, brat. Dove's not...are you?"

"No! I just want to stop this." I unhooked the ear wire so it dangled at my chin and gestured at the mass of Christians and lights. "All of this is wrong. In a few minutes, Reed will stir everyone up like he does, even easier now since he's got that microphone." I clutched my forehead. "I should've stopped Lobo and Jesse. As soon as someone speaks to those two in Amhebran and they don't understand—"

"Stay out of the light and keep the cloak on." Trinity knotted the cloth under my chin so the hood stayed in place. "Go wait in the trees. I'll talk to Lobo and get them to ditch their TV plan and leave before the rally starts. C'mon, Micah. You can protect me."

She shoved herself between the glaring, war-painted women, towing an open-mouthed Micah behind her.

A small hand patted my hood. "Don't worry, Dove. I can fix this whole thing. I'll stop the guy's microphone and the radio and TV and make them all go home."

Jezebel, still perched on Wolfe's shoulders, pulled her hand out of her purse. Her fingers clenched a small black object. It was Wolfe's last EMP.

"Ready, you guys? Hold hands if you're afraid of the dark. Because the lights are going off."

49

Jezebel knocked my elbow with her shoe. Wolfe jerked his hand from my grip. And the lights continued to blare.

"Let her go, Stone!" Wolfe shouted.

"Gimme back my EMP," Jezebel demanded. "Let me go."

I yanked back my obscuring hood. Jezebel had disappeared from her brother's shoulders and was now trapped under Stone's arm. Carrying the girl, he darted into the mass of gathered believers.

I hurled myself after them, worming through tight spaces in the crowd. When I hesitated at a wall of fur-clad bodies, Wolfe's hand pressed my back, bulldozing me forward. We left angry mutterings in our wake.

"Don't shove."

"Watch it, Girl."

"Look, it's the dove."

Stone, the tallest figure in sight, sliced deeper into the mass of standing Christians, and the crowd closed quickly behind him. I locked my gaze on his tangle of ashy hair, visible above the sea of heads. He paused, and Wolfe and I gained a few yards, almost catching up. Then Stone forged on.

Jezebel's kicking legs appeared in a break between groups. I lunged forward and latched onto her ankle. Unnecessarily—because Stone had halted.

Melody stood before us. She was buffeted by the

surrounding crowd, who watched with crossed arms as Wolfe and I wrestled Stone's bicep. Her deer eyes focused on Jezebel's captor then flicked to me.

"Whew, Dove, you didn't drown!" She eased closer and attempted to hook her arm through mine, as she had a thousand times in the past. I relaxed my hold on Jezebel, though my heart thumped harder. Melody was finally choosing to stand with me—choosing what was right. It didn't matter that Wolfe and I couldn't pry his sister from the strong grasp. With Melody on my side, Stone would release her.

"Dove, you can't believe the trouble you've given us this last week." She tightened her grip on my blanketed extremity. "Sorry—we just have to hold you until the rally is over. Stone, you better go tell Reed she's here...but why do you have that little Heathen girl?"

"For bait." I scowled into his light eyes ringed by shadowed hollows. Was his conscience pricking him awake at night? Good. "He has her as bait to bring me into this crowd so I don't escape into the trees since I can outclimb him."

"No. It's because he's a coward," Gilead growled at my back.

My brother moved me aside and swept Wolfe from his path. "You keep picking on girls—young girls who aren't trained to fight. I don't care if you are Commander Reed's brother. Or Dove's old boyfriend. Let—the kid—go!"

"I don't pick on...I'm not hurting her. I just need to keep Dove—"

Stone careened backward from my brother's fist and released Jezebel. He scrambled to his feet, swiped at the blood on his lip and returned the punch. Again,

Gilead was quicker. He trapped the giant's offending arm. Then, with a grunt, he slammed Stone onto his back.

"Dove, you idiot. Take the kid and scram!"

A circle of bodies jostled as they pressed around the fighters. One crouched as if eager to join in. Next to me, Jezebel flattened herself against her brother's chest with her eyes squeezed shut. I pulled my hood over my head and followed them through a sudden gap in the packed bodies.

"We've got to get out of this light, Dove, like Trinity said. It's dangerous. If only Stone hadn't stolen my EMP. It's funny, though..."

I threw him a dagger-like glare. Melody's continued betrayal ached worse than a kick to my gut. And Stone might mangle Gilead beyond repair...or vice versa.

"OK. Not funny. Odd. I didn't realize your brother liked Jez so much."

I shrugged. He hadn't fought Stone only for Jezebel's sake. He'd fought for his own macho pride. And to distract onlookers—Christians who might otherwise have turned their unhappy attention to me.

Our chase after Stone had brought us near the very center of the crowd. How many of the ten minutes had we wasted? How many were left until Reed began the rally? Four minutes? Three?

I pointed past the light posts to the dark patch of woods far beyond. "Head that way, Wolfe. To the trees."

He struggled forward, throwing words over his shoulder at me. "And I bet he likes Diamond. Did you see how he glanced around before he swung, as if hoping to see someone? Maybe Diamond? Maybe he's decided that he likes nonbelievers. I bet he won't attack, even if the rest do."

"He'll attack. Aim toward the posts so we can see if the others got out. C'mon, move faster." My heart slammed against my sternum, beating away the seconds.

The grassy terrain began to rise under my frustrated feet. More bodies crowded the slope leading to the source of light ahead where bulbs blazed from poles. If the people would only move aside, I'd be able to see the platform, the generator, and radio equipment...I threw up a desperate plea.

Let Trinity have gotten Lobo and Jessica out of here.

"Brothers and Sisters! So many of us sacrificed, becoming the Sent our Councils asked us to be. And for the past few months, we've lived peacefully among our enemies. We've stood unflinchingly against their violence and their hate."

I froze, and my hood fell back. Two Christians, Frog Face and another from the cave, lifted Reed and set him on his feet on the elevated platform. He didn't hold a microphone. Yet his voice swelled like thunder, drowning out every noise in the crowd.

"But while we were away from home, sacrificing all, our enemies swooped down. They invaded our homes and stole away our mothers and fathers. They took our aunts and uncles. Even our grandparents."

Jezebel flicked my hat brim and pointed up. Lobo clung to a light pole just beyond Reed. His twisted legs anchored his body yards above the crowd. His dark eyes sought mine. One hand gestured first at his ear, then to his lips. *Speak,* he mouthed. He slashed the air. *No TV.* He pointed at his mouth again. *Speak.*

Wolfe grabbed the wire dangling at my chin and

fitted it back around my ear. "Lobo's a genius! You're wearing a microphone—this thing! He's got it working with the speakers. C'mon, Dove, talk! Speak! You can fight Reed with your words, tell everyone the truth. Just stay incognito while you do it." He yanked up my hood.

Me? Fight with words? Words weren't my gift. I was bad with words. The few syllables I'd shouted in the camps were proof.

A group of Christians threatened Lobo's hold on the light pole, attempting to yank him off. I heard their Amhebran shouts—questions and accusations that Lobo wouldn't understand.

His grip slipped. Slipped again. Then he fell.

My gasp echoed. I craned to catch sight of him behind the platform, but people blocked me. Was Jessica nearby? Could she help him, or had she ditched him and escaped? *Oh no.* I bit my lip. Her petite figure appeared in the crowd. It lolled over a stranger's fur-clad shoulder.

Blood roared in my ears, muffling Reed's next words.

"You...you are here tonight because the Councils planned for us to unite in order to mourn and to pray. But God has already answered our prayers."

I ripped my gaze from the victors carrying Lobo's sagging form down the hill and focused on Reed. He'd recovered his bravado that'd faltered during Lobo's interruption. Excitement radiated from his thin body that leaned over the crowd.

Molten anger burned my cheeks as I fingered my tiny microphone. If I spoke, would my voice project to rival his? Would believers even listen? Or would they fall over themselves, competing to see who could silence me first?

I swallowed and lifted my chin. *I'm ready, Lord. Words?*

Commander Reed's fist struck the air. "Good news! Our lost people are not hidden in California. Instead they are close. Very close. And I have seen them with my own eyes. My soldiers and I have battled for their freedom. And we've won it...freedom for part of our people!"

"You lie, Reed Bender." My accusation blasted across the crowd. "You. Lie. Who did you battle? When?"

Reed's amplified choke resonated through the sudden silence. Then murmurs from hundreds of people started up.

I braced for the hands that would grab or strike me down. But my immediate neighbors had their backs to me. I'd shouted from inches away, yet their shoulders shrugged. One rubbed his neck saying, "It sounded like the crazy girl who yelled at us in the camp."

A miracle.

Thank you for hiding me.

Wolfe dumped Jezebel onto the ground. "Froggy just spotted me. Me and Jez are taking off. Don't follow. Stay covered and get to the trees." He hustled me onto my knees.

"But—"

"He's coming, Dove. Go!"

I reached for Wolfe and Jezebel, who seemed to melt into the crowd.

Reed forced a guffaw. "Ignore the false accusation. Let me assure you that I'm not lying. In a few minutes, I will present you with proof that I tell the truth."

My amplified, "Ha!" shattered my own eardrums.

"Find her," Reed whispered, no doubt a command to some of his hovering, deluded followers to search for me...and shut me up. At least Wolfe and Jezebel had separated from me. Maybe they'd stay unharmed.

He continued in a louder voice. "Yes, we've obtained freedom for some of our people. Yet our enemies dare to still hold another portion of us as prisoner. The Heathen refuse to release our few from their evil grip. Satan's workers attempt to suppress us because they are afraid of us—afraid of the power we yield. And they should be afraid! Because our power is from Almighty God who says it's time for us—His people—to take back this nation!"

I quit crawling around amongst people wearing homespun shoes and lifted my head. "Sky alive, people! Plug your ears against his lies. Stop a moment and use your brains. Does God want us to slaughter other humans for land? Of course not. That's what Satan wants."

A youth with a waxy face and missing teeth leered down at me, and I recoiled. Two more smudged, pale complexions loomed over. The mole family I'd eaten crackers with surrounded me.

The fatherly man I'd prayed with in a camp tent whispered, "Shalom, Warrior Dove. Quick, your hunters are close. Become a boulder so we can sit."

Become a boulder...*what*? His hands pushed me down and molded my gray covering until I hunkered on my hands and knees in stuffy darkness. The full weight of at least one body settled down on my spine. Someone else leaned against my shoulder...using me as a boulder to rest against. Hiding me.

As my exhausted limbs trembled under their load, Reed's eloquent falsehoods trickled through the blanket's woven strands. "You, the Sent who've obeyed God in the past...will you obey God again? Listen, the freed are on their way to us. I hear their footsteps approaching—"

The crowd's rumblings multiplied.

The weight against me lifted. A jab at my back prodded me forward. "Your hunters have moved past. Carefully now, Dove Strong. Follow us to safer ground."

Still covered by the blanket, I crawled—a goat being herded—responding to the taps against my body steering me to the right or left.

The crowd finally calmed, and Reed again spoke. "When they arrive, what will you do? Will you slip away and return home with your loved ones? If you do, you're turning a blind eye, allowing your enemies to hold other brothers and sisters captive."

"Don't believe him, people!" Neither the blanket nor the stuffy air muffled my microphone's capability. "This Bender you call Commander is the one who has held your families captive all this time. Not the godless."

"I won't abandon my brothers and sisters who are in need!" Reed shouted. "I claim God's promises. Claim them too. Join me. Walk with me. Fight with me!"

My guide eased his body down on my shoulder blade, and I froze. Another searcher approached. Seconds later, the load lightened, someone nudged, and I crawled forward.

I wrenched my thoughts away from my bruised palms and kneecaps. Away from the memory of Lobo and Jessica's limp bodies...and the probability that Wolfe and Jezebel had been caught and were now suffering. And what about Trinity? Mom and Grandpa?

Sweat trickled down my ribs. How long had I been crawling? Hours? Shouldn't I be out of the light by now? No matter, I must hear Reed...listen to God...and be ready with words. Even if they fell out of my mouth sharp and ugly as thistles. Even if no one cared.

Reed spoke again.

"The Heathen who carry out Satan's plans feast together tonight. These evildoers reside in one of those worldly buildings over these hills. They don't know we are gathered. And they are ignorant of our great power and—"

"They are ignorant of all of this." My voice was quieter now, yet it still swallowed up his. "Because the nonbelievers are innocent. Reed Bender planned this whole deception. He—"

"Storm their fortress with me!" Reed half-shrieked. "Together we will hold the responsible Heathen hostage until they release every single imprisoned Christian. And if the pagan stay firm in their evil schemes and decide to fight us, who here will step boldly forward to meet them?"

A bobcat's scream answered from close by. I paused. My fingers tensed, digging into the dust and tree debris over a thick root.

A tree root.

I groped the air in front of my blanket and touched rough-ridged bark. My hands tore the covering off my sweat-drenched head, casting its veiling material into some bushes. I clung to the cedar's base while my lungs drew in fresh air. The solitude of a gloomy forest outside the circle of light welcomed me.

"Dove!"

Wolfe reached around one of my guides and pulled me up. When he ended his hug, one arm stayed latched around my waist.

There was a flurry of movement from the tree. Ten feet above eye level, Jezebel kicked her legs in a hello from a sturdy limb. Safe.

My sudden smile died. The chant that'd sparked in the crowd now grew like wildfire across the clearing.

"Free our brothers! Fight for freedom! Free our brothers! Fight for freedom!"

"No!" The solo shout registered like a whisper compared to the crowd's roar. "No!"

Who wouldn't fight? I ascended the fifteen-feet to Jezebel's limb and leaned off.

"No!" A male with red hair flung himself onto his knees next to Danny D, who spread his arms in protection over his jumble of cables and radio equipment.

Ben, I mouthed. He was the security leader I'd met in Chaff's tent.

Crack. "Whoa!" Wolfe threw his arms around the trunk next to me and gave me a sheepish grin. I glared at his shoe that had dislodged a limb below. When I turned back to the crowd, Ben had vanished. Where? Had Reed's followers silenced him?

"Free our brothers! Fight for freedom!"

"No!"

The chant to fight wavered as a handful of other faded nos peeped out from different areas in the throng. Again, I leaned toward the light. Who else rebelled?

I huffed in frustration. The bodies below were too tight. I couldn't tell. I ruffled through images in my brain until I conjured up the faces of those I'd prayed with in the camps. The prayer warriors had spent time with God. Did they have the courage to speak out about what God wanted?

"No!" The father of the mole family who'd herded me to safety fell to his knees. His body spilled into the fringe of light within spitting distance of my cedar.

A half-dozen Christians in gray garments on the hill past the platform turned toward his bellowed protest. I recognized Reed's closest followers. The guy with the frog mouth shielded his brow and pointed his knife. Not at the kneeler but at my branch. *There. She's up there in the tree.*

"No!"

Reed's henchmen frowned up. Trinity had shimmied up the light pole above their heads and now clung to a spot next to their commander.

"No," she repeated.

As my hand pressed my lips, hers reached up to the sky as if to pluck a star. Her fingers balled into a fist of defiance. She shook it at Commander Reed.

A tiny projectile flashed as if released from a skilled hand or sling. Trinity's blonde head jerked forward from the hit. Then, as if in slow motion, she freefell backward to where Micah poised with outstretched arms below.

50

Was she alive or dead? I didn't know. It was Micah's fault she'd hit the ground since he hadn't caught her. But everything leading up to her fall was mine. My fault.

"Stay at the camps, Trinity."

"Help sabotage the explosives, Trinity."

"Sacrifice yourself to publicly defy Reed, Trinity."

I might as well have suggested that last one. Because that's what my cousin had heard tonight when I shouted truths over Reed's lies.

"Don't go down to her. Dove, no." Wolfe panted, struggling to keep me in the tree. He released my shirt and locked my cheekbones between his palms. "You can't help her."

"Let go—"

His fingers dropped. "It's Saul. I...I can't believe it! Saul's here. And he's got Trinity."

Uncle Saul? I took a shuddering breath and quit trying to drop onto the branches below.

Jezebel kept her face against my chest as my uncle, who'd appeared out from nowhere like so many times before, carried my broken cousin down the far side of the hill. Micah tagged after like a puppy until the crowd swallowed him too.

My uncle...

A flea's amount of hope pricked through my horror and nausea. Uncle Saul had arrived. Had Reed's guards released our missing families?

"Behold," Reed boomed. "My proof. Please welcome our arrivals."

The chanting had grown strong as if fueled by the attack on Trinity. Now it subsided.

I held still. There were muffled footsteps...too many to distinguish...and the thud and swish of feet over lush grass. Indistinct silhouettes emerged in the night over a hill far from where I balanced. Dozens of people were walking toward the fluorescent light.

A low, continuous undertone of anxious voices started up. But I'd seen my uncle. I knew the arrivals weren't Heathen.

The adult figures that neared the fringes of light were stooped and clutched walking sticks—no, not sticks but spears. Weapons. The closest group of newcomers hesitated. The glow illuminated their haggard faces, blinking eyes, and angular bodies that seemed to creak stiffly from disuse. The men were unshaven. The women stooped under their heavy hair coils.

An animal's yowl rang out near the lake, and the threatening sound broke the invisible barrier. The freed Christians surged forward, mixing into the mass. More weary groups trudged over the golf course, blinked in the light, then joined. Amhebran cries broke out.

My aunt! My stomach lurched up to greet my heart. Trinity's mom stood in the light with her hand to her brow, no doubt searching the sea of bodies for someone familiar.

I hunted the vicinity around my aunt, and my stomach began to sink. My mom hadn't been released. Or my grandpa. If they had, they'd be clustered near her. Which meant they were being kept behind, locked up for being suspicious.

The flow of freed captives coming down the hill had become a trickle, and Reed's voice barreled on. I caught snatches.

"Follow my soldiers...use force if necessary...bargain for the rest of our people's release...best perimeter offensive route..."

My eyes strayed over joy-filled scenes as family members reunited. Their joy was temporary. Reed's plans would lead them from relief to regret in a matter of minutes.

Jezebel pulled my face in alignment with the dark golf course. "Josh does run fast!"

Just beyond the circle of light, a black-haired kid rocketed through the gloom toward a limping figure supported by two others. Joshua tackled the injured person in the middle.

Rebecca threw off Brooke's and Hunter's supporting arms, and the siblings staggered backward, almost colliding with two more stragglers.

My cedar bough bounced as I struggled up. I cupped my hands. "Mom! Grandpa!"

They couldn't hear me. They were more than a hundred feet away, and my voice was weak, swallowed up in the hundreds of others. My microphone didn't work. I must have broken it—probably while grappling with Wolfe. I had to get down there.

"Grandpa! Grandpa!"

"Wait, Dove—" Wolfe latched onto me. "It's not safe. Reed's followers have seen you. They've divided up and are heading this way. We're trapped. Maybe if we get into the woods—"

I batted and pointed. "Gilead!"

Wolfe's hand tightened around mine as Gilead left

the crowd and joined my relatives. Mom sighted him first and staggered forward. She clasped his shoulder with both thin hands then rested her forehead against it. Was she crying?

My brother broke away to gesture with his knife at the out-of-sight village. He seemed to be speaking, possibly recounting Reed's lies that he believed to be truths. Blaming the innocent godless for Reed's kidnappings. Explaining that now was the moment for an uprising if we wanted to stay free.

"Don't believe him," I whispered.

Gilead stopped. The three stood still, as if contemplating Reed's barrage of instructions and encouragement. My grandpa, a skinnier version of himself, raised his spear in the direction of the village buildings. He nodded.

My blood turned to ice. "Grandpa!" Fumbling, I grabbed the wire and lifted it off my ear. "Fix my microphone, Wolfe! So I can call to him—and tell him the truth."

"Fix it, Woof!" Jezebel shouted.

"I...I can't. Half of it's gone. Dove, we need to get you out of here. Jezebel, too."

My hands pressed my ears. If only Reed would stop talking. The fight mantra had started up again. If only the chant would quit...

My eyes skimmed the crowd. Like Wolfe had said, Frog Face and his cronies had split up. Here and there their gray-uniformed bodies were struggling to get through the chaotic mass, inching in my direction. Eli was farthest away, blocked by a group chanting near the radio equipment.

The radio. For the first time since I'd climbed this cedar, I remembered the broadcast. This nightmare was only the first wave of violence, the beginning of which would trigger a storm of other nightmares in other places.

As Jezebel hugged me, my mom and grandpa continued to hesitate with their backs to me. There was movement in the darkness behind them. Joshua and his sister and friends scurrying away? Or curious villagers arriving who were disturbed by our noise?

Sirens sounded in the distance, evidence that godless with weapons were hurrying toward us. Within minutes, they'd force a fight.

Wolfe recaptured my hand. He leaned over Jezebel's round head, speaking faster than hummingbird wings. "Dove, your family...it's not going to end well for them. They're going to d...die."

He choked on the word, then rushed on. "Or end up in a CTDC forever. You can't help them because we'll be caught before we get halfway to them. Reed's soldiers are waiting for you to climb down. They haven't taken their eyes off you since Trinity f-fell."

His mouth was inches away, moving faster with a new intensity. "But we don't have to die with them or grow old in a CTDC. We can slip away—we'll get into these woods fast, hide in the trees. You, me and Jezebel, we can make it. We'll start a new life. Marry me. I love you, and you're my best friend—"

I flung my arm around his neck and pressed my lips to his.

His lips were warm. They were sunshine, laughter, and doughnuts. Everything good. Everything I wanted.

My other arm ditched the branch and came around his shoulder.

It was OK to love him. To kiss my best friend. To

kiss the guy I could be equally yoked with...if I chose not to die.

I broke off and scooted away. My eyes lifted to where the moonless sky stretched above the cedar boughs. When I stood, the springy limb under my feet tried to buck me off.

I had three choices.

I could slip into the safety of these woods with the Picketts and begin a new life as Dove Pickett.

I could make an impossible dash for my grandpa and mom in an attempt to stop them from joining an attack based on lies.

Or I could try to stop this whole nation of violence-obsessed, pigheaded Christians from making a huge mistake.

My fist pressed an ache in my chest. No matter how much my brother—and Christians like him—annoyed me, I loved them. I loved my people. I couldn't stand by and let them sin...not if I could stop them.

Could I stop them?

"Dove, what—"

I thrust my palm outwards at Jezebel. I'd heard what I'd waited for—an abnormal hush as the distant sirens died. The crowd's chanting became moth wings. And Reed's commands for the attack muted.

Then came the clear directive from Heaven.

Have faith.

I squinted at the crowd, an ankle-breaking distance below. Right there was the spot where I'd land if I jumped.

The branch groaned behind me. Wolfe's shout retreated into the sky.

"Dove, no! Stone...no! Catch her!"

51

Stone plucked me out of the air and held me for a moment. "Your cousin. I thought at first it was you...that you'd fallen. Died. And it was my fault because I didn't listen to you. I should never have..."

He set me on my feet and spoke to the ones wearing gray grouped around us. "She's in my control. Go."

Frog Face and two others slunk back toward their commander.

I spoke fast, shouting through the crushing noise. "You let all the Christian captives go tonight—all of them. Even the suspicious."

"Yes."

I shook his arm. "You went against Reed on that. Because you're sick of following him...of hurting people."

"Yes."

"So, quick, give me back the EMP!"

The swollen lids of both bruised eyes slid shut. "I would if I could. But it's in the lake."

"Dove!" Melody cowered beside me. "I'm...I'm sorry. You know, for being dumb. I heard what you said tonight. It's true. Everything. And I shouldn't have ditched you—"

I gripped her sleeve and pointed at the platform and Reed's back. His fist punched the air to accentuate another lie. "The truth—is he danger? Or no danger?"

"Danger."

I jerked her closer. "Then help me shut down the Reclaim."

She held up her hands, palms up. "Sorry, but it's too late."

"It's not too late for everyone. Not for believers in other parts of the nation who are following. And maybe not for us."

I whirled her around to face the unreachable plasma generator on the slope, Reed's power source. Silent but potent with energy, like every other generator I'd encountered since I'd left home. Yet Bull had mentioned chipmunks could kill their power. And I was stronger than a chipmunk. And maybe I had help.

I glared at the technology that powered the key to Commander Reed's communication with believers in this clearing and beyond. His microphone. His lights. His radio broadcast.

"Be my muscle, Stone. Help me. No more hurting. No more war. We end this."

I didn't wait for his response. My gaze latched onto the distant spot where the generator existed in the tight-packed crowd, and I flung myself toward it.

I got held up at my first obstacle of a happy reunion, but I didn't have to slow for long. Stone went before me and cleared my path. I sensed bodies and weapons flung aside. Shouts and pointing fingers followed as I wormed past.

I skidded to a stop, panting. The generator.

I fell onto my knees in the grass. A thick cable snaked from its smooth side. My fingers wrapped around the cord that gave life to everything Reed depended on. My muscles tensed as Melody clamped a warm hand over mine.

"Ready, partner?"

"Ready. And Stone, smash it. Beyond repair."

Together we pulled, and a crash of plastic breaking into a thousand pieces rent the air.

Pitch darkness fell like an eclipse. There was a lull in the crowd's noise. Then a rush of voices began, swelling like the ocean until the constant roar drowned out the sirens...and Reed Bender, who'd become invisible and powerless.

Melody's hand continued to grip mine. Together, with Stone, we'd assassinated—or at least disabled—this dangerous leader's ability to command. We'd killed his radio broadcast, hopefully discouraging other zealous Christians who'd been waiting for the broadcast of his attack. I raised our hands in victory … and then screamed.

A hundred pounds of warm-blooded fur slammed against my back, bowling me forward. Searing pain sliced my ribs. A guttural purr sounded. And something like knives stabbed my skull.

52

"Darcy!" Stone shouted. "No! No...retreat! Get off!"

A bellow like a million train horns blasted my eardrums and rattled the ground I'd collapsed against. The earth shook with such bone-rattling force that Darcy screamed. Her claws retracted, and her weight rolled off.

I tried to reach out a hand in the direction where I'd left Wolfe in the cedar, but I couldn't move. My body throbbed against the quaking grass that'd grown damp with blood. I choked on the heavy, metallic-tinged air. My gaze lifted to the moonless, pitch-black sky.

The noise wasn't a train, but a trumpet. Somehow a trumpet's blast had saved me from Darcy, Reed's most lethal follower I hadn't expected tonight, and it continued to jolt every cell in my body.

Lord? Is that You?

Light slammed down, brighter than my eyeballs could handle. Brighter than the sun. I squeezed my lids shut, and the whole world became stained red.

Red...a red stain that spread across the nation...

My blood.

Truth pierced through my dizzying pain, the blaring horn, and the blinding light.

I smiled and would've laughed out loud if I'd had strength.

So many times, I'd visualized a dove flying, spreading red in its wake. Yes, I was the dove...but I'd been wrong about the red. The symbolic color wasn't from an earthly bloodbath or a war. It was Jesus's blood. The red meant His perfect blood He'd already shed in order to cover us sinful humans with his righteousness. His blood, the only source of eternal life. The Red.

I sprawled on my stomach in the grass, too weak to move. Still I smiled.

I'd been God's messenger. Maybe He'd used me for peace, but more importantly He'd used me to spread His eternal life-giving blood to those who hadn't yet accepted it. I, God's dove, had expanded the reach of His salvation to those who hadn't known about Him.

Wolfe, Jezebel, Lobo, Bull, Grandma Pickett, maybe thousands of strangers with televisions...

A sudden surge of joy exploded through my mind and body, the wave erasing my heart-wrenching despair about Trinity, my mom, and Grandpa. The crippling pain from Darcy ended. I relaxed in sweet relief, and I exhaled.

My lids fluttered open.

I wasn't on my belly anymore but on my knees in the emerald grass. There was no more red or blood in sight. Wolfe and Jezebel weren't in the tree but knelt next to me with their eyes shut. Beyond them was Melody and Stone; Mom, Gilead, and Grandpa; the Joyners; the Braes; and a clearing filled with hundreds of kneelers.

A ripple of excitement drew my eyes upward to the source of light.

I cried out, though no sound escaped.

Jesus's face. Sky alive, I couldn't look away! I never wanted to look away, even though Gran was nearby. She was the same grandma I'd known—yet different. Strong and unwrinkled, she traveled without hesitation in the direction I longed to go. Upwards.

An airy giddiness spread through my body. I raised my arms.

My feet left the ground, and I rose. I didn't unglue my eyes from my Savior who radiated light, but I felt the presence of thousands—maybe more—traveling with me. Jezebel was rising on my left and Wolfe on my right.

Wolfe Pickett, my best friend, squeezed my hand. I gripped his tight.

Together we rose, hand-in-hand, to spend eternity with our Savior, with our families, and with each other.

A perfect eternity, united together. Forever.

Acts 2:17-21

"In the last days," God says,
"I will pour out my Spirit upon all people.
Your sons and daughters will prophesy.
Your young men will see visions,
and your old men will dream dreams.
In those days I will pour out my Spirit
even on my servants—men and women alike—
and they will prophesy.
And I will cause wonders in the heavens above
and signs on the earth below—
blood and fire and clouds of smoke.
The sun will become dark,
and the moon will turn blood red
before that great and glorious day of the Lord arrives.
But everyone who calls on the name of the Lord
will be saved."

Thank you…

for purchasing this Watershed Books title. For other inspirational stories, please visit our on-line bookstore at www.pelicanbookgroup.com.

For questions or more information, contact us at customer@pelicanbookgroup.com.

Watershed Books
Make a Splash!™
an imprint of Pelican Book Group
www.PelicanBookGroup.com

Connect with Us
www.facebook.com/Pelicanbookgroup
www.twitter.com/pelicanbookgrp

To receive news and specials, subscribe to our bulletin
http://pelink.us/bulletin

May God's glory shine through
this inspirational work of fiction.

AMDG

God Can Help!

Are you in need? The Almighty can do great things for you. Holy is His Name! He has mercy in every generation. He can lift up the lowly and accomplish all things. Reach out today.

Do not fear: I am with you; do not be anxious: I am your God. I will strengthen you, I will help you, I will uphold you with my victorious right hand.

~Isaiah 41:10 (NAB)

We pray daily, and we especially pray for everyone connected to Pelican Book Group—that includes you! If you have a specific need, we welcome the opportunity to pray for you. Share your needs or praise reports at http://pelink.us/pray4us

Here's a sneak peek at another great futuristic novel from Pelican Book Group

***Vanquished**, by Katie Clark*

Book one in the Enslaved Series

1

The old hospital looms in front of me like some ancient castle from the Early Days. This is where they keep people with the mutation. My heart races at the thought of going inside.

I've never been in a hospital before. In fact, I've never been in a building that big at all. I wish I'd taken Jamie's offer to come with me or had come with Dad last night. I wish that Mom hadn't gotten the mutation at all.

I take a deep breath and push through the double doors.

The quiet lobby area is dim, lit by a few small windows and a couple of glowing lamps. I knew the hospital gets extra electricity allowance, but I've almost never seen anyone use manufactured lighting during the day. I'm awed by the sight. In front of me is an abandoned office area, and to my right is an old cafeteria. A sign dangles over the counter by one chain. It seems like someone would have taken it down by now.

I make a split decision and yank it down. Chains clatter as they plunge to the floor. It stays on the ground, and I turn back to the main lobby. My heartbeat calms at regaining this tiny bit of control.

Beyond the cafeteria, several signs hang on the wall. One points me to the stairs.

My dad said Mom was on the third floor. Back in the Early Days, they fought the mutation with chemotherapy drugs and something called radiation. We don't have those things anymore, so we fight it with fruits, vegetables, and herbs. Sometimes it works, but most of the time it doesn't. I don't want to think about what this means for Mom.

The door to the stairs is beside the old elevator shafts. I reach out and feel the cool metal doors. They reflect my image back to me, but I don't pay attention to that. I've seen enough of my short blond hair and not-so-tall stature, but I've never actually seen elevators before. I wish the doors would open, and I could peek inside. Riding up to the third floor would be even better, but no one has enough electricity allowance to run elevators, not even the hospital I guess.

I make the climb to the third floor without even getting winded, and more manufactured lighting greets me. Long bulbs line the ceiling. These lights are brighter than the lamps downstairs, and they make an odd buzzing noise. I stumbled into a beehive once, and the angry bees buzzed a lot like the lights.

There are so many rooms down the long hallway, I can't imagine there would ever be enough sick people to fill them all, but then I remember what they tell us about the Early Days. There were a lot more people back then. Now there are so few people I think we could all fit in this hospital together. How would it feel to be around so many people, all the time? Would it feel crowded? I don't think so. I think it would feel safe.

The hallway is empty, but a faint beeping comes from down the hall. I pass an old desk on my way toward the beeping. A dumpy computer sits on the desk. People still have those?

I pass one door, two doors, and then an irritated voice stops me in my tracks.

"We could give her chemo at the onset to slow things down a bit, and then start the natural healing. The least we can do is to give her a fighting chance. She's a Middle, after all." It's a woman's voice, coming from the room with the faint beeping. Her tone is hushed and angry.

I look at the piece of paper that's been tacked to the wall outside the room.

Maya Norfolk.

I suck in a tight breath. They're talking about Mom? What do they mean by 'a fighting chance'? My heart picks up speed, and I step closer to the room, careful to stay out of view.

"It takes time to get approval for chemo drugs, and what if she talks? Everyone who gets the mutation will start demanding them. What's her occupation?" It's a man's voice, and he sounds just as angry.

Papers shuffle and the woman says, "Professor at the military academy. I say we do it. She knows how to keep secrets if she's worked in the military. What chance does she have otherwise?"

The pause in conversation is excruciating as Mom's life hangs in the balance. Meanwhile my mind spins. Chemo drugs? They're not even supposed to exist. How can they be talking about this so casually? Have the rest of us been lied to all this time?

"Do you need some help?"

I jerk around, my heart thumping like the rain during a torrential downpour. A boy stands in front of me. He doesn't look much older than my seventeen years, but definitely old enough to have taken the Test.

"I was looking for my mom's room," I say quickly. "I've never been here before." I hope that sounded innocent and confused, and not like I'm scared to be caught eavesdropping.

"What's her name?" His dark hair is short, but it has a little curl to it. His chocolaty brown eyes aren't suspicious, not like they'd be if he suspected me of listening to the doctors…

To continue reading, grab a paperback copy or download the e-book today